LaPlata Law

by David Rotthoff

While the characters in this story are strictly figments of the writer's imagination, the geography is quite accurate, thanks partly to a DeLorme gazetteer of Colorado and partly to personal experience with the area acquired during several visits to my older daughter and her family when they lived in Bayfield. The only really drastic liberty taken with geography has been to exercise a little literary license and add a mile and more to county highway 501 between the traffic light at the U.S. 160 intersection and Ludwig Road in Bayfield. This extra mile or so is added to account for the location of the Diamond F ranch. Other than that, the geography, as stated, is pretty darned accurate.

A dedication? For my daughters and their families, and for my wife, Patricia, always for Patricia.

Commentary: visitors to the Durango area absolutely must ride the Durango and Silverton. The scenery is some of the most magnificent in all of North America. The high point of the ride is passing along the 'high line', where the railroad runs on a shelf some four hundred feet above the tumultuous waters of the Animas River gorge. The whole line is on the National Register of Historic Sites.........as well it should be.

INTRODUCTION

Meet Tony Frye......Air Force Academy graduate, former active duty USAF officer but now both a rancher and millionaire, by virtue of an unexpected inheritance, and deputy sheriff, strictly by virtue of accident. You might think of Tony as sort of an Archie Goodwin, but without a Nero Wolfe in the picture. He's young, occasionally impulsive, and has a variety of interests. He's bright and good-looking. He's attracted to women.....and vice versa. Tony is equally at home in jeans or Air Force mess dress [and virtually anything in between] though he is honest about being much happier in informal attire.

Tony would freely admit that he's a mite snobbish about certain things. He likes good coffee, brewed military strength, though he's willing to drink a lesser brew if necessary.......but absolutely NO flavored coffee. And he certainly does like good food. He prefers specialty sandwiches, and he'd certainly turn his nose up at watercress on oat bread or anything else that's way high up on the crunch scale. "Yuppy" foods just don't turn him on. Good kosher corned beef and high quality Swiss cheese, chopped liver, jerked pork, Philly cheesesteak, or a well-made Reuben are much more his style. He enjoys good cheeseburgers and loves pizza. Prime rib, or any good cut of beef, for that matter, is a weakness; even more of a weakness is a good home-cooked ham dinner. He isn't so much of a food snob that he would prefer presentation over substance, though. He's been known to say more than once, "You can't eat presentation."

Above all, he's a good cop. He enjoys police work, and that's something that initially surprised him when the Air Force turned him from a would-be fighter jockey in to a criminal investigator. Tony is also a good rancher. He spent much of his youth on his grandfather's cattle ranch and loves ranch life and the hard work that goes with it. Tony's father, on the other hand, never liked life on the ranch on which he grew up. As a result, when Tony's grandfather died, Tony inherited the ranch.....and a whopping load of the financial wherewithal that made it possible for him to leave the military and begin a life as a very affluent rancher.....and deputy sheriff, though the latter was totally unplanned.

People who know him well will testify that being rich, actually being a millionaire many times over, hasn't spoiled him. He's quick to grab a check and doesn't hesitate to spend liberally, especially if it contributes to getting a job done. One of his standard lines is that his lawyers and accountants are always happy to see him come up with another tax deductible expense or two. He doesn't waste money, but spends pretty much what he wants to when the occasion happens to call for doing so.

Chapter One

Tony Frye ran a little over a mile that warm, sunny late spring Thursday morning. The exertion left him panting and sweating. His normal morning run, three or more days a week, for the last seven years and somewhat longer, had been at least three miles, weather and work schedule permitting, but for the last five of those years and a bit more, the great majority of his morning runs had been done a lot closer to sea level than the roughly seven thousand feet in altitude where he'd run the last two mornings. Running at that high altitude where the air was considerably more than somewhat thin, in excess of a mile above sea level, resulted in a considerable amount of huffing and puffing, true for anyone not used to strenuous exertion at altitude.

Until his lungs got used to breathing the thin Colorado mountain air again, Tony knew that running three miles was out of the question; He was going to have to gradually work up to the three mile mark. He also knew from previous experiences that it would only take a week or two to readjust to the altitude, providing, of course, that he exercised frequently. He'd made the altitude adjustment several times before. He knew he'd be able to do it again. It was just a matter of physical discomfort, time, and effort, effort being the key item.

After showering, getting dressed in comfortable blue jeans, an L.L. Bean cotton shirt, and an old but soft and well broken-in pair of western boots, walking variety rather than riding ones, Tony fixed himself a light breakfast of coffee, tomato juice, toast, butter, peanut butter and red raspberry preserves and while he ate, he went over in his mind some of the things he needed to do that day. He needed to move the last few boxes and bins from the back of his pickup truck to the house, then empty a variety of those boxes and bins, organize the contents thereof, and put all the items away.....or throw them out if they didn't strike him as being essential.

For the most part, he had postponed the decision as to what would get saved and what would have to be pitched out until after he moved back from Washington, D.C., to Colorado, figuring that he'd deal with it when he got to back to where he'd always thought of as home and had more time to deal with decisions of this nature. Of course, this meant that he ended up packing a lot more things than he would have packed if he'd decided what to throw out before heading west. But doing otherwise would have involved making decisions that he wasn't quite ready to make......not yet, at least. All in good time. Besides, the good old USAF had paid to ship a considerable amount of Tony's personal effects back to his home of record. Content of those boxes would have to be dealt with, too, when they finally arrived, but all in good time. No need to rush.

When he traded his two year old Ford Mustang in on the crew cab truck a couple months earlier, something he'd done knowing that he'd be packing up and leaving Washington for Colorado, he'd also bought a matching cap for the cargo bed, so anything that was left in the truck was protected from the elements and, depending on where the truck was parked, was relatively safe from miscreants who might wish to liberate a thing or two. As a result, Tony knew he could take his time about unloading, if that were his wish. It wasn't, but he wasn't in any burning hurry to finish the job either. And if the weather really went south before he finished unloading the truck, he could always put the truck inside one of the hay barns until he managed to finish the chore.

Still, all procrastination aside, all of his accumulated possessions really did need to be moved in to the house. Within a few days, he knew he'd have to unpack the rest of the boxes and bins and get the contents either properly situated in the large ranch house he'd inherited from his grandfather or, as was likely to be true in some instances, tossed out. But there was no real great rush; as he lived alone, a little disorganization around the house was not of major concern, especially with entertaining guests not being an item under consideration, at least not for a while.

He could do bits and pieces of the work over a few more days. Most of his clothing and other important things had been unloaded and unpacked yesterday and the day before. His train models, books, magazines, and the accumulation of what he thought of as "personal junk" could wait a day or even maybe longer....or maybe even a few weeks longer for unpacking some of the really nonessential things.

Once he got the truck completely unloaded, some things could be put off for a bit longer. At least he'd had the foresight to label the boxes and bins with the specifics of the contents, though one of the bins was actually, and quite accurately, labeled *miscellaneous junk*. Tony somehow knew when he packed it and loaded it in to his pickup truck that it'd be the last bin he'd unload and the last one he'd unpack. It was a conclusion that did not take a person with a doctorate in astronautical engineering to reach. When he reached that decision a couple of weeks earlier, Tony had chuckled and mentally tagged it as a no-brainer.

So Tony spent close to an hour moving a couple of boxes of books and a bin from the truck to the house and then doing a little unpacking. It wasn't the bringing things in from the pickup that took time, it was deciding where the contents of the boxes and bins were to be put. He took the time to decide which room each box or bin should be moved to, a task made easier by his having taken the trouble to tape a condensed list of contents to each box or bin. At least this made it possible to decide whether to unpack a box or bin now, or to put it off until later.

The back of the pickup was well over three-quarters empty when he decided he'd better sit down and go over more of the paperwork he needed to take care of before he consulted with his grandfather's attorneys again.....he surmised that they were *his* attorneys now. That consultation he would have to save for Tuesday or even later the next week, seeing that he was looking at a holiday weekend. There was no real rush to get it over with. He made a mental note to spend the upcoming Memorial Day weekend catching up on some of what he needed to learn from the large stack of papers piled up on what had been his grandfather's desk. Fortunately, the team of lawyers working on the estate settlement had done an excellent job of organizing the paperwork, despite probate in this case being quite complicated. *God willin' and Pine River stays within its banks*, Tony thought, he might even have time for a short horseback ride.

He also needed, he decided, to drive the few miles in to Bayfield and see what mail, if any, had collected in the ranch's post office box. His foreman had picked up the mail the day before yesterday, but Tony hoped that by now a few of his magazine subscriptions had progressed through the change of address process. But first, he forced himself to spend a little over an hour working his way through a part of that stack of legal and financial papers.

Then he walked down to the horse barn, for maybe the tenth time since arriving at the ranch late the previous Monday afternoon, just to look around again. There were things he wanted to do in the barn, but those things would have to wait anywhere from a few days to a few months. So, after a cursory look around the barn and at the dozen or so horses in the big pasture between the barn and the river, he got in his truck and drove the roughly half dozen miles in to the village; Bayfield is just a mite small to honestly be called a town.

Much later, when he'd had time to reflect back on what happened that Thursday, Tony Frye was struck by how one simple decision, insignificant in itself, could end up altering the course of several people's lives, his own included. If he had not wanted something different for lunch that Thursday, a change from the ham and American cheese sandwich on white bread that he'd tolerated, but had not really enjoyed, for the last few days, the odds were very much against him ever getting involved in a series of events that seriously impacted not only upon his life, but on the lives of a number of other people as well. If he'd not wanted to pick up a few food items more to his liking, he'd have driven right back to the ranch instead of making a spur of the moment detour to the grocery store in Bayfield's small shopping plaza. And that simple decision, as things turned out, made a world of difference in the lives of a good many people.

As he pulled out of the post office parking lot, he decided, more as an act of gastronomic desperation than anything else, to stop at Bayfield's one and only grocery store on his way back to the ranch in hopes of finding a loaf of rye bread. Lew Barnes, his grandfather's closest friend and ranch foreman, had stocked the kitchen cupboards and the refrigerator at the ranch house with a limited assortment of foodstuffs the day before Tony arrived back in Colorado, late Monday afternoon, but the plain white sandwich bread Lew bought wasn't quite to Tony's liking. Nor was he really fond of sliced pressed ham and American cheese sandwiches, at least not as a daily noontime meal. *That got old really quickly,* he'd thought as he drove toward the small shopping plaza.

As a result, a little before eleven o'clock that morning and after having picked up his mail, Tony was sitting in his pickup truck in the parking lot outside the grocery store in the little strip mall on the north side of U.S. Highway 160 in Bayfield, Colorado. A few minutes earlier. he'd picked up a goodly assortment of mail at the Bayfield Post Office a half mile or so south of the main road, in what passed for "downtown" Bayfield, and had tossed it in the passenger side bucket seat of the pickup. From the size of the pile of envelopes and assorted other mail, magazines and such, that the postal employee had handed to him, Tony concluded that at least a few of the change of address forms he'd mailed out a few weeks before he left the Washington, D.C., area must have worked.

"Damn, some rye bread sure would taste good," Tony muttered to himself as he leafed through the stack of accumulated mail. "Any if I'm lucky, I can get some decent liverwurst and maybe even some good imported Swiss cheese. If I can't get the stuff here, maybe I'll run in to Durango tomorrow."

In the twelve years or thereabouts since Tony left his grandfather's ranch, his off and on home since he was in grade school, and gone off to the Air Force Academy, his gastronomic horizons had been considerably broadened. He'd come to the conclusion that many, if not most, sandwiches were at their best when made with something slightly more exotic than white bread and that there were other sandwich varieties besides ham, ham and cheese, and peanut butter and jelly.

He particularly favored rye in any of its varieties and had cultivated a particular liking for liverwurst and Swiss cheese sandwiches on rye, pinwheel rye if it were available, with a slice or two of red onion, mayonnaise, and just a dash of horseradish. His second choice would be kosher corned beef on rye, done up the same way. He'd even become quite fond of chopped chicken liver spread, also on rye; however, expecting to find this delicacy or any other of the more esoteric sandwich makings he'd come to favor, in Bayfield's one and only grocery store was probably stretching optimism to the breaking point.....and then some.

Another favorite, though one which he'd not yet developed enough courage to try making himself, was a well-made Reuben. Fortunately, Tony remembered that there was at least one restaurant in Durango that served a decent Reuben and mentally noted that it might be nice to arrange to be in town come lunch time within the next day or two. The truth of the matter was that Tony, by his own admission, had grown in to somewhat of a food snob, though he preferred rather to think of it as his tastes having both expanded and matured over the years.

Tony figured he just might get lucky and find a few of the items he wanted in the grocery store. He also realized that it would be just a mite overly optimistic to hope to find some of the things he craved, chopped chicken liver or real kosher corned beef, for example, in Bayfield. But hope does tend to spring eternal from the human breast; nothing ventured, nothing gained. Maybe in a good Jewish deli in Durango, if such a thing existed there.

The odds of finding a good deli in Durango, though, didn't give him any warm, fuzzy feelings either. But he could always hope. He was absolutely certain that he wouldn't find one in the small town of Bayfield. Truth be told, Tony was pretty skeptical about finding a Jewish deli, good or otherwise, in all of southwest Colorado. Maybe in Santa Fe or Albuquerque, but odds are that looking for a really good deli in Durango was going to be a waste of time.

While Durango and some of the other area towns such as Pagosa Springs, Mancos, and Telluride weren't quite wild West communities any more, and hadn't been for several decades, neither were they really centers of gastronomic sophistication, save for a few really good up-scale restaurants that largely catered to tourists and the large number of affluent newcomers to the area. At least those towns hadn't been bastions of fine food when Tony left the area to enter the Air Force Academy. But back then, Tony's gastronomic horizons had also been pretty limited. Several years of living in Washington, D.C., had brought about a culinary awakening. He'd actually become sort of picky about things such as rye bread, cheesecake, escargot, French onion soup, and prime rib with horseradish.

As he looked through the stack of mail, there were a few items that tempted him. He'd hoping that a couple of his hobby magazines would have caught up with him, and he was delighted to find out that this had happened. There was also one thing he was afraid he'd find in the mail, even though he really didn't want it to be there. And in leafing through the pile, he found in it just what he'd really not wanted to find.......letters from Marissa Montgomery.

A couple of years earlier, Tony's father and stepmother had dragooned him in to escorting Marissa Montgomery to some sort of artsy-fartsy tie-and-tails social function at the Kennedy Center. It wasn't something Tony really wanted to do.....parent-arranged blind dates didn't strike him as a really neat idea, but seeing that it would make his step-mother happy..... He tended to think of his step-mother in close to Cinderella-like terms, or even to being close to the wicked witch in *The Wizard of Oz*. But, within reason, to keep her happy. Tony skipped wearing his tux for that occasion, opting instead for his Air Force mess dress uniform.

Given what the uniform had cost him, he tried to get at least occasional use out of it, other than having to wear it on the all too frequent occasions when he would get drafted as an escort or a canapé passer at Pentagon or White House social functions. This was an occupational hazard for junior officers stationed in the nation's capital, especially those who were socially well-connected, as Tony just happened to be. This was a thing that Tony hated; he tried to arrange to be out of town on duty whenever it looked as if he might be tapped for social duty. Unfortunately, this was something he was frequently unable to avoid. No longer being subject to this call of duty was something that Tony looked upon as a positive return for leaving active military service. Getting out from under Marissa's thumb, though, was something about which he had mixed feelings.

The lovely Miss Marissa Montgomery, daughter of an influential member of the United States House of Representatives, liked what she saw on her first date with Tony, and quickly managed to co-opt him as her semi-regular escort for a variety of social functions. One thing sort of led to another, and before he knew it, he found himself dating her on a steady basis, an *extremely* steady basis, if truth be told. He also found Marissa making decisions for him, a state of affairs that he really didn't care for, but tolerated for a considerable amount of time because he really didn't wish to get on her bad side.

Disagreements with Marissa could be considerably less than pleasant, something Tony had learned from painful personal experience. Sometimes he asked himself why he put up with her. Ample experience with the young lady proved that she certainly had earned an advanced degree in bitchiness. When he left the nation's capital a week and a half earlier, though, he had parted with Congressman Bradford Montgomery's lovely raven-haired daughter on considerably less than good terms.

What Marissa expected, even demanded, of Tony, at the minimum, was that he would go to Colorado, do what had to be done to enable him manage his inheritance from a considerable distance, and then return to the city, and to her, as quickly as humanly possible. What she really wanted Tony to do, so he'd concluded, was to divest himself of the Colorado property he'd inherited as quickly as possible and return east so she could micromanage his life. Marissa, or so Tony thought, must have also done graduate study in micromanagement. If it were an Olympic event, he thought, she'd be a strong contender for the gold.

There were some major problems with what Marissa wanted, actually what Marissa *demanded.* In Tony's mind, selling the ranch was absolutely out of the question. It had been in the Frye family since the early 1880's and he wanted to keep it in the family.....which, he realized when he started to give the matter serious thought, pretty much meant that somewhere along the line he'd better think about marrying and having children.

Tony knew his father had no interest in the ranch, even though he'd grown up on it, which certainly explained why Tony had inherited it. His dad had been delighted to escape the ranch to study international affairs at Harvard, get advanced degrees in the same field, and then work for the federal government in Washington and other places around the world, eventually ending up with a Ph. D. in the subject and a very senior position in the State Department. Grandpa Pete had often told Tony that, even as a grade school student, his father had hated life on the ranch and the chores that went with it. Tony, on the other hand, loved it.

His much older sister, Doctor Elizabeth Anne Frye - Moore, MD, Ph.D., and a few other sets of letters, had even less interest in the ranch than did their father. Liz was firmly entrenched in a high society marriage, a lucrative medical practice in Baltimore, and teaching at the Johns Hopkins Medical School. As a child, she'd never enjoyed her infrequent visits to her grandfather's ranch. In this respect, she was her father's child. Tony didn't see that state of affairs changing any time soon.....if ever. *Her loss; my gain,* he thought.

Tony was adamant that under no circumstances would he be an absentee ranch owner, no matter what Marissa Montgomery wanted. The considerable time he'd spent living with his grandfather after his mother's death gave him a highly favorable slant on ranch life. When he turned in his Air Force regular commission on a reserve commission on separating from active military service, he'd done so with the intention of being a working cattle rancher, despite the fact that the very substantial fortune that had passed to him through the trust funds set up years before by his grandfather had put him in the position of never having to so much as lift a finger for the rest of his life, should he choose to go that route. But doing that would mean becoming what both he and his grandfather had always thought of as a social parasite; spending the rest of his life as a playboy, making major investments in fast women and slow horses, was certainly NOT an option as far as Tony was concerned.

He had been brought up believing that there was no shame in working, In fact, he'd been brought up to believe that doing honest work conferred a considerable amount of respect and dignity on those who did it. Tony knew two things as far as work went: how to be an Air Force officer, to be more specific how to be an Air Force criminal investigator, and how to be a rancher. He had cheerfully given up one to become the other. This was no hardship; he loved ranch life and the hard work that went with it. Leaving the D.C. area and returning to Colorado was something he thought of as a homecoming. However, the decision to return to his roots did not sit well, to make a massive understatement, with the lovely and demanding Marissa Montgomery.

Tony and Marissa had gone out to dinner the night before he left Washington. To say that it had not been a pleasant evening would be making a molehill out of a mountain. Before they'd even finished their pre-prandial cocktails, Marissa, who saw the evening as a last ditch chance to mold Tony to her will, had been enumerating the reasons for Tony to change his plans, divest himself of his grandfather's ranch, stay in the Washington area, and go to work as a Congressional staff member in her father's office, or, at the very least, arrange to be an absentee ranch owner so he could stay in Washington and do all the things Marissa had planned for him.

When, as they were eating their salads, Tony once again explained that anything of this nature was absolutely NOT an option. Marissa began to seethe and sputter. By the time their waiter had delivered the main course, Tony was not speaking to her and she was shouting at him, something that had caused their waiter to request that Marissa tone things down a bit. Marissa's vocally profane refusal to do any such thing had prompted a visit from the restaurant manager, who made mention of the threat of a visit by the local police force......if the young lady continued making a major disturbance. Mention was even made of a possible charge of disturbing the peace.

This resulted in them leaving the restaurant, more or less still hungry and more than somewhat thirsty, at management's strongly-worded specific request.....or threat. By the time Tony delivered Marissa to the door of her parents' apartment, neither of them was speaking, other than for Marissa telling him in very graphic terms that she never wanted to hear from him or to see him again. Any lingering hope, however faint, for a good-night kiss, not to mention anything more substantial than a peck on the cheek, had evaporated quite a while before she slammed the apartment door in his face.

Tony refused to let Marissa's snit deprive him of a chance to get something of substance in to his stomach. On the way back to his condominium at the Watergate Complex, he made a detour to a Five Guys burger emporium, where he had a large diet soda, a large bacon cheeseburger, with two beef patties instead of just one, and fries....LOTS of fries. On more than one occasion, Tony had jokingly said that a large order of fries at a Five Guys was enough to feed a small third world nation.

Having eaten a considerable number of both calories and carbohydrates while he stewed about the sequence of events that had him eating his last dinner in D.C. at a Five Guys [as much as he liked their burgers and fries] instead of eating the prime rib that he'd ordered before he and Marissa had been requested to vacate the restaurant, Tony's attitude as far as Marissa Montgomery was concerned was pretty much *screw her*, figuratively speaking, of course.

Very early the next morning, just as the sun was starting to give a tinge of pinkish-orange to the eastern sky and after a not very good night's sleep, Tony called the car rental agency and told them where they could pick up the car he'd rented for the past several weeks; the rental car was a result of his not wanting to drive his new crew cab truck around the D.C. area, especially once he'd started to load it in anticipation of heading west. He showered and got dressed, threw his wet towel, facecloth, sheets, blanket, and other dirty clothing in a plastic bag, which he knotted and threw on the back seat of the pickup, finished putting the last odds and ends of his possessions in the cargo bed, the final item to be loaded being his personal handgun, a Browning 9 mm.

He was under official orders allowing him to carry a handgun, in or out of uniform, at his sole discretion, so he could cheerfully give a middle digit salute at the District of Columbia's draconian anti-firearms statutes .A district cop tried to rattle his cage about carrying a couple months ago; the cop ended up getting a new anal orifice as a result, threatened with a federal charge of interfering with a federal officer in the performance of his duty. With the condo empty and the truck loaded, he turned the keys to his grandfather's condo unit, now his by virtue of inheritance, and the key to the rental car over to the complex's night concierge, and cheerfully kissed Washington, D.C., goodbye.

He had already hired a cleaning service to ready the condo for the next occupant, to whom he would cheerfully lease it out. Tony's grandfather had bought and furnished the condo years ago for the occasions when business took him to D.C. Grandpa Pete had put the title to the condo unit in the name of Frye Enterprises, Inc., the privately held corporation that controlled virtually all of the assets that he owned. There were ten thousand shares in the corporation. On his twenty-first birthday and on each birthday following, Tony received from his grandfather a block of one hundred shares, par value of a hundred dollars per share, as a birthday gift. The same day that he received his first one hundred shares, he was elected as both the vice president and a member of the three person board of directors of the corporation, thanks also to his grandfather, who owned the remaining 9,900 shares as of that birthday. Nominal voting control of two of the shares had been assigned to other corporate officers, though Grandpa Pete retained ownership of them. Now, since his grandfather's death, Tony owned those shares as well.

When Tony got assigned to Washington, Grandpa Pete gave him the use of the place, including maid service, for a very reasonable rent.....the monthly housing allowance Tony got from the Air Force. Actually, as a corporate officer, Tony could have lived in the unit rent-free, as technically speaking the corporation maintained the unit for the use of corporate officers visiting the capital city and Tony, as corporate vice-president, certainly qualified as such. However, the corporate tax attorneys pointed out that having Tony pay his quarters allowance to the corporation would create a situation far less questionable and thus one that was not liable to raise red flags on the part of the I.R.S. Tony was delighted to hand over his quarters allowance to the corporation, especially given the financial benefits he received as an officer thereof. Damned few junior officers in the military were able to afford any kind of luxury living conditions in the D.C. area. What the military paid to a junior captain as a housing allowance would not provide for anything remotely close to a high standard of living, at least not in Washington, D.C. and the surrounding area.

Now that he was, so to speak, burning his bridges, and with no intention of returning to the nation's capital city except to visit family, he saw no need to leave the unit empty. A little extra income for Frye Enterprises, Inc., certainly wouldn't do a bit of harm. He'd briefly considered selling the unit, but decided that this was a decision that could be put off for a while. It was also a decision that would require much careful thought on Tony's part. His grandfather had said many a time that any piece of property should be held virtually forever providing, of course, that it was not losing money. Grandpa Pete had stressed that this particularly applied to ranch land. Ranch land owned by the family was something that had never been for sale, at least not in his lifetime, according to Grandpa Pete. His motto as far as ranch land was concerned was *Buy it; don't sell it.* And Grandpa Pete sure practiced what he preached.

Not long after sunup, a mile or so over the D.C./Maryland line, and before the start of the worst of the area's morning rush hour traffic, he made a quick stop at a Dunkin Donuts, then got on Interstate 270 with a toasted bagel and cream cheese, two butter crunch donuts, and a large carry-out cup of black coffee heavily laced with sugar to keep him company. The donuts were bought on impulse; Tony figured the extra calories and sugar wouldn't do any harm, given that he needed to stay alert while behind the steering wheel. Breakfast in hand, in more ways than one, he'd headed for the closest ramp on to the interstate heading west. Once he'd eaten the bagel and donuts, downed most of the coffee, and had driven fifty or so miles, his mood became quite a bit brighter.

He realized he wasn't missing Marissa Montgomery one tiny bit. He mentally kicked back and relaxed, knowing that he was really going to enjoy the drive to Colorado. It would serve as a mini vacation, one which Tony thought he richly deserved, especially as he hadn't taken any of his annual leave for well over a year, save to attend his grandfather's funeral. He arranged his actual separation from the military to take effect when his accrued leave and travel time back to the place from which he'd entered the military ran out. Until this actually happened, he technically remained in an active duty status, drawing full pay and allowances.

On the morning of his first day heading west, Tony managed to get as far as Hagerstown, Maryland, where, on the spur of the moment, he decided to stop for a quick and quite early nine holes of golf. After an enjoyable round in the company of two very pleasant grey-haired, upper middle-aged ladies, both of whom flirted with him shamelessly, he made an early lunch stop at a Subway before he got back on the road, and, acting on a whim, drove north to Breezewood, Pennsylvania, and then west on the Pennsylvania Turnpike to Bedford, in order to tour the historic Bedford Village living museum.

Tony had read about Bedford's history when he'd done some casual research on the French and Indian War and had flown over the area several times while taking advantage of relatively uncrowded airspace on the occasional weekend's recreational flying he was able to squeeze in. As the most convenient routing to Colorado was going to force him to head north to pick up the Pennsylvania Turnpike anyhow, doing so when it gave him an opportunity to visit a place that interested him was a no-brainer. He enjoyed his tour of the village, then got back on the Pennsylvania Turnpike heading west.

Though he would normally have travelled another hundred or so more miles before calling it a day, Tony was tired from lack of sleep the night before. This being the case, he got off the toll road a fair distance outside of Pittsburgh, where I-70 and I-76 split, and, driving a few more miles west, stopped in Washington, Pennsylvania, at a Comfort Inn, then went out for a good steak dinner before turning in for the night. The lack of pressure and doing what he damned well pleased gave him a considerable sense of freedom. That night he slept well, much better than he'd slept the previous night after the considerable dose of unpleasantness that resulted from dealing with Marissa and her hissy fit.

The next day, Tony ran for perhaps a mile around the motel parking lot, then showered, dressed, and breakfasted at the motel. He stopped for a mid-morning cup of coffee an hour or so west of the Ohio/West Virginia border, and later, about an hour or so before he planned on stopping for lunch, made a comfort stop at a rest area on I-70 not too far east of the border between Indiana and Ohio. The thought of more golf had crossed his mind, but he'd not made a decision about stopping to play when he stopped at the rest area. When he returned to his pickup, his cell phone was making the 'missed call' noise. He had a voice mail....a call from Marissa. Apparently Marissa's stated desire never to speak to him again lasted less than two days. He mentally cringed as he listened to the strident recording: "Tony, I need to talk to you. Call me immediately as soon as you get this message!"

Tony swore in three languages, none of which was English; the string of profanities included a particularly vile and nasty oath in Russian, one that he reserved for occasions when he was really seriously pissed off. Marissa did tend to have that effect on him, he admitted to himself, not for the first time. He turned the cell phone off, and tossed it in the glove box. He was in no mood to talk to Marissa Montgomery. He was in even less of a mood to listen to her bitching. If bitching ability were rated, he was certain that Marissa Montgomery would hold world-class ranking.

Eight pleasant days later, after stopping at a few more historical sites, the Eisenhower museum in Abilene, Kansas, being the one that fascinated him the most, spending a couple days visiting old friends at the Air Force Academy in

Colorado Springs, and taking time along the way to play a couple more rounds of golf, Tony arrived at the ranch where he'd spent much of his youth during the frequent times when State Department business had taken his father to places where it was impractical or impossible to take children.

The cell phone was still in the glove box, unused since western Ohio except to call a couple friends in Colorado Springs and to call Lew Barnes as he pulled off Interstate 25 and on to U.S. Route 160 at Walsenburg, stopping just off the interstate to fill the truck's gas tank before making the call. Given that cell phone service in the mountains was spotty at best, Tony figured he'd better make the call while he was within range of a tower. Heading west of Walsenburg on U.S. 160, cell phone coverage, as he knew from experience, was most certainly not something to be relied on. He did notice that there were voicemail messages awaiting his attention, but decided to ignore them, at least for the time being.

He'd made the call to give Barnes, his grandfather's ranch foreman, a fairly decent estimate of his arrival time at the ranch. Tony had an excellent idea of how long it would take to drive from Walsenburg to Bayfield, even allowing a half hour and more for a sandwich, pie, and coffee at the Hungry Logger in South Fork, a stop that had become sort of a tradition when he and his grandfather had occasion to drive over that way. Years earlier, the two of them had decided that a slice of homemade pie in South Fork ought to be a part of any trip east from Bayfield.

His disinclination to talk to Marissa had not lessened since he arrived in Bayfield. Two full enjoyable days of starting to settle in to what he had, with some initial difficulty, begun to think of as *his* ranch caused Tony's attitude toward Marissa to mellow, but only just a little. Had it not, chances are he'd have thrown her two letters out of the window of the pickup.....unopened. Probably the only thing that kept him from doing so on the spur of the moment was his being unwilling to litter the Colorado countryside, especially with some things that had his address on them.

He put the two letters from Marissa back on the pile of mail. "Oh, hell!" he sighed. "I'll read them when I get back to the ranch, I guess. Either that or maybe just toss them out." He opened the driver's side door of the truck, but before he could get out of the truck, he heard a loud, strident noise coming from the Bank of Bayfield building at the north end of the shopping plaza parking lot.

"Damnation!" he exclaimed. "That's gotta be the bank alarm!"

Tony reacted strictly on instinct. He slid out of the truck and without talking his eyes off the bank building, reached under the driver's seat and grabbed the holster holding his Browning Hi-Power 9 mm. automatic pistol. He pulled the pistol out of the holster and worked the action to chamber a round. As he did so, two men, each holding revolvers in one hand and large cloth bags in the other, ran out of the bank. At the same time, a man wearing the uniform of a La Plata County deputy sheriff, pistol drawn, came running around the corner of the hardware store at the east end of the strip mall, perhaps a hundred and fifty feet east of where Tony was parked.

The bank robbers, or so Tony mentally tagged them, saw the deputy as he reached the corner of the convenience store adjoining the hardware store. Despite the distance, long for a pistol shot, one of them fired three shots at the deputy. Tony doubted that the shots were aimed. More than likely, the shooter was shooting to discourage any activity the deputy might have had in mind. One of those shots, if not more, obviously hit the law officer. *Lucky shot,* Tony thought.

Tony saw the deputy stagger backward, then fall flat on the parking lot. As the deputy fell, both robbers ran to a car parked near the bank, opened the two doors on the right side, and got in. As the two doors slammed shut, the driver put the vehicle in gear and stepped hard on the gas pedal. With a squeal of tires against pavement, and the large puff of dense black smoke that resulted, the robbers' car gained speed and headed toward the parking lot exit, Tony stepped around the back of his truck, dropped to one knee, and raised his weapon. As he did so, the man in the rear passenger seat of the car saw him, poked his revolver out the open car window, and fired at him.

Tony heard the bullet whiz over his head and smash through the plate glass window of the grocery store behind him, but neither the sound of the gunshot nor the sound of falling glass distracted him. Using both hands to steady his weapon and taking aim as best he could at the rapidly moving automobile, he fired five shots at the car, resisting the temptation to get all thirteen rounds in the pistol's magazine off because of the potential harm that might come from indiscriminately spraying lead all over the landscape. Tony's first shot shattered the car's rear window, and he heard the other four rounds hit either metal or glass, but without visible effect on the car or what little Tony could see of its occupants.

Gaining speed, and with tires still smoking and screaming in protest, the car sped out of the parking lot and turned east on highway 160, forcing an old pickup truck in to the ditch on the south side of the highway as it did so. By now, several people had come out of the grocery store. Tony turned to them. "Somebody call the sheriff's office," he shouted.

"Officer down! Bank robbers heading east on 160 in a blue Ford Taurus with New Mexico plates!" He stood, slipped his Browning in to the waistband at the back of his slacks, reached under the driver's seat of the truck to get the small first aid kit he habitually kept in any vehicle he owned, and ran across the parking lot toward where the deputy sheriff lay.

As he reached the deputy, Tony realized that the man was alive, wounded in the chest, but alive and moaning. "Captain Frye, Air Force," Tony said as he dropped to the pavement beside the wounded deputy. There was no answer other than moans of agony. Taking his Swiss Army knife from his pants pocket, Tony opened it and began cutting away the man's uniform shirt just as a girl came out of the convenience store and ran across the parking lot.

"I called a doctor and the sheriff's office," she called. "The doctor will be here in a couple of minutes. His office is less than a mile from here."

As she spoke, Tony heard the sound of sirens off in the distance. "Hang on, buddy," he said to the wounded man. "Help's on the way." The deputy didn't hear Tony's words. He had fainted, probably from a combination of shock and loss of blood. By this time he'd cut away the man's shirt and undershirt. "What a mess! Tony muttered. "At least it doesn't look like he took a hit in a vital spot. But I bet he's got a couple busted ribs, at least."

A few moments later, while Tony was still kneeling over the wounded man and trying to stop the bleeding, a sheriff's department Jeep Cherokee, siren blaring, pulled to a stop about thirty feet away. Two other Cherokees sped east on the main road. Tony heard car doors slam and then a gruff voice shouted, "Drop the knife, stand up and put your hands in the air! Then turn around real slow."

Tony let his knife fall to the pavement. Raising his hands high above his head, he slowly and awkwardly got to his feet. Then, very slowly, he turned to face the direction from which the command had come, finding himself staring down the barrel of an automatic pistol held by a very large officer wearing a La Plata County Sheriff's Department uniform. The man must have been close to six and a half feet tall, close to four inches taller than Tony. His brown hair was close-cropped and starting to go gray around the temples. Tony's initial reaction was that he'd met the man before, but with the stress of the moment, couldn't for the life of him immediately remember where or when.

"Identify yourself, mister," snarled the smaller of the two men in uniform, smaller but not considerably so, as he moved behind Tony and took his pistol from the belt where he'd stuck it a few moments before.

"Frye, Anthony, Captain, Air Force OSI," Tony called out, hands held high. *"Well, technically it's true,"* Tony thought. *"I'm still in a leave status for another three weeks, but technically I'm on active duty until my leave runs out and my transfer to the reserves officially takes effect."*

There was a somewhat pregnant pause lasting for perhaps as much as five seconds. "By God, I thought you looked familiar," laughed the larger of the two officers, holstering his weapon as he spoke. "Sam," he continued with a smile as he spoke to the other officer, "give the captain back his piece." Then he turned to Tony again, smiled, and held out his hand. "We met at old Pete's funeral. I'm Jack Matson, La Plata County sheriff."

By this time, there were a considerable number of people from the various businesses in the shopping complex gawking at Tony and the two law enforcement officers. Tony took the proffered hand and shook it. "Of course! Now I remember, Sheriff," he said. "I thought your face looked pretty familiar, too, but I don't remember you being in uniform at the funeral. You and your department sure were very helpful when Grandpa Pete's died." He took the firearm handed back to him by the other officer, who the sheriff introduced as Sam Culbertson, made sure the safety was in the 'on' position, stuck it in the waistband at the back of his slacks, then shook the deputy's hand, too.

As Tony spoke, there was a flurry of activity in the parking lot. A car stopped and a grey-haired man carrying a medical bag ran up to them. A few seconds later, the Pine River Rescue Service ambulance pulled up next to the doctor's car and two ambulance attendants jumped out. Tony and the two law officers moved aside so that the doctor and ambulance crew could treat the wounded deputy. A second Sheriff's Department vehicle pulled up, but before the driver could bring the vehicle to a complete stop, the sheriff waved it on with one hand, while pointing toward the bank with the other. The deputy driving the vehicle got the message and headed for the bank

After watching the doctor work for a few minutes, the sheriff spoke. "Doc, what kind of shape is Barry in?"

"He'll live, Sheriff," the doctor said without either looking up or stopping work, "absent unforeseen complications, but he's going to be out of action for a good long while. Right now it looks like at least broken three ribs and a collapsed lung. It'll take a good spell in surgery putting him back together, not to mention getting that lung inflated. You two," he said, pointing to the ambulance crew, "let's get him loaded and to the Durango hospital, pronto! First orders of business are to stop the bleeding and get this lung pumped back up. I'll ride in back with the patient."

"You take real good care of him, Doc," the sheriff said as the ambulance crew gently lifted the deputy on to a wheeled gurney. "He's a good man... good cop, too." Then, as the deputy was loaded in to the back of the ambulance, the sheriff turned back to Tony. "All right, son, what happened?"

Tony remembered a little of the sheriff's background from things he'd read in some of the newspaper articles his grandfather had sent to him. La Plata County's sheriff was a retired army lieutenant colonel who'd been awarded the Congressional Medal of Honor in Vietnam as an eighteen year old enlisted man, then earned a commission through college ROTC before returning to active duty and a career, first as a junior infantry officer and then in a variety of security and law enforcement positions. Quickly and precisely, Tony told what had happened. The telling took not much more than a minute.

When he finished, the sheriff said, "Well, that's just about what the man that called from the grocery store said, about the car heading east on 160, at least. Fortunately we had three units, including mine, at an accident site not too very far west of here, just this side of Gem Village to be exact. That's why we got here so fast." He looked at Tony for a moment, then asked, "You back here just for a visit or are you figuring on being here permanent, like?"

"Permanent, if I have it my way," Tony answered. "Got back a couple or three days ago and I'm still getting my pickup unloaded and settled in."

Matson paused for a moment, frowned, then continued, "You're carrying." It was a statement, not a question. "Got a concealed weapons permit? I hate to ask, but........."

"I'm still carried on OSI's active duty roster as being on terminal leave. I'll be on leave status for another three weeks or so," Tony answered. "Until my leave runs out......"

"Until your leave runs out and you're officially a civilian, you're a commissioned federal officer in a law enforcement position and most likely authorized to carry just about anything you want in the weapons department," Matson finished Tony's train of thought. "Short of tactical nukes, of course," the sheriff said with a slight smile, making a somewhat feeble attempt at humor. "Good," he said, smiling as he spoke. "I'd hate to have to rattle your cage even a tiny bit about carrying a concealed weapon. With the new laws and all, that's kinda legally discouraged, even out here in the wild, wild West."

The sheriff paused, smiled and put his right hand on Tony's left shoulder, then continued, "Matter of fact, come in to the office before your leave runs out and we'll do the paperwork to make it legal and get you a concealed weapons permit. Ought not to take more than five minutes. I don't see much chance of anyone expressing doubt about you being of good character, you being old Pete's grandson, and all that. Plus there's no doubt that a former military officer knows how to handle a firearm." He paused again, then said, "Heard a rumor yesterday that you'd decided to come back to Colorado. Old Pete'd be happy, I 'spect."

"Guess he would, at that," Tony replied, then changed the subject. "Sheriff, what do you figure the chances of catching those robbers?"

"Pretty good, I think," the sheriff answered after barely a second's thought. "On the way here, I radioed Archeluta County and they said they'd set up a roadblock at Chimney Rock. The sheriff over that way said he had a patrol car within a few miles of Chimney Rock and that he'd send out two or three other units. They most likely will have their road block set up well before the robbers can make it that far."

He went on to say, "Except for ranch roads, National Forest access roads, and a couple housing developments like that Elk Meadows development about six miles or so east of here on the south side of 160, there's no place between here and Chimney Rock to turn off, either, except to cut back past the Catholic church on the other side of the rise over there and head south toward Ignacio. If they try turning in to those housing developments off 160, they'll most likely have trouble with the locked gates."

"We can see the road past the church from here," Tony said. "I know they didn't go that way. They headed east on 160, no doubt of that."

The sheriff smiled. "And there sure ain't any safe place to cut off between here and where Archuleta's going to put up the roadblock. No road that leads anywhere, at least. Everything dead ends or peters out in to trails suitable for four wheel drive vehicles, horses or ATV's."

Matson paused and thought for a second. "Well, there is a turnoff at Lower Piedra," he said, "that'd eventually get you down to the Navajo recreation area, but there's a wash out about two hundred feet off the main road. Archeluta County has getting it on their to-fix list, but it ain't happened yet and won't even be started for a couple more weeks. Even with four wheel drive, like as not nobody can get past that washed out spot. A person would need a horse or an ATV to get past the washed out area.

"So the odds are good that they'll have to stay on the main road," Tony said,

Matson nodded his head affirmatively, then continued. "That's why I radioed dispatch to coordinate with the Ute Tribal Police on our way up from Gem Village. They'll set up a roadblock this side of Ignacio. And if Archeluta County doesn't stop them on U.S. 160, we'll just cover every side road between here and Chimney Rock. I figure they're pretty well boxed in".

He paused again and looked off in the direction the robbers had taken. "Like I said, they're all either ranch roads or National Forest access roads, except for a couple roads leading in to those residential developments, and those have security gates. If you don't know the gate combination, you can't get through the gate, short of crashing through it. It'll take a while to search every side road, if it comes to that, but if they're around here, we'll get them. Unless they somehow manage to make the Chimney Rock turnoff before Archuleta gets their roadblock set up, and the odds of that happening are damned slim without driving a car that can exceed the speed of sound. Those critters are pretty well boxed in, barring some sort of an unexpected miracle."

"I hope so," Tony said. "And when you find the car, you just might find some blood in it. Between the round I put through the rear window and the ones that hit the right side door and the back of the car, there's a small chance I just might have got a piece of at least one of them. I got five shots off and saw the first round shatter glass and heard the other four hit the car."

"Sure wouldn't be upset if you did," the sheriff muttered, getting in to his Cherokee. "I damn well hope so, too"! As soon as the door slammed shut, the deputy behind the wheel floored the gas pedal and the cruiser shot out of the parking lot, siren blaring and lights flashing, as it sped east on the main highway.

Tony walked back toward the grocery store. He stopped at his truck, opened the door, slid his Browning out of his waistband, and put it back in the holster, which he then slid back under the driver's seat. "Welcome home, Tony Frye," he muttered wryly. "Nothing like a nice quiet morning in a sleepy little Colorado town. I'm home for not much more than three days and look what happens. Maybe I should have stayed in Washington!" He closed and locked the truck's door, then headed toward the entrance to the grocery store.

A good bit less than half an hour later, his grocery shopping completed with only a limited amount of success, Tony drove north on county 501. He chuckled as he drove around the traffic circle that some of the local politicians, the prime instigator of which happened to be a female who his grandfather had once accurately, but somewhat less than charitably, described as being "totally clueless", had insisted on putting in on the road. According to his grandfather, that chief instigator for the building of the rotary insisted it be of a certain size.....too small for large trucks to negotiate. So tractor-trailer drivers just drove across the grass in the center of the rotary as if it weren't there, cheerfully doing considerable damage to the grass as they did so.

A few minutes later, he turned off county 501 in to the chokecherry tree lined lane leading toward the Pine River and the Diamond F ranch buildings, including his grandfather's sprawling house, his house ever since his grandfather had dropped dead from a massive heart attack in the terminal building of the La Plata County Airport the previous October. He decided he'd make lunch first, then deal with the letters from Marissa Montgomery. He wasn't looking forward to having to contend with her bickering and her demands that he drop everything and return to Washington. But he was looking forward to the pumpernickel bread, kosher style dill pickles, domestic liverwurst, horseradish sauce, and Swiss cheese he'd managed to buy at the grocery store. Real gourmet sandwich fixing's they weren't, a fact that Tony was well aware of, but right now, they were a welcome and more than an acceptable substitute for what he'd eaten the past few of days. Tony planned on really enjoying his lunch.

****

***

The car slowed as it turned off the forest service trail. A few hundred feet into the woods, and a good half mile off the main highway, it stopped. The driver and back seat passenger opened their doors, got out, and stood, looking around as if they expected to see something in particular. After a few moments, a small man dressed in camouflage and carrying a pistol stood up from where he'd been hiding.

"What the hell happened?" the small man asked, looking at the missing rear window and the obvious bullet holes on the car's right-hand body, as he walked downhill to the car and the two men.

"Got shot up some pulling out of the parking lot," the driver, a beefy man with close-cropped brown hair, said. "There was a deputy around the corner somewhere. Buford or Jim Bob, one or the other, dropped him. Then as we were heading out of the parking lot, someone opened up on us with a pistol."

"Yeah," the somewhat older appearing man who'd been riding in the rear seat said as he hauled two bank bags out of the car. "He shot out the back window and got a couple hits on the car's body. The bullet that came through the rear window hit Jim Bob in the head and must have only missed me by a couple inches. Damn, blood and brains went everywhere! The inside of the car's a mess."

The short man peered through the right front window of the car. "Looks like ol' Jim Bob's had it, all right. And I'd say he got hit twice, not once. Gawd almighty! There's blood all over in there! He's dead for sure."

"Sure is," the driver replied, peeling the rubber gloves off his hands. "I stopped and checked his pulse just after we turned off the highway. Nothing."

"Were you followed?" the small man asked. "Anybody see you pull off the highway?"

"Naw," the driver replied. "I told you we'd pull it off OK, Mike. Nobody followed us and there was nobody in sight when we pulled off the main road on to the forest service road."

"What about fingerprints?" Mike, asked.

Buford answered, "Why do you think we wore these rubber gloves, just like we planned. He held up the pair he'd just pulled off so Mike could see them, then put them in his pocket. "I don't think there's a single print of any of us in the car." He hefted one of the bags, which, from the way he lifted it was obviously heavy. "Better get out of here, though. Where's the horses?"

"About two hundred feet from here," Mike answered. "In ten minutes we'll be out of here."

"Good," the man who'd driven the car said, taking the gas cap off and stuffing a rag down the filler pipe. He pulled a pack of matches out of his pocket. "I'll take care of the car and Jim Bob."

"Holy....!" Mike exclaimed. "Cletus, don't do that! If you torch that car, it'll just attract attention. We don't need that, man! It'll take the fuzz a while to find the car. By the time they do, we're going to be long gone. Don't need to give the cops any help. Don't need to start a forest fire either."

The man addressed as Cletus stopped. Then he put the matches back in his pocket. "You're right, Mike," he said, picking up the second bag. "If nobody saw us turn off the road, we sure don't want to advertise where we are. Don't matter how many cops come out searching for us, it'll take a while before the find the car up here. With a few hours head start, nobody'll find us."

"Unless they get damn lucky. Any way the cops can connect us with Jim Bob?" Mike asked.

"Don't think so," Buford answered. "He said he was clean. No criminal record, as far as I know. And he said he'd never been fingerprinted."

The three men headed up the hill. Buford and Cletus each carried a heavy bag. Mike followed, walking backwards and using a pine bough to wipe out any sign of their footprints.

CHAPTER TWO

A little before four that afternoon, as he sat in the large kitchen of his ranch house, Tony was listening to the news on the Durango radio station. He still hadn't opened the letters from Marissa Montgomery. In fact, they were still in the glove box of the pickup, along with his cell phone and he was considering consigning them, the letters, that is, to the trash without opening them. The cell phone, of course, wouldn't end up in the trash.

The feature story on the news broadcast was about the bank robbery, of course, and Tony's name was briefly mentioned, but the broadcast didn't give any new information. He'd spent a couple hours after lunch bringing in from his truck more of the things he'd brought west from Washington and then unpacking several more boxes of assorted odd and ends and finding places in the house to put things.

Carrying the heavier boxes, especially those filled with books, resulted in some huffing and puffing. Tony smiled at his own discomfort, remembering once again that, after being away for a spell, he'd always had a little trouble adjusting to the thin air at the ranch's altitude of well over six thousand feet above sea level. "Big difference from Washington," he muttered." I guess I'm glad I skimped on running again these last few mornings. Need to start working back up to the three mile mark soon, I guess." His clothing and personal effects went to the master bedroom, the bedroom where his grandfather had slept. Books and other items went in the den or the living room.

Mary Barnes, Lew's wife, who had served as his grandfather's housekeeper and occasional cook for as long as Tony could remember and who had more than once been jokingly accused of looking on Tony as the grandson she'd never had, had moved his grandfather's personal effects from the master bedroom to one of the smaller bedrooms. Tony knew that eventually he'd have to go through Grandpa Pete's clothes and other things and decide what to keep and what to throw out, or most likely give to Good Will or the Salvation Army, but that chore could wait until a lot of other things were taken care of. At first, Tony thought of keeping the bedroom he'd always used when he lived on the ranch, but Mary Barnes convinced him that his grandfather would have wanted him to use the master bedroom, with its king size bed, huge walk-in closet, and attached, well-appointed master bath.

Once he'd unloaded a bit more of the pickup and put a few things away, Tony made another pot of coffee, decaf this time, then sat down at the kitchen table to take care of unfinished business. He'd fired about a third of a clip of bullets from his Browning 9 mm earlier in the day. Now it was time to clean the weapon. Firing a weapon and then putting it away without cleaning it went against everything Tony had learned from his grandfather about caring for firearms. Grandpa Pete had been a fanatic about the subject; Tony had learned the lesson well. Cleaning any weapon that had been fired, by Grandpa Pete's rules, was a task that shouldn't be put off any longer than absolutely necessary.

Any firearm got stripped and cleaned the day it was fired; no exceptions! Any firearm that was touched got wiped down with a silicone-impregnated cloth before being put away, again no exceptions. The rule was to leave no fingerprints. Acid from human hands could literally etch fingerprints in to the blued metal of a firearm.

Later, say in a day or two, Tony reminded himself once again, he'd have to give serious thought to sorting through his grandfather's things. Old Pete's clothes, a lot of them at least, had already been given to the Salvation Army. What should be done with Grandpa Pete's tux and dinner jackets was another consideration. Tony also needed to get in to town to see his grandfather's lawyer and visit a few banks, but those chores, or most of them, would have to be put off until the following week, after the holiday weekend. Right now, cleaning his pistol and getting settled in to living on the ranch again was Tony's top priority.

Tony had just finished putting a patch coated with Hoppe's cleaning solvent through the bore of his pistol when he heard a knock at the door. Laying the pistol on the newspaper he'd placed on the kitchen table, he stood, walked across the kitchen and through the dining room into the living room. Through the large glass window of the front door, he saw the bulk of a large man in uniform and instantly recognized the sheriff. He opened the door and said, "Come in, Sheriff."

"Afternoon, Captain," the sheriff responded as he crossed the doorsill into the living room. He looked around the room, taking in the furniture and the several pictures handing on the pine paneled walls, one of which was a Charlie Russell original worth a small fortune. "Well, this hasn't changed since I was here last, Captain."

"Drop the 'Captain'," Tony said. "The name's Tony, Sheriff, and there's coffee in the kitchen if you're thirsty. It's even more or less fresh."

The sheriff smiled. "God, I'd just about kill for a cup of coffee, fresh or otherwise, Tony! Lead me to it. It's been a damn long day."

Tony led the way to the kitchen, motioned the sheriff to a chair, cleared the pistol and cleaning supplies from the table, got two mugs from the cupboard, and poured coffee into them. "It's decaf," he explained. "I try not to drink high test after noontime.....it sometimes makes it hard for me to fall asleep. Cream and sugar?" he asked as he poured. "And I'm assuming you're here about this morning rather than socially. Did you catch them?"

"Just sugar, thanks, and you're right about why I want to see you. Well, sort of." He hesitated a moment "Truth is, I came to ask a favor," the sheriff said, picking up a spoon and then reaching first for the coffee and then for the sugar bowl Tony had placed in front of him. Matson hesitated again before he continued. "I talked to General Carpenter on the phone a couple hours ago. He told me you're a damn good man, and that he hated to lose you. He also said for me to remind you that you can have your job and your regular commission back any time you want them."

"Yeah," Tony said. "He told me that, too, about a week or two ago, the day I before I signed out on terminal leave. Thanks, but I'm realizing I never did really care for living in Washington. Too damned much traffic, for one thing; too many bleeding-heart liberals for another." He paused for a second, then continued, "Liked the work, though. Most of the time it was real interesting, even the paper-pushing part." Tony stopped for a second, then continued. "So how do you happen to know the general I used to work for?"

"I don't, actually," the sheriff replied, "but I do know his opposite number in Army Security. Worked under him, actually, when I was a brown bar and he was a brand new captain. So I called Mike Stevens, told him what I wanted, and he got your former boss on the horn. From what General Carpenter says, you walk six inches above the water."

The sheriff stopped speaking for a second, put his coffee mug down, then he continued, "By the way, you were right about getting a piece of one of those guys. You got a piece, all right, a real big piece. We found the car on a National Forest road about two miles off 160, and that took a good bit of searching, I can tell you. You called it spot on when you said you hit the car five times. One through the window and four more in metal. Darned good shooting, considering. The round you put through the back window apparently caught the guy in the right front seat in the head. One of the rounds that went through the door may have done the same thing.....we'll know more after the autopsy. He bled out all over the seat and....., "Matson paused briefly before going on. "Well, let's just say it was quite a mess! That stolen car's sure gonna need a damned good cleaning, not to mention some body work."

Tony frowned. "Oh!" he said softly. He sat quietly, lost in thought for a second.

"First time you ever killed someone, son?" the sheriff asked, concern heavy in his voice.

"No, the second time, actually," Tony answered. "I didn't much like it the first time, either. Actually, I hated it. I would have rather taken the man in alive, but he got stupid and pulled a gun. I didn't have much choice but to take him down, but there was nothing' written in stone that said I had to enjoy it, either." Tony poured a little more coffee into their cups, if for no other reason than to give him a chance to get control of his emotions. When he'd settled down, he continued, intent on changing the topic, "Sheriff, you said something about a favor. What is it that you need?"

"What I'm going to ask you is really what I called Washington about. My department's in kind of a bind," he said. "I already had one deputy slot unfilled, another out with a busted leg, and now Barry Morgan's out of action for at least three months, and probably more. I'm shorthanded, three deputy positions vacant for one reason or another and people due to take their summer vacations, which I can't refuse, according to the contract. God's honest truth is that I'm between a rock and a really hard place."

Matson frowned, pulled his left earlobe, and then continued. "And even when I'm at full strength, the department is a good half dozen patrol deputies under what we realistically need to do a decent job of covering the county, and that's because of budget cuts. I can't cut personnel at the jail and the judges have given me a hard time about cutting deputies working as process servers and such. So I've had to cut patrol and investigations just about to the bone. This bank robbery is just going to make things worse."

Matson pulled his other earlobe. "Knowing you were with OSI, I checked you out, then I spoke to the county commissioners. I asked if I could offer you a job, on a temporary basis. Considering the way things are going right now and with the bank robbery added to my list of headaches, they couldn't very well refuse that request."

"Good God!" Tony exclaimed, putting his mug down on the table. "I wouldn't have the faintest idea of how to be a deputy sheriff."

"Son, you react like a cop." the sheriff responded. "This morning proved that. You're also an experienced criminal investigator, and right now that's what I really need more than anything else in the world....'cept maybe a bigger department budget and a bigger staff, of course. Those two things are right up at the top of my Christmas wish list."

The sheriff took another sip of coffee, then went on. "You're not a dude, and I suspect you probably know La Plata County fairly well, considering you spent one whole lot of time here as a kid, according to the things your grandpa said about you. More important, your old boss said you've got a good head for contingency planning and that you're real good at thinking outside the box."

He continued, "And I'm going to need all the help I can get. The Bureau should be working this case, seeing that bank robbery is a federal crime, but they won't touch it, except for talking to the folks who were in the bank when it was robbed, playing with their computer data resources, and looking at security camera film, unless somebody with a lot of political pull puts a gun to their heads."

"Why not?" Tony asked.

The sheriff hesitated for a few seconds before answering Tony's question. "A while back there was a case over in Montezuma County involving three crazy survivalists and a stolen water truck. A Cortez town officer got killed. "You hear anything of that?"

Tony thought for a moment. "Yeah, I remember something about that," he said. "Granddad sent me the clippings from the paper. It even made the news back in D.C., both TV and newspapers," Tony said. "The Bureau didn't earn any brownie points with that mess, as I remember."

"The Bureau screwed the pooch so badly on that case that no federal agent with half a brain and a desire to retire with a federal pension is going to touch anything that looks even remotely like it, at least not out here in sagebrush and canyon country. Mountain country, too, for that matter," he said.

"Officially, due to 'higher priority cases and a manpower shortage on the Federal level in the local area', as the man said, my office has been asked to work the case. The Bureau promises what they call 'all possible assistance and cooperation,' but I'm not going to hold my breath. Just between you and me and the lamppost, I suspect there isn't a FBI office within five hundred miles, and maybe even more, that would risk having its staff being involved in another potential screw-up like that Cortez mess." Matson hesitated a second, "I could call in the Colorado Bureau of Investigation, but it's something I really want to avoid, if possible."

The sheriff took another sip of coffee, then continued. ""At least Carl Herrin, the local SAC, is a pretty good guy. He's real close to retirement, though, a matter of a few weeks, and knows his department's limitations, one of which is that he and his six or ten agents, more or less, are city folk and tend to get lost when they get more that fifty feet away from paved streets and sidewalks, and that's on a good day. On a bad day, one or two of them, the new hires, probably need guide dogs to get across the Denny's parking lot from where they've parked to the restaurant's front door. I don't think Herrin would give us the shaft, at least seeing that he's heading for retirement in a few weeks. But most of the higher-ups in the Denver and Santa Fe offices would cheat their own mothers out of credit for solving a major case, or even a minor one, for that matter."

Matson sighed, took another sip of coffee, and then continued again, "About the job. I won't push for an answer right now. Think it over some before you make a decision." The sheriff pulled a business card and a pen from his shirt pocket and wrote something on it. "Here's my home and office numbers. Think about it, then let me know, one way or the other, by tomorrow morning, if possible. To be real honest, the department's really in a bind. I could use your help, for sure."

He stood, pushed back his chair, and walked to the kitchen sink and rinsed out his cup. When he finished, he took two steps toward the front of the house, then turned. "Thanks for the coffee, Tony. It's nice to see signs of life in Pete's house again."

The sheriff stopped again. Pointing a finger toward the jade and ivory chess set on a small table in the corner of the large kitchen, he continued, "By the way, Pete said you played a pretty decent game. Whenever you feel up to it, I play well enough to have given your grandfather some halfway decent competition, I think." He paused, then said, "And, like I said, if possible, I'd appreciate it if you could make a decision by tomorrow morning, considering the job offer, that is, not playing chess. I really need a trained investigator and I need one as of yesterday."

Tony walked the sheriff to the door. Neither said anything else. Tony stood in the doorway and watched the sheriff get into his Jeep Cherokee and drive up the driveway. Then he turned and slammed his fist against the door jamb before closing the door. "Son of a bitch!" he swore. "I don't need this. I *really* don't need this!"

Tony was miserable the rest of that afternoon and on in to the evening. He couldn't get the sheriff's job offer out of his mind. It was an offer that, in some ways, he didn't want to take. But in other ways, he really didn't mind the idea of being a working cop again, at least not for a while, if he could work it in with running the ranch. Truth be known, Tony enjoyed investigative work. But his job with OSI had been one of the several bones of contention, and a very large one at that, between him and Marissa Montgomery. She tolerated Tony's work only because Tony was politically and socially well-connected through his father and stepmother. She was really impressed that his stepmother, as Tony had been known to say on many occasions, had more money than God.

Her father, who sat as a member of the House Armed Services Subcommittee, had frequently told him to leave the military and get a meaningful job. When he decided to leave the service to take up running the ranch, Marissa had assumed, at the worst, that he would be a gentleman rancher, one who would spend much of his time in the big city, either Washington or Philadelphia, where he could be an asset to her daddy's next reelection campaign as well as taking an active part in Washington's social scene. And she was overjoyed that Tony was giving up what she called "pig work."

What Tony hadn't told her until the night before he left Washington was that he had no intention of being a gentleman rancher. He wanted to delay breaking this news as long as humanly possible. When he decided to leave the Air Force, it was with the intention of being a dirty-hands, run-your-own-spread rancher. Before he retired, Grandpa Pete had been a highly respected petroleum geologist and even in retirement had sat on the boards of several major corporations. He'd been comfortable in bow tie and tails at a variety of social functions, but even more at home in blue jeans and scuffed, down-at-the-heels riding boots. Wealth hadn't kept him from rounding up his own cattle, making his own hay, and mucking out his barns with a pitchfork.

Tony had learned ranching from his grandfather. Grandpa Pete's way had been the hard, dirty-hands way, and Tony intended to follow in his grandfather's footsteps. He intended to be a working rancher rather than a "gentleman" who let someone else do the dirty work and didn't get blisters or calluses on his own hands. Truth was, Tony enjoyed ranch life and the hard work that went along with it. A hard day's ranch work made him sleep well. There wasn't much, if anything, in the way of ranch-type jobs that he couldn't handle and handle pretty darned well, if truth be told. The one exception to this was putting shoes on horses. That chore was hired out.

In his heart, he knew what this meant. Marissa would dump him immediately, once she found out for sure that he intended to stay in Colorado and be a working rancher. Marissa Montgomery was a product of Capitol Hill and Philadelphia's Main Line. Five years of working in her father's congressional office made her even more of a big city, high society woman. "Just like my stepmother," Tony mused. "The kind of woman who can ruin a good man."

Unfortunately, Tony also thought of Marissa as being the kind of woman who could make a man enjoy being ruined, at least up to a certain point. She'd often spoken of the two of them getting married and then running for congress from two adjoining Pennsylvania congressional districts and making history by doing so. At first, Tony thought she was joking; after a while, he realized that she was quite serious. And then came to the realization that marriage to Marissa Montgomery, or anyone like her, would be a very big mistake.

Because of this, and for a variety of other reasons, he still hadn't opened the two letters from Marissa. Being a politician, especially a member of Congress, was right down at the bottom of his career goals, somewhere slightly south of being a cat burglar. He wanted to do what he thought of as honest work. Besides, Marissa and her father were staunch liberal Democrats, a good bit too liberal on many social issues; Tony strongly favored the opposite political persuasion; that, too, was a product of his western Colorado upbringing, coupled with his years in uniform.

The hell of it was that Tony really had enjoyed his Air Force job; he enjoyed the mental challenge of criminal investigation. The work was interesting, and his superiors thought he was good at it, to the point that he was fast-tracked for major as soon as he completed Squadron Officers' School and had the bare minimum time in grade required for promotion. When he returned to Washington from Grandpa Pete's funeral, General Carpenter told him this, and more.

The general had told him that he could reasonably expect to spend most of his career in the OSI or in other security and/or intelligence assignments, except for one or two career-broadening assignments, probably in the administrative or personnel fields, and that he could also reasonable expect to retire with at least one star, if not more, despite not being rated as a pilot. The general, Tony realized, was, to put it in police terms, acting as Tony's rabbi; grooming him for bigger and better things.

Tony knew that much of this was because of his family connections; he also knew his boss wouldn't bullshit him; at least he didn't think so. He further knew the general did not want to see him leave the military. In addition, he knew that Marissa would possibly consider having a potential general as a husband as maybe a somewhat acceptable alternate to being married to a congressman.

But that star on his shoulder, or maybe even two stars, would have been a long time in the future. Marissa wasn't a patient person. And, he admitted to himself, being married to the daughter of a member of the House Armed Services Subcommittee might well enhance his career prospects. Then he had second thoughts about that; the notation *Political Influence* on one's personnel jacket was not always a career enhancement, especially when the person with the influence tended to be a pushy loud mouthed individual, as was the case with Marissa's father. Add to this that marriage to Marissa would certainly have its unpleasant aspects and.....................

The whole situation angered Tony. He always intended to rise or fall in the Air Force on his own merits. On the other hand, Marissa was a lovely, bright, talented woman, and Tony was, or at least had been for quite some time, enchanted with her. "The only problem," Tony muttered to himself as he pitched old straw out of a stall in the horse barn, "is that I'm not really sure if I care for her or whether I've been overwhelmed by the way she fits in to the D.C. social whirl. She really can't abide the things I think are important, and the things that are important to her really don't turn me on. And she's a first class bitch when she's crossed."

Tony's decision to actually *work* his ranch would jeopardize his relationship with Marissa. If he went back to "pig work", to use Marissa's terminology for police work, even for a limited period of time, Marissa might totally terminate their relationship. He'd still not opened the two letters she'd sent, partly because he didn't want to be subjected to more demands that he return to Washington and partly because he feared that he'd learn that she really was terminating their relationship. He didn't want her trying to manage his life but he was infatuated with her to the point that he really wasn't totally sure that he was willing to lose her. There was a bit of doubt, but more than anything else, Tony was pretty well ready to ditch Marissa and cut his losses.

"Damn"! Tony swore, for perhaps the fifteenth time since Sheriff Matson unloaded the request on him. Tony had decided not to cook his own dinner. Instead, he drove up to Vallecito Reservoir and ate at the Lakeshore restaurant. He'd always enjoyed the food there, but tonight's steak dinner just didn't seem to taste right, something that Tony knew was because he was torn between doing two things, both of which he enjoyed. Then, too, he had to consider the matter of Marissa Montgomery. That issue could not be ignored forever.

. After finishing his meal, he drove back to the ranch, where, despite making a valiant effort, he just could not get involved in the ranch paperwork he needed to tend to. Finally, an hour or so after getting back from dinner, he left the living room of the ranch house and stepped out on to the wide covered porch that ran around three sides of the building. He walked around to the west side, the side facing the Pine River, sat down in one of the old rocking chairs that had been on the porch for as long as he could remember, after first removing a small stray yellow and white cat, really not much more than a large kitten, from the chair, and lit a cigarette.

The kitten, displaying no resentment at being evicted from its seat in the chair, jumped up in Tony's lap, curled up, and began to purr. Tony scratched the cat between its ears, noticing as he did that it had on a worn-looking flea collar. Scratching it between its ears caused the critter to purr all the louder. He sighed, reconciling himself to the probability that he was being adopted, something that really did not distress him, though, as he had a long-standing fondness for cats. Besides, he thought, there are always mice around farms and ranches. A cat can earn its keep by providing rodent extermination services. There were already a couple cats hanging around the barn.....strictly barn cats, feral and skittish as all get out. But they earned their keep. Always had been cats around the barn, he remembered, so why not have one as a house guest?

He glanced at the evening sky, as much as he could see of it above the steep, high hills on the far side of the river. At this hour, there was only a slight tinge of pink remaining from the sunset. As he rested, he noticed that there was a build-up of heavy, dark clouds off to the southwest. "Might be some rain later tonight", he muttered as he made himself comfortable in what he thought of as his grandfather's favorite chair, "we could sure use some rain."

Without being really conscious of it, Tony heard the gentle sound the Pine River made as it flowed south from Vallecito Reservoir to where it would eventually flow in to the Colorado River and then on to the Gulf of Lower California and the soft noises made by night insects, birds, and bats flying around the house and yard. Nor was he really conscious of the noise made by the occasional car or truck passing on County 501. Tony was wrapped up in his thoughts, trying to come to a decision. Two and a half cigarettes later, Tony had the answer to the question that had been bugging him. He knew what he had to do.

He stood quickly, causing the cat to fall to the porch floor, ground the last half of his third cigarette out in the ash tray that sat on the porch railing, opened the door and walked in to the living room. The kitten followed, head-bumping Tony's leg when he stopped at the desk upon which a telephone rested. Taking the phone in hand, he picked up the sheriff's business card, looked at it, and dialed the sheriff's home phone number. On the third ring, he heard a click as the phone was picked up, followed by a voice.

"Matson residence. Jill speaking."

"May I speak with the sheriff, please," Tony replied.

"May I ask who is calling?" the voice on the other end responded pleasantly.

"Certainly, Mrs. Matson. This is Tony Frye. The sheriff asked me to call."

"Oh, hi, Mr. Frye. Daddy's been sort of expecting you to call. And, by the way, that's *Miss* Matson. Hang on while I get him."

Tony heard a click as the phone was put down. *Wow! Nice voice*, he thought. *Wonder what the rest of her is like?* He didn't have enough time to form a mental image that was anything more than a blur before the sheriff picked up the phone.

"Hey, Tony," the sheriff said as he picked up the phone. "I kind of expected to hear from you this evening. I'm betting you're calling to take me up on that job offer."

"I didn't make a decision until less than three minutes ago. What made you so sure you'd con me in to working for you, Sheriff?" Tony asked, slipping the sheriff's business card under the phone for future reference.

"Simple," the sheriff answered. "Knee-jerk reaction. You've been an investigator too long. That's one thing. The other thing is that you already got yourself involved yesterday when you shot up that getaway car."

"Now what in heck does that have to do with it?" Tony asked.

"Just something Pete once told me about you. He said that when you start something, you never liked to put it down until you finished it." The sheriff chuckled. "Get a good night's sleep and meet me at my office first thing in the morning. Things have shifted around a bit since you moved away from here to go to the Academy. The new jail and sheriff's office are now on Turner Drive, in the Bodo industrial park area, between Carbon Junction and downtown. I assume you know where Bodo is"?

"Yep", he answered, "unless it's been moved, too. I haven't been away *that* long!"

"Good", the sheriff replied with a chuckle. "See you at eight, Tony. This time I'll make the coffee. Once you're sworn in, I'll go over ever thing we have on this sorry mess, most of which we've withheld from the press. Hell, I haven't told the newshounds we've found the car and a body yet." Matson paused briefly before concluding the conversation. "Don't know how much longer we can keep that hushed up, though. See you in the morning. 'Night." The phone clicked as the sheriff, apparently having nothing more to contribute to the conversation, hung up.

"Good night," Tony said, as the phone line went dead. Once he'd made his decision and had made the phone call that went with it, Tony realized that he was exhausted. It had been a long day. After putting the cat back outside, he turned out the lights in the living room and kitchen after locking the doors, went to his bedroom, and prepared to turn in for the night. He thought for a moment, then giving in to the inevitable, resolved to buy a litter box, litter, a supply of cat food, and a package of fresh flea collars the next day. Truth be told, Tony liked having a cat around the ranch house and didn't object to being adopted by this one. His grandfather often referred to housecats as four footed, fur-covered 'rodent control agents'. They tended to earn their room and board. Besides, they tended to be affectionate. There was something soul-satisfying about petting a lap full of purring cat. After undressing, he brushed his teeth and turned in for the night.

The good night's sleep the sheriff had wished him failed to materialize. Tony spent much of the night tossing and turning, due largely to a succession of dreams, some of which involved shooting at moving cars and the rest of which involved an irate and overtly hostile Marissa Montgomery or a succession of hundreds of barn cats with bad attitudes invading every room of the ranch house. Only toward morning did he slept soundly, dreaming of the voice of Jill Matson. It was the only really pleasant dream of the entire night.

****

***

Cletus poured a second cup of coffee and lit a cigarette. He stretched his legs, which were still stiff from having spent most of the day in the saddle. After taking a puff on the cigarette, he spoke. "Mike, are you real sure it's safe to have a fire? Won't somebody in one of the fire towers spot it?"

"Don't sweat it, man," Mike replied, pushing his hat off his face and rolling onto his right side to face Cletus. "The wood's dry as a bone and won't smoke hardly at all. Sure not enough to be spotted. There's no fire tower anywhere near here. It's pretty dark so even if somebody in a fire tower is looking this way, it's too dark to see the smoke. I wouldn't risk a fire in the daytime, though, not even a small one."

Buford walked out of the deeper darkness of the woods and approached the fire. "Mike's right, Cletus. I was about a hundred feet back in the woods and couldn't see a thing." He paused. "But I sure could smell the smoke. Bet anybody within a half mile could smell it, too."

Mike grinned. "Bufe, chances are there's nobody within a good five miles of here, and probably more. It's springtime. And it's a little too early for a lot of campers and fishermen. That'll change this weekend, though. The odds of running in to anyone out here are damn slim. That's why we pulled this off now. My sister and brother-in-law planned it this way. It wouldn't work in the fall, though," he mused, "too many hunters."

"How much you figure we got?" Cletus asked, changing the subject.

"Don't know," Mike answered. "We'll count it when we're back at the guest ranch. But from the heft of those bags," he continued, "I bet we can afford to buy a lot of firepower."

"Hot damn!" Buford exclaimed. "We get us some automatic weapons and those government bastards'll sit up and pay attention!"

"They'll be put in storage until the time's ripe for the movement to act, Bufe," Cletus said. Militia ain't going to risk acting too soon, and we won't risk using a lot of firepower hitting banks, that's fer sure. The idea's to get the money, then buy the weapons, and eventually....."

Mike finished the sentence for him. "...eventually to set up our own free country here in the San Juans without all the silly ass regulations those bastards in Washington keep laying on us."

CHAPTER THREE

Durango, though far from being a major city, is the largest of the communities in southwestern Colorado. The heart of the downtown area, the business district, is some six thousand feet above sea level. It is bisected by the Animas River and sits at the south end of a longish stretch of flat land hemmed in by mountains on the north, east, and west sides, and just north of a narrow gorge between Smelter Mountain and Florida Mesa. The river, and until they were torn up in the mid-1900's the Denver and Rio Grande Railroad's lines from Durango south to Farmington, New Mexico, and east to Antonito, just a few miles on the Colorado side of the Colorado/New Mexico border, ran through the gorge, diverging there; one heading east and the other south. Both of Durango's main highways merge into a single road here, heading toward the city from the south and east along the hillside above the river.

In the vicinity of Carbon Junction, where the old Denver & Rio Grande tracks heading toward Denver once diverged from what had been the branch line running south to Farmington, New Mexico, the highway passes both the new Walmart shopping complex and the older Durango Mall on the other side of the highway, and runs past a goodly number of other commercial establishments as well, including those in the Bodo Industrial Park, where the La Plata County Sheriff's office is located.

At just after half past seven the following morning, Tony was parked in a visitor's parking spot in front of the La Plata County sheriff's office, roughly two miles south and east of downtown Durango. Still somewhat bleary-eyed from having had less than a comfortable night's sleep, he finishing the dregs of a cup of bad convenience store coffee, making a wry face at the bad taste, and, rationalizing that bad coffee was just barely better than no coffee at all, watched the rays of the morning sun creep down the side of Smelter Mountain.

The few puddles of water left from the night's brief rainfall would soon be gone, he thought. From the KREZ-TV mobile news unit parked in the spot next to him, plus the crowd of people standing near the walkway leading up to the front entrance of the sheriff's office, he guessed that word of the finding of the getaway car, and probably of the dead body in it, had managed to leak out. Parked as he was, Tony had the driveway entrance visible in his rearview mirror, and when what he tentatively identified as the sheriff's Jeep Cherokee turned in to the parking lot, Tony got out of his truck, closed and locked the door, and casually walked through the mass of waiting newshounds [as he'd mentally tagged them] to the front door of the building. Opening the door, he stepped into the lobby of the sheriff's office and walked to the counter. A motherly-looking woman, her salt and pepper hair pulled back and fastened in a bun, sat at a desk behind the counter, talking on the phone.

When the woman finished her call, she turned to Tony. He said, "Tony Frye, here for an appointment with Sheriff Matson. From the looks of things out front, he might be a while. I suspect he's being bushwhacked by the media."

"That was him on the phone, Mr. Frye, calling from his car phone. He told me to take you in to his office, make you comfortable, and get you a cup of coffee. If you'll follow me...."

The matron walked to the end of the counter and lifted a hinged gate, allowing Tony to pass through. She led him down a corridor and through a door in to what obviously was the sheriff's office. As she walked over to the coffee pot on the low table near the wall, she said, "Have a seat, Mr. Frye. Sheriff Matson'll be in just as soon as he can brush off those reporters that have been lying in ambush for the last half hour and more.

"By the way," the woman said with a smile, "I'm Maggie Miller. I'm the sheriff's coffee maker, secretary, chief dispatcher, and occasional female matron, at least when there's no female deputy handy and we need to do a search of a female suspect. From what he was saying on the phone yesterday, I've got a hunch you're going to be joining us, at least for a while, from what Jack said." By the time she'd finished this speech, she had a cup of coffee poured for Tony. "Cream and sugar?" she asked, handing him the cup.

"Just sugar, please, Mrs. Miller," Tony answered, "or diet sweetener, and thank you." He took the proffered cup and the two packets of sugar. "The sheriff's asked me to fill in, on a temporary basis, for a little while. Told him I'd consider it."

"Well," she said, "we could sure use the help. I guess the boss told you we're already short-handed, and now with Barry out...," her voice trailed off. "Anyhow, like I said, we sure could use the help." She gave him a motherly pat of his right shoulder and continued, "Now you sit here and relax until the boss gets in. I've got to get back to work. And the name's Maggie. Mrs. Miller was my mother. Nice meeting you, Mr. Frye." She paused slightly, then went on. "Oh, by the way, I knew your grandfather. Knew him pretty well, as a matter of fact." She turned, and walked into the corridor, shutting the office door behind her.

Is there anyone in La Plata County who didn't know Grandpa Pete, Tony wondered. He sat and sipped his coffee, which was considerably better than the cup he'd just finished in his truck, looking around the office as he did so. One of the first things he noticed was a cluster of framed certificates hanging on the wall directly across from him. He stood, and walked over to the wall so he could examine them up close. Two of them he recognized, course completion certificates from FBI courses that he, too, had attended, though not at the same time the sheriff attended them. A foot or so from the certificates was a framed and autographed photograph of the sheriff, considerably younger and in military uniform. The picture showed him shaking hands with a former U.S. President and one-time navy pilot.

"That's right," Tony muttered under his breath, "I remember reading somewhere that Sheriff Matson did duty escorting the President a couple of times." Tony then muttered aloud, "And I've got to ask him how he knew Grandpa Pete. They had to know each other fairly well. Gramps didn't play chess with just anyone."

The office door opened just as Tony finished his musing, and the sheriff walked in. "Good, I'm glad you're here. And you can be thankful you got inside before that gaggle of reporters realized just who you are. I thought the gal from the Durango *Herald* would never shut up! I finally just walked away from her.....guess I pissed her off, too, from the language she used." He paused, then went on, thoughtfully, "Women really shouldn't talk like that." Matson said, holding his hand out for Tony to shake. "It ain't lady-like."

"The coffee's ready. But then it always is," he continued. "Maggie's kind of our departmental den mother. She sort of spoils me." He walked to the carafe Maggie Miller had left on a warmer that sat on a table near the sheriff's desk, poured himself a cup, and crossed to his desk. Seating himself, he continued, "Grab a seat, Tony, and tell me what you're willing to do as far as working for the department."

Tony seated himself in the chair across from the sheriff. "Well, you said you need an investigator, and that you're a few men short. I'm willing to work as an investigator, but I'm not too keen on being a highway patrolman.....no experience, and no real burning desire to learn the job through OJT. The doctor said your deputy would be out about three months, as I understand things. I'm willing to work until he recovers, but only as an investigator and on an as-needed basis. I'm not looking for a full-time job; I've got a ranch to run," he concluded. "Of course," he continued, "in an emergency....."

"I wouldn't fret too much about the ranch, Tony," the sheriff replied. "Lew Barnes has been pretty much running it for a couple years now. Pete's docs told him he needed to cut back on working. His health hadn't been that great for a good piece of time before he died and he hadn't been too active around the spread for a while," the sheriff responded. "As for only working in an investigative capacity, that's what I really need most, especially right now, with this mess that you walked in on yesterday. Until it's solved, that's going to be your full time job. No working in the jail and no hanging paper on people that the court system has business with. Much as I could use another couple of patrol cars out on the highways, I need somebody with experience as a criminal investigator a hell of a lot worse."

"That's just about what I figured," Tony said. "Now, if you don't mind," he continued, "I've got a personal question. I know you knew Grandpa Pete well. He didn't play chess too often with folks he didn't know fairly well, and never with strangers. How'd you get to know him?"

The sheriff leaned back in his chair, raised his arms and laced his fingers together behind his neck, then smiled and said, "Just after I was elected sheriff the first time, I was out on patrol one afternoon, just swinging through the airport parking lot, oh, it must have been close to six, maybe seven years ago now. Saw an old man with a flat tire on his beat-up old pickup truck, stopped, and offered to help with the tire. As it happened, the old man was your grandfather. I changed the tire for him. Two mornings later, a check for ten thousand dollars for our yearly Christmas fund for needy kids showed up in the mail. When I went out to thank him for it, we ended up having coffee and playing a game of chess. "

"Well, one thing sort of led to another, I guess. We'd play chess every once in a while. Got so we'd even go fishing occasionally, too. We'd just sit in Pete's boat and talk and fish…..mostly talk, actually. Pete needed to get out of the house and I guess he needed the company. I know I needed the relaxation. It was sort of therapeutic for us both, I guess. Plus he had dinner at the house with my family several times. A few times he took us out to one or another of Durango's better eating establishments. He was a good friend. I miss having him around." The sheriff had a wistful smile on his face by the time he finished speaking. It was obvious that he'd thought a lot of Tony's grandfather.

Tony smiled, too. The story the sheriff told was typical of his grandfather. The check to the sheriff's department charity was just another example of Grandpa Pete returning a kindness many times over. As for the fishing, well, Tony had spent more than a few hours out on Vallecito Reservoir in the fishing boat with his grandfather. They were good times. *Come to think of it*, Tony thought, *I guess the boat's mine, now. Have to ask Lou about it. But now that I'm working......* The thought snapped Tony out of his daydream.

"Sorry, Sheriff," he said. "Got lost in a couple old memories for a second." He paused for a brief moment, then continued. "I'm yours if you want me, I guess, at least until your shot-up deputy is fit to go back to work." He paused. "But no jail duty....or process serving either."

Matson smile widened in to a grin. "Deal, Tony," he said, holding out his hand to seal the bargain. "Now let me fill you in on what we know so far." He leaned back in his chair and began to fill Tony in on the details of the case.

The filling in took the better part of an hour. One of the first things the sheriff's department did when they found the car was to run both the license plate and the VIN number. They didn't get a match. The plate, as it turned out, had been stolen from a car parked in long term parking at the Farmington, New Mexico, airport, some sixty miles south of Durango.

The car, on the other hand, had been stolen the morning of the robbery from the long term parking lot at the La Plata County airport, just a few miles outside of Durango. The car had just been parking in the lot the morning of the bank robbery. The car from which the plate had been taken had been parked at the Farmington airport for three days. Both the car and the license plate had been thoroughly dusted for fingerprints, with absolutely no results. They were both a clean as a hound's tooth. Someone had gone to a lot of work to deny finger-print evidence to the authorities.

The corpse the law officers had found in the front seat had died of a 9 mm bullet wound in the head. In addition, a second bullet penetrating his neck, severing the right carotid artery. Death had been, according to the coroner, a very quick one, the primary cause being massive trauma of the brain, plus considerable loss of blood, both from the head wound and the severed carotid artery. From the photos the sheriff showed Tony, it had also been quite messy. The man had been wearing rubber surgical gloves when he died, a fact that helped explain the lack of fingerprints in the car. From fingerprints taken from the corpse, and from dental records...fortunately the lower part of the skull had been intact...the sheriff's office, with assistance from the FBI, had identified the dead man as James Robert Tolliver, age 31, commonly known as Jim Bob.

Tolliver was not unknown in law enforcement circles. He had finished serving a three year sentence in a federal penitentiary the previous October, having been convicted of possession of stolen weapons, and of having transported them across a state line. One of the facts that Tony mentally noted as he listed to the sheriff's narrative was that Tolliver was not from the Four Corners area, but was a native of Kansas who most recently had been living in Oklahoma. He also made a mental note to ask if Tolliver had been involved, or was suspected of being involved, in any militia group.

It had taken several hours of searching roads and trails on either side of U.S. 160 east of Bayfield before one of the sheriff's deputies found, not more than an hour before darkness fell, the getaway car and Tolliver's body. It had been driven up a forest service trail on the north side of 160, heading up toward Wickerson Mountain, and then driven off the trail and up a gulch into some thick brush. Someone had gone to a peck of trouble trying to erase all sign of the car being driven off the road. At least someone had tried...but had not succeeded. Mike Carson, one of the deputies, had noticed a portion of a tire track leading off the trail. In less than five minutes he and his partner discovered the car, and its contents. By this time, one hell of a lot of flies had discovered it, too.

The contents, of course, had consisted mostly of Tolliver's body and a lot of blood, quite dry and covered with flies. The people who had been at the bank with Tolliver, the other criminals, were nowhere to be found. Darkness terminated the search Wednesday night, but at first light Thursday, sheriff's department members resumed the investigation. They followed footprints of three men about a tenth of a mile up the gulch to a small meadow. There the footprints disappeared, but there was a wealth of evidence at the meadow to indicate what had happened to the bank robbers.

At least five horses, and perhaps six, had been pastured in the meadow for about two days. From what the deputies discovered, they probably had been tended by a single person, who had made camp at the edge of the meadow, close to the spring which had provided drinking water for both man and beasts. From the tracks, it was obvious that the horses had been brought in across country rather than having been brought in by horse trailer. The man who camped there tending the horses had built a small fire, and had dined upon government surplus MRE's. There were a few fingerprints on the MRE wrappers. That was the good news. The bad news was that there was no record of the prints that lead to any person by name. The FBI did have a record of one set of the prints from another crime scene, a major firearms theft at a sporting goods dealer in Oklahoma, but did not have a name to go with them.

From what the deputies determined, the surviving bank robbers made their getaway from the meadow on horseback. By the time the deputies had called in on a cellular phone and had arranged for horses and other equipment to be brought to them, it was after noon on Friday. The robbers had about a twenty-four hour head start on horseback. The deputies followed their trail for about three hours, then had to call a halt due to darkness. By six o'clock Saturday morning, they were back in the saddle following the trail again, and periodically calling in their location as cell phone coverage allowed. Unfortunately, as far away from civilization as the deputies were, cell phone coverage was very spotty. Thanks to a sophisticated GPS unit, though, one with a readout in both latitude and longitude, they could pinpoint their location with a very high degree of accuracy.

By the time Sheriff Matson finished filling Tony in on the details, it was well after nine o'clock, and the coffee pot had long since been emptied. Matson picked up the phone on his desk, pushed a button, and spoke, "Maggie, when you get a minute, could you brew up another pot of coffee?" He waited a second, then hung up the phone. In a matter of seconds, Maggie Miller opened the door and walked in to the room, a small stack of papers in her left hand.

"Jack Matson," she said with a smile, "what are you ever going to do if I retire? Who'd you get to make your coffee and keep you out of trouble?" She handed the sheriff the papers she'd brought with her. "Here's everything in the way of paperwork you need to put Deputy Frye to work. Everything," she added, "except his ID card. When you two boys are done, I'll do a quick photo and I'll have the card ready in a flash. It's all finished except for the picture, a signature, and a Social Security number."

Tony's eyes widened. "Maggie," he said, "how'd you know I'd take this job?"

She looked at Tony and laughed. "First," she answered, "you boys are all alike, and pretty darned predictable, at that. Nary a one of you can resist something that might be interesting, not to mention being a little on the macho side.

Second, the sheriff said you wouldn't be able to turn it down. He's a pretty good judge of people.

"Besides," she continued after a brief pause, "like I told you earlier, I knew your grandfather. He talked about you a lot. Heck, from what all Pete said about you, I probably could have done all this paperwork yesterday right after Jack told me he'd offered you a job." Having said this, she walked to the coffee service and began the task of brewing a fresh pot.

Tony turned to the sheriff. "What the heck do the two of you know that I don't?" he demanded. "You told me I wouldn't be able to turn it down because of something my grandfather said. Now Maggie says you told her I wouldn't be able to turn it down. Come on, Sheriff! Give! I'm getting darn curious. And what the heck did she mean when she said, 'I knew your grandfather'?"

Matson and Maggie both laughed. "Your grandfather had kind of a high opinion of you, Tony," the sheriff answered. "And he did considerable bragging about you. He and Maggie were both on the county historical society's board of directors. Knowing your granddaddy and the braggin' he did on you, I can pretty much flat guarantee that anybody on that board, and just about every other civic organization Pete worked on, knows quite a lot about you," he replied, then paused a moment before going on.

"I've got a suggestion," he said, "actually an invitation. Why don't you come out to the house to dinner tonight? My wife said if I was going to drag you in to this mess, the least I could do would be to see you get a good Friday night home-cooked dinner under your belt. I'll even tell you some of the things old Pete said about you. Think a bit about what he'd have said about you this afternoon and see how close you can come to guessing. Maybe wondering about it will get your mind warmed up for figuring out how we can catch those bank robbers."

Frye smiled. "Thank you, and thank your wife. I most graciously accept. Looks like it might be the only way I'll satisfy my curiosity." Tony thought that his curiosity might get satisfied in more ways than one. The sheriff's daughter might be at dinner, too. If he was lucky, Tony would be able to put a face to the very interesting voice he'd heard on the phone the previous evening. If the rest of her proved to be as enchanting as the voice.....

Matson spoke again. "OK, I've given you most of the background. What do you think I left out, and what else do you need to dig in to?"

"First, how much money did they get away with?" Tony asked.

"Enough to make it worthwhile, that's for damned sure! The bank had just got a Federal Reserve shipment in earlier in the day. Today is payday for most of the area employers, early because of the holiday weekend, and the bank needed extra cash to take care of people who needed their checks cashed. The robbers got on the high side of a quarter of a million, most of it in larger bills, twenties and on up to hundreds. They missed close to an equal amount that had been slid under a desk."

"Whew!" Tony whistled. "A quarter mil.....and more! I should say it was worthwhile!" He hesitated a second, then continued. "How much FBI cooperation can you count on?"

"Probably not a hell of a lot. Like I told you yesterday, they really don't want to touch anything like this, even though bank robbery is something they're responsible for investigating. If they wanted to, they could bring agents in from Farmington, Santa Fe, and Denver and other places, but..."

Tony interrupted him. "City slickers, most of them, from what I've seen of FBI agents in D.C. and other places. Dudes!" The tone of his voice certainly got the idea across that he was using the word *dude* in a pejorative sense. "Get them out in sagebrush and canyon country." he went on, "and they wouldn't be able to find their backsides with both hands and a roadmap! And they'd be just about useless, if not a hell of a lot more so, blundering about out in the National Forest, either on foot or on horseback. And that's assuming you'd get agents who knew how to mount a horse, which I don't think I'd count on. Hell, you'd need some extra deputies to babysit them and keep them out of trouble." He thought for a second, then smiled. "Might be fun to watch, though," he said with a grin.

"The official position, " Matson said, smiling at Tony's last observation, "is that they will provide all possible assistance. Of course, once we catch the perps, assuming we do, the Bureau probably will step in and hog the glory, or at least try to. On the bright side, the state has loaned me four men for up to a week. Of course, the department has to cover their pay and expenses. They'll be here in a few hours and I'm going to ship them up to guard the roads the crooks might take down out of the mountains."

"And if we don't catch the baddies," Tony continued the train of thought, "the Bureau will disclaim responsibility. I've heard that song and dance before in some of the cases I worked for OSI." He lightly hammered his right hand on his right knee, then finished speaking. "All right, Sheriff. Swear me in or whatever it is you have to do before I go to work. I hope you've got a cubbyhole I can call home for a while. I'll need a computer with internet access, a phone, and a bunch of Coast and Geodetic Survey maps of the whole county and surrounding area...as big a scale as is available, 1:25,000 if possible. I sure hope that cubbyhole or whatever has a big enough wall to map out the whole of LaPlata County, and even part of Archuleta."

The sheriff swore Tony in, a brief ceremony interrupted by Maggie Miller bringing a Polaroid camera in to the office to take Tony's picture. Then the sheriff led Tony to the next office down the corridor. The room was small, but had everything Tony had asked for and more, filing cabinets, a cellular phone, a fax machine, and even a television set hooked up to cable. Either they were standard equipment or someone, Maggie Miller, most likely, had anticipated Tony's requests. Most of one wall was already covered with maps butted together to cover all of La Plata County and more.

Looking at it made Tony think that someone must have anticipated his request for maps, either that or maybe hanging maps on office walls was standard operating procedure in La Plata County law enforcement circles. Further consideration caused him to realize his second thought was probably the correct one. Army people, he knew, had a thing about maps; so did Air Force people, though to a somewhat lesser extent. Looking at the map-covered wall, even from a distance, he noticed that one of the maps had several pins stuck in it in various places.

Matson took Tony to the map-covered wall. He pointed to one of the pins, a red one. "This," he said, "is where we found the car and the body. And this," pointing to another pin right next to it," is where the robbers got the horses, the meadow where the person who led them in camped while waiting for the robbers. And this," he said, pointing to three pins in a row, "is the positions my deputies have called in to

Maggie as they follow the tracks. It's up to date as of the last call. I think the robbers will come out of the woods on the east side of Vallecito Reservoir." He pointed to a spot on the map just a few miles north of Tony's ranch. "At least it's too early for a lot of tourists to be camping back in there," Matson continued. "That ought to make it easier to figure out who's who. Right now I've got two deputies in there, and that's where I'll put the state troopers when they get here from Denver, which ought to be real soon now."

Tony looked at the map for a couple minutes. "Huh? Sheriff, I hate to rain on your parade, but I don't think I'd count on the bad guys showing up at Vallecito," Tony said, a frown on his face.

Matson looked at Tony, a puzzled look on his face. "No? OK, tell me why not? It's the obvious thing for them to do," the sheriff replied.

"Right. And that's why I'm betting they don't go there. Look at what you have so far," Tony said. "Car stolen in one place and plates stolen in another. Then there's the fact that the car was wiped clean. So was the stolen license plate. We've got no prints to go on, except those of the corpse. The dead robber was wearing rubber gloves. That plus no prints in the car indicates that maybe everybody else wore them, too. In fact, I'd say that's probably gospel."

"Then there's the horses for the getaway. That's something that had to be organized well in advance, right? Besides, there's only one easy way out of Vallecito. Putting in a roadblock would be like putting a cork in a bottle." He paused, then finished his thought. "Providing, of course, that the bad guys cooperate and use the one easy way out of the area." He paused for a moment. "But I don't think I'd count on that. Looks like they intend to pull a vanishing act. And seeing they're on horseback, that opens up a whole raft of possibilities."

"Well," Matson said thoughtfully, "I can't dispute any of that. I guess what you're saying is that this whole thing has been too well-planned for the bad guys to blow it by doing the obvious. I guess you're probably right, too. Besides, the fact that there was someone with horses and supplies waiting for them sort of indicates that they might be too bright to take the easy way out. What ticks me off," he continued, "is that I should have figured that one out on my own."

"Maybe. But maybe not, Sometimes people just don't figure they might screw up by doing something that's pretty obvious. And as for you not figuring it out, aren't two heads sometimes better than one?" Tony said in reply. "It's obvious that Vallecito is the closest place they could conveniently come down out of the hills, ditch the horses, and disappear. It's the closest place in the direction they're heading where they could have a car stashed. And. it's obvious from the way they're heading that they could be making for the lake. And that's the problem. It's too obvious, at least that's the way I see it. Maybe they assume we'll consider just that, and that we'd discard Vallecito as being too obvious. On that theory, they'd expect us to be anywhere else besides the Vallecito area, and figuring it that way, they just might head there to where they've stashed a car. The hell of it is that it's not totally likely, but we can't toss it out completely. That means keeping men in the area, and that's going to stretch your resources pretty thin, won't it?"

"It sure will," Matson muttered. "Won't be writing too many speeding tickets. And we won't be doing a lot of other highway patrol work until this gets resolved. Damnation!" he swore. "All right, you figure out what you need to do and get to work. Anything you need, just ask Maggie and she'll take care of it. Meanwhile, I better figure out how to get some supplies to Mike and Eddie. Better get some plaster of paris in to them, too. It just might be handy to have plaster casts of the horseshoe marks of those horses they're tracking." Matson sighed, "It looks like they might be riding horseback for a lot longer than I originally figured. That's two more deputies I can't count on for routine patrol." The sheriff turned toward the door, then stopped. "Oh, and Tony, it'll make things easier if you call me Jack. Everybody else does. I'll check back with you about lunchtime." He turned again and headed out into the corridor.

"OK," he said. "'Jack' it is. One last question, Jack," Tony called after him. Matson stopped and turned. "There are lots of trails out there in the National Forest. Are the robbers using them at all or are they staying off to the side? And are they staying in woods or are they riding out into meadows where they might be spotted from the air?"

"Damned if I know," the sheriff called from the corridor. "But I'll damn sure ask when my people call in next. Let you know as soon as I find out."

CHAPTER FOUR

Tony closed the office door. Then he walked back to the map-covered wall, dragging his desk chair with him. He spun the chair so that the back faced the wall, then straddled it, leaning his arms on the back as he did so, and stared at the map. He tried hard to imagine himself riding horseback through the mountainous country, trying to evade capture. He considered a variety of possibilities, dismissing those he deemed most unlikely. After nearly ten minutes of intense thinking, he stood, picked up the chair and carried it back to the desk, and sat down in it. "Maybe," he muttered. "Just maybe." After making several notes, he picked up the phone and punched a number. Nothing happened. Again he tried to make a call. Nothing. Finally he walked down to the reception area and asked Maggie how to get an outside line. Returning to his cubbyhole, he then followed her directions and was able to start working on the list of calls he'd decided to make.

For the next hour and a half, Tony made phone call after phone call. Several were to agencies of the federal government, including one call to the Pentagon and one call to Leavenworth Federal Penitentiary. Two of the calls were to Maggie; one to tell her to expect an important incoming call and the other to get answers to several questions and to request a package of index cards, the 5 x 7 size. As he worked, he wrote extensive notes, mostly on a yellow legal-sized pad of paper, but some of them on the note cards that Maggie provided almost immediately after Tony asked for them.

The call to USAF OSI headquarters was profitable. Tony dialed the OSI duty desk number from memory. The phone rang twice, then Tony heard, "OSI duty desk. Sergeant McCorkle."

"Corky," he said, "what'd you do to get stuck with the duty this nice holiday weekend?"

"Well, I shall be eternally honored to handle this call," McCorkle answered, obviously suppressing a laugh. "If it isn't the millionaire cowboy cop himself!"

Tony groaned. "Where in hell did you pick that up?" he asked.

"It's all over page one of this morning's *Post*, Captain Frye, sir," McCorkle answered, "with a major jump on page 2. It's an Associated Press story out of Colorado, with extra material from a couple reporters on the *Post staff. Sounds* like you've really stepped in it this time, Buddy." Despite military regulations about socializing between officers and enlisted personnel, and the customs of the service that discouraged such, Tony and McCorkle had become close friends as well as professional colleagues, about as close as an officer and an enlisted man could be. Each had a high regard for the other's intelligence and professionalism.

Tony explained the series of circumstances to Sergeant McCorkle, who was somewhat less than sympathetic regarding Tony's new nickname. Then Tony explained the favor he was asking.

McCorkle quickly responded to Tony's request. "You just got lucky, The boss called in to say that if you called, we were to move whatever needed moving to assist you. He sort of figured you might need some federal support. Let me start working on it. I'll get back to you ASAP."

At about half past ten, the sheriff knocked on the door and entered. "Parking lot's still infested with those damn news people. Radio, newspaper, and television, they're all out there just waiting for us, like a flock of vultures flying around a dying calf. There's even network people from Denver," he said. "If we go out for lunch, it'll be just plain hell, Tony. What about ordering out for pizza? There's a place right near here that makes a pretty good one, and they're still plenty hot when they're delivered."

"Works for me," Tony answered, "and my treat. Make mine sausage, mushroom, and extra cheese, if you would, please. Oh, and a diet cola, too, if you'd be so kind. Now," he said, "I had a couple ideas, and I've also got some information. If we went out for lunch, we probably couldn't discuss it, could we?"

"No, we couldn't," the sheriff replied. "Not without risking that anything we said might be picked up by damn near every newsperson in the Four Corners area. I'll tell Maggie to order the pizzas brought in. Sodas we got. There's a machine in the break room. Back in a sec." Matson left the office and returned in less than two minutes. "All right," he said when he reentered the room and sat down. "What's up?"

Tony told him, and in detail, something that took nearly twenty-five minutes. The idea that hit him as he looked at the map was that the robbers would probably be out in the National Forest for several more days, unless they came down out of the mountains in the Vallecito area, an event Tony considered increasingly unlikely the more he thought about it. If they stayed in the National Forest, they might be lighting a fire that evening in order to cook their evening meal, but they might not be, either.

Based on the empty packages found at the edge of the meadow where the horses had been kept, the person who brought the horses in had been eating MREs. Problem was, heating MREs didn't require a fire. They were heated in their containers by a chemical reaction. These successors to the old military K rations could be eaten cold, but they were better when heated, though only marginally so, according to many veterans who'd had to eat them. Tony, who had some close personal experiences with MREs, was of two minds. Some varieties were not bad, especially if one happened to be hungry, like *really* hungry. Others were so bad that even maggots would turn noses up at them, or so many soldiers said forcefully.

If the crooks subsisted totally on MREs, they wouldn't need a fire, unless they would light one for warmth. Evenings in the mountains were still fairly chilly, especially at higher elevations so they just might risk lighting a fire to keep warm. Thinking about MREs caused Tony to smile; he couldn't help smiling as he remembered two of the commonly-used alternate names for MREs: "Meals Rarely Edible" and "Meals Rejected by Everybody."

Thinking about military meals caused Tony to think about other items of a military nature, which resulted in him forming the outline of a plan. He called the Pentagon, confirmed the current location of his former commander, and then called the general's home number. Tony asked, he almost begged, the general to pull some strings and arrange for a military photo-reconnaissance aircraft to make at least three flights over the area east of Vallecito Reservoir at half hour intervals early that evening.

"No sweat," Tony," the general said. "Corky just called to tell me he'd anticipated this and is already working to set up what you want." He laughed. "The good Sergeant

McCorkle's efficiency is legendary." More laughter. "You may assume he has used my name and rank more than once to finagle things for you. Let me know how things work out. I can do commendation letters to the units and personnel involved if the things Corky worked out help you."

Tony spent a couple more minutes exchanging chit chat with the general, thanked him, and hung up.

Another call was to the FBI office in Durango, to ask the Special Agent in Charge to urgently forward the same request to the Pentagon. In less than a half hour after hanging up with the general, Tony received calls from both Sergeant McCorkle and the National Guard office at the Pentagon. That evening, a Texas Air National Guard photo reconnaissance aircraft would overfly the Vallecito area and would do infrared photography of the area. The film would be processed overnight and stereo pair prints would be flown to the La Plata County airport early the following morning. General officers could move small mountains with a simple request; even moving large mountains rarely required a serious pulling of rank.

"And once we get the photos," Tony told the sheriff, "we ought to be able to see any location where somebody has a campfire going. The Guard will fly another mission for us on Sunday, but only if they can schedule an aircrew plus the maintenance staff and photo lab people they'll need, which probably isn't going to be a problem, at least I hope not. We got lucky. This is a drill weekend for that unit and they'll have a few troops in tonight to get ready for the weekend's work, which is why we get a flight tonight. If nothing goes wrong, and if the bad guys do light a fire, we ought to be able to pinpoint where they are from the photos. Also ought to be able to see how far behind them your deputies are."

"I would have never thought of that," Matson said. "And I used Air Force recce info quite a few times when I was in the service."

"It was just dumb luck that I had some contacts who could set it up, not to mention setting it up right quickly," Tony said. "Fortunately, a sergeant friend of mine knows where a lot of bodies are buried and my general likes me. I think the general might have made a couple phone calls to speed things up. And I set something else up. If you're not tied up with other things, I think it might be a good idea for the two of us to fly over that area this afternoon. If nothing else, it might give the bad guys the notion that people are looking for them. I'm a licensed pilot, and I have a plane rental scheduled for about half past one o'clock."

"Ouch!" Matson said. "I don't know if the department can afford it. My budget's damn tight right now, and I already spent a bundle today getting supplies air lifted into Mike and Eddie."

Just then, Maggie walked in with two pizza boxes and two cans of cold soda. When the men got settled on either side of the desk with their lunch between them, Tony picked up the conversation again. "Money's no problem," he said. "Like I said, I'm a pilot and I wanted to arrange for some flying time anyhow, so I figured I could kill two birds with one stone."

He picked a piece of sausage off a slice of pizza, popped it in his mouth, chewed and swallowed it, and then continued. "I need about a half hour for the rental service to do the paperwork and check me out in the plane, and then we're off. It's a really good deal. I get to fly, which is something I love doing. I get a tax write-off as a business expense, which is going to keep my accountants and lawyers happy. Plus we get a close-up look at the area we're concerned about, and at no cost to the country.....except for our time, of course. Unless you don't want to go," he concluded, taking another bite out of a slice of pizza.

"Oh, I want to go, all right," the sheriff responded. "I'd just like for the department's budget to pay for the plane rental, but we've been paying a lot of overtime the last few weeks, and it's not going to get any better for a while, especially with having to cover the expenses of those four state cops."

Tony swallowed the pizza he was chewing on. "Don't sweat it. Money is something I don't have to worry about." Before he took another bite, he said, "As the saying goes, 'what the hell, it's only money."

"Mmmmm," Matson mumbled around a mouth full of pizza. "I guess I gotta warn you about something. It was bound to happen sooner or later, and it did....sooner, that is. Somehow the news people caught on to you being hired as a deputy. That ain't all. They know who you are, your background and all that, and one of those idiots from the Durango newspaper christened you the 'Millionaire Cowboy Cop.' Seems like other papers have picked up on the term, TV networks, too."

"Oh, shit!" Tony swore. "So that's what Corky was talking about. Apparently the word's been spread as far as D.C. That's all I need!"

"It gets worse, though you might not think it could!" Matson said grimly. "The county commissioners' office called. I got orders for you and me to hold a news conference. It starts in about twenty minutes or so, right after we finish lunch. The TV news folks asked for the conference to be held early enough to use some of the videotape on the noon news. And I flat guarantee you the media is going to be all over you like flies on a moist cow pat. Maybe half the questions I had to dodge on the way in concerned you and what you're going to be doing for the department."

Hearing this caused Tony to utter several other terms, the mildest of which was another, "Oh, shit!" A moment later, he said, "Can I resign?"

Matson wasn't at all sure that he was kidding. Not wanting to mess up what he saw as a good deal, he didn't reply.

Less than an hour later, the news conference, most thankfully, in Tony's opinion, was over and Frye and Matson were on their way to Animas Air Park, the airfield where the charter service was based, a matter of a few miles' drive south of Durango from the sheriff's office. The news conference had not gone well. The first question, other than those of a personal nature, asked of him concerned what he was contributing to the investigation. His answer was that he would not comment on an investigation in progress. This did not sit well with the members of the press. They continued to push for information until the sheriff made it plain that freedom of the press only went so far.

He did throw them a couple crumbs, one of which was the identity of the dead robber. The other was a promise of another press conference at noon on Monday, coupled with a stipulation that no member of the department would comment further on the case until then. Tony's statement that he felt unqualified to comment on anything at all relative to the case did not sit well with the press corps either. They were even less happy about his refusal to answer questions about his personal life.

Checking out the plane didn't take long. Tony showed his pilot's license and logbook to Logan Bennett, the owner of the charter service, who then had Tony do a takeoff and landing with Bennett riding in the plane to observe. Shortly afterward, having satisfied Bennett as to his flying ability, Tony and Matson were airborne. Tony's face sported a contented look; he loved to fly. The look on the sheriff's face, however, was not one of great joy. Sheriff Matson looked just a mite scared.

Tony listened to the plane's engine as he climbed up to altitude. It was purring like a kitten. He thought for a moment about how much he enjoyed piloting a small plane and how long it had been since he had last flown. *Too long,* he thought, resolving to fly at least a couple times a month, weather permitting. Realistically, though, he figured he'd not be flying small planes in Colorado's mountain areas during the winter, except on very clear days.....too many rock-filled clouds.

He leveled the little Cessna 172 off at about three thousand feet above the terrain, flying parallel to U.S. Route 160 as they headed east from Durango. "Boy, this is the life!" he exclaimed happily. "I never was able to get enough flying time in D.C. to keep me happy. Besides, there was always too much air traffic in the area. I used to drive close to three hours and more up to Pennsylvania occasionally just for an hour or two in the air in some relatively peaceful air space. Then I'd have a three hour drive back to D.C. Getting a couple hours flying time would pretty near kill a whole Saturday. Haven't flown in over a month, and I missed it."

"Isn't it a little bumpy?" Matson asked, holding on to his seat with both hands, despite the fact that he was securely strapped in. Tony looked over at him and decided that the sheriff was getting just a bit green around the gills.

"Not really," Tony answered. "Wait 'til we get up over Vallecito. The mountains are higher there, so I'll have to climb another thousand feet or two. And the higher mountains will make for more rising and falling air currents, so we'll probably bounce around a bit more. There's a paper bag or two under the seat, just in case."

The tone of his voice changed to being major serious. "I don't mind paying for the plane rental, but I'm damned if I'm going to clean up after you, Jack. You barf, you take care of the mess!" The way Jack looked, Tony thought that the odds of the sheriff having to use one or more of the barf bags was verging on a definite possibility.

The plane bounced again, losing a couple hundred feet of altitude. Matson grimly clenched his teeth as he fumbled under his seat for one of the bags Tony had mentioned, without trying to reply. The look on his face indicated that he, too, considered tossing his cookies to be a very real possibility. Matson was also mentally regretting having ordered pepperoni on his pizza, though Tony was not aware of that.

In a few moments, Tony pointed off to the left of the aircraft. "There's Bayfield and the bank," he said. "Now let's find the road the robbers took up into the hills"

Less than a minute later Matson pointed this landmark out. Tony banked the plane and flew in a circle, then rolled out of the turn heading roughly north. A few seconds later, the sheriff pointed out the small meadow where the robbers picked up the horses, and shortly afterward, the opening in the trees where supplies had been dropped for the deputies an hour or two earlier.

"That's Middle Spring," Matson said. "It's about 8,100 feet above sea level, and about 1,800 feet above Vallecito."

"Got it!" Tony replied. "From the looks of it, the lake is about two miles straight line from that clearing."

"Right," the sheriff called over the engine noise. "And if they headed that way, they just might have bumped into two of my boys. And you can see the roadblock the state troopers have set up on the far side of the dam. If I can swing it, I'm going to put two more where the pavement ends, up north of the lake a ways."

"I see the roadblock," Tony answered. "Nothing can get out of the lake area by road without passing it?"

"That's right," the sheriff replied. "Everything else is just trails, and a lot of them even four wheel drive won't do any good. Most of that's horse country...or hiking country. Some of it.......well, let's say there are places where you'll find stuff growing on both sides of the same acre. We're talkin' really steep slopes; damn rough country down there."

Tony flew two loops around the reservoir. Before beginning the second loop, he advanced the throttle and pulled back slightly on the control column, gaining a thousand feet or so more altitude. When he reached the point in the second loop where he was flying north, he straightened out the course and flew until he was six or seven miles north of the reservoir, banking the plane occasionally so that both he and Matson could get a clear view of the landscape below, much of which was tree-covered, except for some high meadows and the considerable number of places so high in altitude as to be above the tree line. Then he headed due west for approximately twenty straight line miles before turning south to head back toward Durango. Just as he turned south, he banked the plane and pointed toward the ground.

"If I had to pick a point where they'll come out of the woods," Tony said, "that's the area I'd pick, based on what I've seen from up here and what I picked up from reading the topographic maps. There's enough side roads and drives feeding out on to the main road that someone could pick them up without attracting too much attention. There's also enough streams flowing down out of the mountains to make for fairly easy downhill travel on foot or on horseback, just by following the stream banks. Only thing is, it'd take them a couple or three days of rough country riding to get that far, and maybe even a day more.....at least."

"You just might have something there," the sheriff agreed from the left hand seat. Apparently he must be getting more used to the flying, as the color of his face was not quite as pale as it had been less than fifteen minutes earlier. "There's no way we can check all those side roads and trails, and there also no way we can stop and check every car moving along U.S. 550 north of where the road heads up into the mountains. If they come out much further south, they'll be in a pretty inhabited area. Too much further north, and they'll be in some really wild and rough country. That area up around Molas and Coal Bank Passes is damn rough country, even by Colorado standards!"

"Which is something that makes the idea of heading through the mountains to Silverton or beyond a little unlikely," Tony said.

"Right," Matson said. "Hard hiking country and doing it on horseback isn't much easier. So how do we catch them?"

"Now that's something I haven't totally figured out," Tony replied. "Let me sleep on it."

A few moments later, Tony landed the Cessna at the airpark. He greased the landing and then taxied to the parking apron, shut down the engine, got out and chocked the wheels, wrote the details of the flight in the new logbook he'd bought just before the flight, returned the aircraft's ignition key to the owner of the charter service, and picking up his charge card receipt for future reference. Then he and Matson headed for the sheriff's Jeep Cherokee.

On the way back to the office, Matson pulled a set of keys out of his shirt pocket. "Here," he said, handing the keys to Tony. "You'll have exclusive use of Unit 6 until this is over. It's just out of the shop and all gassed up and ready to go. There's a list of radio channels on the front seat. Consider yourself on duty twenty-four hours a day, so use the vehicle for anything, including personal use."

"I'd rather use my truck," Tony said, "except it doesn't have radios. Anyhow, it's parked at the office. What do I do with two vehicles?"

"Give me the keys to your truck when we get back," the sheriff answered. "I'll have one of the deputies going up to the lake drop it off at your ranch and leave the keys with Lou."

"All right. I'll just have to get my pistol out of the truck. Suppose I should be carrying one, all things considered."

"You certainly should, both on duty and off. That's departmental regulation. I didn't tell you there was a department pistol for you in your desk, in the locked drawer, did I?" Matson queried. "Maggie's got the desk key."

"Nope. And I probably wouldn't want to use it anyhow, unless I have to. I'm really comfortable with my old Browning. Grandpa Pete gave it to me back when I was in high school, and he taught me to use it pretty darn good. I carried a Beretta 9 mm. for the Air Force, but never really felt comfortable with it because I'm so used to the Browning. I'm not really anxious to start carrying a new weapon right about now, considering that I might have to use it. Like I said, I'm comfortable with the Browning. Can I have permission to carry my personal weapon?"

"The department issues Berettas, and we're thinking about converting to Glocks but suit yourself, Tony. Hell, it's against department regs when folks are on duty hours but, like you just said, 'all things considered...' Guess there has to be an exception for damn near every rule. Truth to tell, I gave myself permission to carry my own Colt .45. Got used to it in the service a whole bunch of years ago and sort of hate to carry anything else. Wasn't really comfortable when the army went to the 9 mm. It just doesn't have the stopping power of the .45. Shoot someone with a .45 and they sorta lose all interest in doing anything nasty. Besides, my hands are too damned big to be comfortable with the Beretta." He paused for a second, then continued. "I'll write up a memorandum granting you an exception for on-duty use of your personal firearm before I leave for the day."

Matson uttered a soft belch, begged Tony's pardon, then continued. "What you carry off duty is your own business, but departmental policy is that you pack a weapon twenty-four hours a day when you're off your own property, unless you're doing something like skinny dippin'." As he pulled off the street and in to the sheriff's department parking lot he said, "Take the rest of the day off, unless there's something you need to take care of. Looks like you'll be doing some work tomorrow with those recce photos. Come on in for a minute and I'll draw you a map of how to get to the house. Dinner'll be about half past six or so and if you get to the house an hour or so before, we might have time for that game of chess." He pulled the Cherokee into his reserved parking spot.

"There's one thing I do need to check," Tony said, as he got out of the Jeep, "but I don't expect the information to arrive until tomorrow and there's not a heck of a lot I can think of to do until it arrives, except make a quick run to Walmart to buy a litter box, cat litter, flea collars, and cat food."

This comment produced a quizzical look on Matson's face. "I've been adopted by a kitten," Tony said, by way of explanation. "At least it looks that way." He recounted the story of the cat on the porch the previous night. "Always been a sucker for cats," he said. "By the way," he continued, "is this a coat and tie affair tonight?"

"Coat and tie!" the sheriff almost choked. "Are you kidding? This is out-west Colorado! Just scrape the cow flop off your boots before you pass through our front door. Pat sort of discourages manure tracks on the wall-to-wall carpeting."

CHAPTER FIVE

By the time he pulled Unit Six into the Matson family's driveway at a quarter past five, Tony had managed to shower and change into something presentable but casual. He'd already unpacked quite a bit of his casual civilian clothes, and from the items hanging in the closet of the master bedroom, he'd selected a pair of tan chino slacks and a light blue pima cotton shirt with button-down collar. He set out a nearly new denim jacket, but only because he wanted to cover up the pistol he planned to tuck in the waistband at the back of the slacks. He touched up the garments with an iron, dressed, and then checked his appearance in the floor length mirror. Satisfied that he was presentable, he headed from the ranch in to town, stopped at a supermarket to pick up both flowers and a bottle of wine, and then headed west out of Durango to the sheriff's house. The pressure of his pistol being pushed against his back as he drove convinced him that a shoulder holster rig was probably going to be a necessary investment. He'd used a holster on a belt clip while wearing civvies on duty, but really didn't like the holster. Because of this, he'd been considering a shoulder holster for some time, but hadn't made a decision about getting one. Then he left active military duty and the point became moot.....up until now.

The Matson home, a large and attractive ranch house on a large, well landscaped lot, was located about five miles or so outside of downtown, in the residential area called Wildcat Canyon. The grounds were neatly tended; the driveway and walk lined with variegated flowers. Tony couldn't come up with names for them, except for several rose bushes, but he vaguely remembered that his mother had planted some of the same flowers, or ones that looked like them, in a large bed in front of their home in Virginia in the years before she died. "Nice house, and a very nice neighborhood, too," Tony said to himself as he walked to the front door. He pushed the doorbell, and a moment later the door opened.

Tony found himself face to face with a tall young woman of about his own age, an absolutely stunning young woman whose head was crowned with a mass of long, naturally curly, bright red hair and whose eyes were the brightest green that Tony could remember ever seeing. They reminded him of glittering pieces of jade, much like the jade of his grandfather's chess set. She had the fair peaches and cream skin typical of redheads, with just a few freckles on her face and neck. His jaw dropped momentarily; he hadn't expected to come face to face with such a drop-dead beautiful woman. Knowing how much like an idiotic mouth-breather he looked, standing there with his lower jaw down somewhere around his kneecaps, he made the quickest and most graceful recovery possible.

"Hi," she said in the voice Tony remembered so well from calling the sheriff's home the evening before as she offered Tony her hand. "You must be Mister Frye."

Jill Matson, the sheriff's daughter, took a good look at Tony and liked what she saw. Tony Frye stood just an inch or so over six feet in height, about four inches taller than she was, weighed, as Jill estimated, pretty close to one hundred seventy pounds, give or take, had bright light blue eyes, and short hair on the blondish side of brown. She graded his facial features as somewhere between very good looking and quite handsome.

"And you must be Miss Matson," Tony answered, gently shaking the proffered hand while trying very hard to regain the composure he knew he'd lost when he caught sight of the young lady and at the same time trying his best not to drop the flowers and the bottle of wine. "Please call me Tony."

Good God! he thought. *This is one absolutely stunningly beautiful girl!* He smiled, then continued, "When people call me Mister, I can't help looking over my shoulder to see if my dad's standing behind me. Either that or I'm reminded of being in trouble as either a cadet or a very green second lieutenant and being called 'Mister' when I was being chewed out. Especially in that particular context, the word kind of has some pretty unpleasant connotations I'd just as soon forget. Call me Tony, please."

The young woman laughed, a lovely, tinkling sound. "OK, Tony," she said, laughter still ringing her voice. "But only if you call me Jill, and," turning to an older version of herself just coming around the corner into the living room, "and this is my mother, Patricia."

"Pleased to meet you, Mrs. Matson," Tony said, as he handed Jill's mother the flowers and then the wine. Pat Matson was an older version of her daughter, tall, red-headed with just a very few strands of gray at the temples, and extremely attractive. Looking at her, Tony was struck by the thought that twenty-five years or so in the future, the odds were very good that, in middle age, Jill Matson would be as stunningly attractive as her mother was now.

"The name's Pat, Tony, and I'm pleased to meet *you*, though hearing your grandfather talk about you I feel as if I've known you for years, " Mrs. Matson said, taking the objects Tony handed her. "How gracious," she continued, "flowers *and* wine. I'll get these flowers in water right away, if you don't mind."

Jill took the wine bottle from her mother. "This is Australian, Mom. I've had it before," she said, after inspecting the label. "It's great! You'll like it." Turning to Tony, she said, "I'm impressed, Mister....., whoops, let me make that just plain 'Tony' Frye. Consider yourself complimented on your excellent taste in wine. Now if you'll come with me," she continued, "Daddy's out in the den." She took Tony lightly by the arm and led him through the living room to the den, where her father was reading a newspaper.

"Hi, Tony," the sheriff said, rising to shake Tony's hand. "I see you've met Carrottop."

"I'll get you for that, Daddy," Jill Matson said, but with a smile on her face.

"And your wife as well, Boss," Tony replied.

"Dinner in about an hour, guys," Jill said. Turning to the guest, she continued, "Tony, I hope you eat ham." She looked at her father. "And that 'carrottop' remark means you're limited to one small serving of ham, Daddy. And no biscuits."

Tony laughed softly at the exchange between Jill and her father. "Like ham? I could smell it even before you opened the front door, Jill. Believe me, the odor of hot cloves was a dead give-away. Only my innate good manners keeps me from drooling on the carpet. Home-cooked ham ranks real high on my list of favorite meals." Tony patted his stomach a couple of times. "My only complaint is that I don't get it anywhere near often enough. Ham served in restaurants just doesn't hack it." He considered this for a few seconds, the continued. "But it's better than no ham at all, of course."

"Then," said the sheriff, "you need to eat around here on a regular basis. It's a family tradition. We have ham just about every other week, and especially for holidays.....Thanksgiving, Christmas, Easter, you-know-who's birthday........" He motioned to a chair opposite the one he'd been sitting in. "Grab a seat, Tony. I've got something to show you."

"Boy, does he ever!" Jill said with a grin. "It's a real hoot, too!" She quickly changed the subject. "Can I get you two something wet and cold before I start making salad? Beer, Daddy, or lemonade, iced tea.....or a cocktail? Tony?"

"Lemonade for me, Hon," her father answered. "Tony, how 'bout you?"

"Lemonade's great, thanks," he replied.

Jill turned and headed for the kitchen as Tony sat. Matson folded the newspaper so that the front page was on top, then handed the paper to Tony. The headline read "Sheriff Hires Millionaire Cowboy Cop." Below it was a three column wide picture of Tony, one of several that had been taken at the news conference earlier in the day.

"I told you this morning the media would eat this up," the sheriff said.

Tony swore softly and passionately, then slowly read the article. He finished reading just as Jill reentered the den, carrying a tray holding two large glasses of lemonade, a bowl of taco chips, and another of salsa verde.

"Well, Mister Millionaire Cowboy Cop, what did you think of the article?" she asked, teasingly as she took a chip and dipped it in the salsa.

"I think I can tell you what he thinks, Kitten," her father said. "At least I know what he said earlier today and again just now when I told him the nickname the press had given him."

"And please don't repeat it," Tony said to his boss. "I'm afraid it was something not entirely fit for mixed company, Jill," he continued. "Actually, I got an inkling when I called the Pentagon earlier today. The 'cowboy cop' bit made the news there, too, including the third word. From the speed it reached the office where I used to work, I kind of assume a certain sergeant that worked with me might have contacts at Washington newspaper offices. And then some idiot from the local rag probably amplified on it," he groaned.

"Oh, joy!" Jill exclaimed. "I can imagine what you must have said," Jill continued. "I know what I'd have said if I were in your shoes, and the first thing probably would have been a word Daddy spanked me good and hard for the first time he heard me using it."

"And a term I sincerely trust that you have not used since, Kitten." Turning to Tony he said, "One of those good old GI terms. I assume you Air Force folks probably use the same cuss words us Army types use. Oh well," he sighed, "I guess it's one of the hazards of raising a couple of military brats. They seem to just naturally talk the lingo, including the cuss words."

Tony grinned, "I'll even bet I can figure out which one." He thumped his fist against the front page of the paper. "Sheer sensationalism," he said. "Why couldn't they have just written something like, "Sheriff hires former military investigator?""

"As the journalism teacher and student newspaper advisor at Durango High, Mister Millionaire Cowboy Cop, I can give you the professional answer to that one," Jill said. "It's simple," she continued. "Sensationalism sells. I hate to tell you this, Tony, but you're going to end up being one of the favorite topics of the local news media until this case ends, and maybe even afterwards. My guess is that for a while, like maybe a week, you're going to be responsible for maybe as much as a ten per cent jump in newspaper sales. Looks very much like you just became an instant celebrity, at least in this part of the Four Corners region." She paused for a second, then continued. "How much you want to bet I can stand you on a corner of the main drag tomorrow and have 95% of the locals recognize you, and by name, at that?"

"Only 95%?" her father asked. "I'd figure it'd be closer to 99%."

"And to think that my goal in life when I left the service was just to run a ranch," Tony moaned. "If I'd stuck around the ranch or gone right home from the post office instead of running to the market, I'd have missed the whole mess at the bank and wouldn't have my picture plastered all over the paper."

"That's probably true," Jill said, turning to leave the room. "But then," she said looking back over her shoulder, "you wouldn't have met my parents and me, and you probably wouldn't be eating ham for dinner tonight, at least not ham the way Mom cooks it."

Matson was laughing softly as a result of the exchange between Tony and his daughter. "Tony," he said as Jill left the room, "something tells me that girl is going to tease you unmercifully." He reached out and pulled a small table into the space between his chair and Tony's. "Gotta warn you, though, the term 'carrottop' probably shouldn't be used.....unless, of course, you have a pretty well developed death wish. I get away with using it occasionally.....but only barely." He paused just long enough to switch topics. "Now, might as well get a game of chess in before dinner, if you're up to it. Let's see if you're as good a player as Pete said you were." He slid open the drawer and began to set up chess pieces on the chess board inlaid on the table's top.

By the time Jill came to call them to dinner close to an hour later, the two men had managed to finish one hard-fought game, a game which Matson won.....but just barely. Neither one was able to totally concentrate on the game. Tony used some of the time to fill the sheriff in on a line of research he'd begun much earlier in the day.

Matson listened attentively, making comments and suggestions as Tony expanded on his idea. One thing that bothered the younger officer was the background of Jim Bob Tolliver. What brought a native of Oklahoma to die as a result of a bank robbery in the small community of Bayfield, Colorado? Tony hoped to have enough background on Tolliver before noon the following day to come up with an answer to that question. If he did not have it by noon on Saturday, he knew he wouldn't get it until Monday. Most government offices in the nation's capital city shut down for the holiday weekend. If he hadn't had some good personal contacts in a variety of federal law enforcement offices, he doubted that he'd have a snowball's chance in hell of getting a little help on a Saturday.

Dinner was delicious, easily exceeding Tony's expectations. Jill and Pat Matson had put on quite a spread. Tony was especially impressed with the biscuits, of which he ate three, praised them highly, and coveted more, though not wanting to be a glutton. Jill blushed, and her mother told

Tony that the biscuits, and the salad, were her daughter's major contributions to dinner. Discussion around the table was lively. The Matson family kept Tony in stitches with a lengthy account of some of the more humorous calls the sheriff's deputies had been called upon to answer.

"This one's funny, too," Jill said after her father had finished telling a story about a man releasing a live skunk, scent apparatus still totally functional, in his former girlfriend's apartment and both the former girlfriend and the owner of the building filing lawsuits to recover damages associated with skunk spray. "Late one night a couple months ago, somebody called in a complaint about a man wearing nothing but a bra and a woman's half slip walking up the white line in the middle of highway 550 out on Florida Mesa."

"There's a law out here against cross dressing?" Tony asked.

"Nope!" the sheriff replied. "But there sure as heck is one against obstructing vehicular traffic. That weirdo was responsible for three or four near accidents. Truth be told, the damn fool was lucky he didn't get himself killed. The deputy who took the call hauled him in and tossed him in jail; two additional charges, one of them being public intoxication and the other being a public nuisance."

"It gets funnier.....or sadder," Jill continued. Turns out the man is, or was, a minister in one of the smaller and more ultra-conservative fundamentalist Christian sects, one that most certainly does not condone the use of alcoholic beverages. Well, the story made the newspaper, of course. I think every reporter on the Durango *Herald* keeps a scanner running day and night to monitor the police frequencies. So a reporter shows up at the station, gets a photo of the preacher getting out of the police unit, attired in what can only be described as something of an out of the ordinary manner, and the story, with the photo, makes the front page of the next morning's paper. Then the poop really hit the fan."

"Yeah," the sheriff said. "We took the parson before a magistrate the next morning, after he'd sobered up, and the judge released him on his own recognizance. We just couldn't turn him loose on the streets of Durango, not dressed the way he was. So I asked one of the city P.D. officers to take him home. His wife, who'd seen the morning paper, took one look at him walking up to the house, threw a pair of pants and a shirt out on to the porch, and then barricaded the door. By noon the next day, she'd filed for divorce, the deacons of his church had fired him, and the governing body of the church denomination had revoked his minister's credentials."

"Wow!" Tony exclaimed. "That poor guy really stepped in it. What happened to him afterwards? I assume he's left the area."

Not hardly," Pat Matson interjected. "He went on the internet, got himself a fifty dollar mail order divinity degree from one of those fly-by-night so-called 'church colleges' out in California. He now works in one of the roadhouses out on Florida Mesa as a bartender. Sunday mornings at 10:30 he holds a church service at the bar for bikers, those who are 'gender disoriented', as he calls it, and other assorted roadhouse patrons. Hard as this may be to believe, he seems to attract a considerable crowd at the services. And from all we've seen there, the bikers and gays tend to get along OK, at least at the services. Given that he draws a really diverse crowd, I think he's probably got a lot going for him. And word is that he's bringing in a goodly amount in the collection basket each Sunday, too, most of which I surmise he's pocketing as salary."

"Well, Mom," Jill said, "maybe the rumor about him using Jack Daniels instead of wine for communion might be true. Then there's the possibility that a lot of them are some of the stranger of the folks who've moved into the area from southern California and Texas, and other places out there that seem to be blessed with more than their fair share of what can only be called weirdoes." she said with a grin. "Now who wants dessert? We have on the dessert menu tonight one item, cherry cheesecake, fresh from Nola's Bakery, accompanied by fresh-brewed Green Mountain Coffee." She looked at Tony and said, "You do have a choice between regular and decaf. I have a pot of decaf made and can do a pot of regular in five minutes."

The cheesecake was exceptionally good, as was the coffee. Over dessert, to Tony's pleasant surprise, he found himself being invited to escort Jill to the theater the following night. Jill and her parents had season's tickets for Durango's community theater, but the older Matsons had to attend some sort of a political social function the following evening. This left Jill with two extra tickets for *Guys and Dolls*, and no one to go with her. Tony accepted, but with two strings attached.

"Strings? What strings?" Jill asked.

"I get to take you to dinner before the play. That's the first one," Tony answered, putting down his coffee cup.

"That sounds swell. I graciously accept. And the second?" she replied, as she took a sip of her coffee.

"Stop teasing me about the newspaper headline. Please!" Tony begged, a smile on his face.

This provoked a laugh from both of the older Matsons. Pat and Jack Matson exchanged looks, both thinking that the two young people were enjoying themselves and that Jill had obviously decided she liked Tony, something that they quickly realized even before Jill invited him to go to the theater with her. The swiftness with which Tony accepted the invitation only served to confirm their assessment that he liked her, too.

Jill agreed to cut down out the teasing about the newspaper article, but warned Tony that she'd just find something else to tease him about. This was a prospect that Tony found not displeasing, as it implied that he might expect to see a lot more of her, and his experiences during the evening so far inclined him to believe that seeing a lot of Jill Matson could only be considered an exceptionally pleasant prospect. Helping her with the dishes was the only time in his whole life that Tony had ever enjoyed wearing an apron, something that resulted in even more teasing when Jack Matson remarked on how good it looked on him and threatened to take a photo of him wearing it.

Shortly after nine o'clock, Tony thanked his hosts and hostess for a most enjoyable evening and said goodnight. Jill walked him to the front door and held his hand for a long moment before they said goodnight. He got a very strong feeling that she would have liked him to stay longer and had it not been for having to meet a plane at the La Plata County airport at half past six in the morning, Tony could have been easily persuaded to linger. But, given having to roll out of bed before the crack of dawn, he figured he'd better get a good night's sleep. Besides, he had a full work day ahead of him after meeting the plane.

Saturday morning's ringing alarm clock came painfully early. The sky in the east was barely beginning to show traces of light when the alarm went off. Tony picked the cat up, dropped it over the side of the bed, and headed for the bathroom. He showered, dressed, made a cup of coffee, poured it in to a travel mug, and left for the airport. At that hour of the morning there was precious little traffic, even on U.S. 160, the main highway, and even less on the back roads he took cutting across Florida Mesa to the airport.

When the Texas Air National Guard T-38 jet trainer taxied up to the terminal building of the La Plata County Airport a few moments before six thirty, Tony was waiting on the tarmac. The plane stopped, and the canopy went up.

"Captain Frye?" the officer in the rear seat had unsnapped his oxygen mask so he could shout over the low roar of idling jet engines.

"That's me, Lieutenant," Tony shouted in reply. The plane's twin jet engines, even though throttled 'way back, made a considerable noise. "Reserve type captain, that is. You have a package for me?"

"Roger that, Captain." The lieutenant tossed down a large plastic-wrapped package. "I packed a stereo viewer in there in case you don't have one. I flew in the back seat on this mission, and then watched the photo techs process the film and make the prints. Let me assure you that you got top-quality service. It's not often we get a tasking like this one, and almost never from as high up the food chain from where the mission order for this came down. You have friends in very high places, Captain Frye."

He paused briefly, then went on. "We shot single frames of IR as well as some stereo pairs on really fast film. There was enough light on the first pass to get good black and white imagery, all things considered, and the IR shows a lot of light or heat sources. We couldn't get anything solid on regular black and white after the first pass, though....not enough light. Hope you find what you're looking for."

Tony thanked the lieutenant and walked to the fence at the edge of the aircraft parking apron. He turned and waved as the aircraft, canopy now closed, turned and slowly taxied out to the taxi way that paralleled the runway. Out of habit, Tony stood watching as the plane taxied to the downwind end of the runway, and then turned into the wind and commenced its takeoff run. He came to attention and saluted as the plane came level with the terminal building, the nose wheel already having rotated off the tarmac. Only when the small jet was no longer visible did Tony turn and walk through the terminal building to where he'd left Unit Six parked in a 'no parking' area on the airport circular drive. *One of the nice advantages of being a cop,* Tony thought, *Cop cars don't get tickets for illegal parking. They don't get towed, either. Sort of on the same theory that says sharks don't bite lawyers.*

As Tony drove across Florida Mesa heading for Durango, he worked on details of a plan he'd thought of the day before. As it was early yet, and as he hadn't had time to eat before leaving the ranch for the airport, Tony decided to drive all the way in to town and treat himself to breakfast. He enjoyed the drive down the hill into the downtown area of Durango. He'd always thought of it as a pretty drive, crossing the Animas River a couple times and swinging past the edge of the yard of the Durango and Silverton Narrow Gauge Railroad.

I haven't ridden the train up to Silverton in years, Tony thought, looking at the old railroad cars in the yard next to the road. *As soon as I have time,* he thought, *I'm going to spend a day riding the train up and back. Maybe I can talk Jill into going with me. There's lots of neat places to eat and some interesting shops on Blair Street.*

The thought of the train rides he'd shared with Grandpa Pete brought other memories of his grandfather into Tony's mind. The train trip was one the two of them had made more than once, and one that they both enjoyed. Tony considered the scenery along the Animas River gorge, as seen from the train, to be the equal of anything he'd seen anywhere else in the entire United States.

Thinking about the train ride resulted in Tony's deciding to eat at the Denny's restaurant just down the street from the depot. He pulled Unit Six into the parking lot and got out, smelling the odor of burning coal that came from the railroad yard and listening to the chuffing noise that came from the steam locomotive being readied for the day's first tourist excursion to Silverton. Tony stood for a moment or two, savoring the smell of burning coal and the sound of steam being released from the locomotive's safety valve, both of which things that brought back pleasant memories of his younger years in the Durango area. Then he entered the restaurant.

After the waitress, who addressed him by name and title, seated him at a booth and took his order, Tony began to mull over the problem the sheriff's department faced. Tracking the bank robbers, he decided, would not lead to their capture. The robbers had the better part of a day's head start over the two deputies chasing them. To boot, the deputies probably couldn't make as good time as the bad guys could; they had to spend time reading 'sign' to follow the bank robbers. All that these men would accomplish would be to confirm the route the robbers were taking through the National Forest.

"It's not having men *behind* the robbers that will put them behind bars," Tony muttered under his breath, "it's figuring exactly where they will head, and then getting a posse in *front* of them. If we can do that and catch them by surprise, we've got them in the bag." As he worked the problem over in his mind, an idea began to form.

The waitress brought his order of scrambled eggs, sausage links, home fries, rye toast, and coffee. Tony put sugar in the coffee, stirred it, and then picked up a fork. *If the photo scan just give me an idea of where those SOB's were last night,* he thought, *we'll know where they'll start from this morning. And if we can get near real-time info on where they are tonight, just maybe I can figure out where to jump them. From the looks of the map, there aren't that many places where they can easily come down from around the nine thousand foot level, which seems to be where they've been staying. At least that's what the reports from the deputies tracking them indicate. And if I can predict the route they take, I think I know how we might be able to block them.*

He considered this train of thought for a few seconds, then muttered, "I need to talk to Jack real quick!" Tony wolfed down what was left of his breakfast, drained his coffee cup, took a ten dollar bill and two singles from his wallet, put them on the table, and walked quickly out of the restaurant.

He crossed the parking lot to his Cherokee, opened the door, got in, started the engine, and headed out of the parking lot. Driving a little over the speed limit, he reached the sheriff's office complex in less than five minutes. Matson's Cherokee was not in the lot. "I'll wait a half hour," he mumbled, "then call him at home if he's not in. In the meantime, maybe some of the other information I asked for yesterday came in." He tucked the package of reconnaissance photos under his arm, got out of the car, walked to the office door, opened it, and entered the building.

The dispatcher on duty at the communications console stood up and walked to the counter. "You're Deputy Frye," the man said. "I recognize you from the TV news and the newspaper. Hi. I'm Mike Rosen." He held out his right hand.

Tony shook the proffered hand. "Hi, Mike, and the name's Tony. Glad to meet you. I guess the sheriff's not in yet?"

"He just called in on the radio not much more than a couple minutes ago," Mike answered. "He's heading for breakfast at Denny's and expects to be here in about forty-five minutes to an hour."

Tony laughed. "And I just left Denny's about five minutes ago. If I'd known.... Oh well, I wouldn't talk business there anyhow. Do me a favor, Mike. When he gets here, let him know I need to talk to him, please." Tony lifted the hinged section of counter and walked through it. Then he headed down the hallway to his office.

Once he was in his office, he opened the package of pictures. Ignoring the stereo pairs for the time being, Tony laid out the infrared pictures from each pass the reconnaissance aircraft made over the area. The heat sources from the homes and camps around Vallecito Reservoir were very distinct. And to the north and east of the reservoir, there were two smaller, less distinct heat blooms. "Bingo!" Tony said to himself. "That has to be what we're looking for." He determined the exact locations of the centers of the heat blooms, then transferred then to the large-scale map on the wall. Having done this, he stepped back a couple of feet and examined the map carefully. "Good," he thought. "Now we're getting somewhere."

The map work having been taken care of, Tony checked the fax machine. There was a large stack of papers awaiting his attention. He took them out of the machine, crossed to his desk, and began reading. From time to time, he would stop reading and make notes on the pad of legal paper on the desk. He was nearly done reading the faxes when Jack Matson stuck his head in the door.

"Coffee?" The sheriff said.

"Morning, Jack," Tony replied. "I could use another cup. It was a short night," Tony answered.

"Rose, the waitress at Denny's, told me I'd just missed you. She said she recognized you from seeing you on last night's TV news. I told her she should have asked for an autograph," Matson said with a chuckle as he headed out for coffee. Then he turned his head back over his shoulder and finished speaking. "She said she'd thought about it, but her autograph book was at home. She also said she'd bring it to work so she can catch you the next time you eat there, though what she said she'd really like is an autographed photo."

"Son of a bitch!" Tony groaned. "Now I'm famous. Just what I really wanted."

In a few moments the sheriff returned, a cup of coffee in each hand. Giving one to Tony, he said, "I have a message for you. Jill says it would be nice if you'd pick her up about five. She also said to tell you she's wearing a cocktail dress, heels, and pearls, and that if you want her to pick a restaurant and make reservations, to please give her a call. I guess she figured you might not be too familiar with places to eat around here any more."

"And she's right," Tony replied. "I'll give her a call in a little while and ask her to decide where to eat. And I guess she's hinting it might be nice if I'd wear a coat and tie. Looks like tonight isn't going to be Colorado casual after all."

"Damn right," Matson said. "I've been to quite a few of these plays with Pat and Jill. We've had season's tickets since we moved back here several years ago. In addition to just plain folks, the Durango Community Theater draws the artsy fartsy crowd, the socially important, and some who really aren't important, but like to think they are, regardless. Well, at least most people try to dress up more than usual. Jeans and cowboy boots would be awful out of place. In fact," he paused to laugh, "I can think of a couple of old biddies who'd chuck a coronary if anyone *dared* show up wearing Colorado casual." He changed the subject. "So what have you been working on this morning?"

Tony led him to the wall map and showed him the reconnaissance photos and the locations he'd pinpointed on the wall map. Then Tony suggested they sit down while he covered the other material. When they were seated, Tony picked up several sheets of fax paper. "The FBI got a lot of data for us," he said. I've been over everything they sent on Tolliver, which is quite a bit. Unfortunately, there's nothing in his personal background that connects him to this area. And there doesn't seem to be any family connection hereabouts, from what the FBI can determine. Now," handing the sheriff a sheet of paper, "here are his known associates from prison. Do you see any names on the list you recognize?"

Matson took the proffered sheet and scanned it carefully. After as minute he said, "No, there's nobody here I've ever....." He stopped and let the rest of the sentence die. "Now wait just a second," he said. Here's a last name I recognize. I know somebody locally named Claibourne. Well," he amended the statement, "her maiden name was Claibourne. At least I think it was." He picked up Tony's phone and pushed a button. "Mike," he asked, "wasn't Gladys Webber's maiden name Claibourne?" He listened to the reply, said, "Thanks, Mike. That's what I thought," and hung the phone up.

"Something interesting?" Tony asked.

"The socially prominent wife of James Webber, our most socially prominent county commissioner, was a Claibourne," Matson said slowly. "By coincidence," he added, "she and her husband both just happen to be originally from Oklahoma, as I recall. And I might add that both the commissioner and his wife are far from being fans of either the United States government or the government of the state of Colorado. Seems both governments make too many rules about what they can't do with land that belongs to the people, like San Juan National Forest land. The commissioner and his wife run sort of a guest ranch, actually it's a working cattle ranch that takes in dudes, and leases a goodly sized hunk of forest grazing land from the Forest Service. They've had a couple legal run-ins because they were running more cattle on the leased land than their lease allowed. Paid a couple hefty fines, too."

Tony put his feet up on the desk and thought a minute. "Militia?" he finally asked.

"Damned if I know, exactly," Matson replied. "But now that you mention it, it wouldn't surprise me too much. He's the type."

"Where's their guest ranch located?"

Matson rose and went to the wall map, Tony following, "It's right here." Matson pointed to a location some distance north of Durango, just on the east side of U.S. highway 550."

"Damn!" Tony exclaimed. "That really fits! And I suppose the commissioner's guest ranch has a string of horses?"

"It sure does, Tony, at least I'd assume that's the case. Don't suppose you could run a dude ranch without horses. Now," he asked, "how do we go about pinning this down? What do we need to do to establish a connection, assuming there is one, between this," he looked at the faxed list of names, "Michael Claibourne and our own Mrs. Gladys Claibourne Webber?"

Tony rubbed the side of his nose with his right index finger, took a moment to gather his thoughts, and then spoke. "You know Jack," he said, "we've both sort of jumped to a conclusion. Just because two people share the same last name doesn't mean there's a connection between them. This could just be a coincidence." He paused again before continuing. "But we can't discount it, either."

"Exactly," the sheriff replied. "It may be just a coincidence, but, like you just said, we can't discount it. So now what?"

"So now I go back to the FBI and request a rundown on this Michael Claibourne.....plus known associates and family members. Especially family members."

"And while you have the FBI digging to find out if there's a connection, then what?"

"Back to the FBI again, I reckon," Tony said. "I worked through Agent Howard yesterday. He was very helpful. Even gave me his home phone number in case I needed to reach him after office hours. So I ask him to light a fire under the people at the Bureau's office in Oklahoma City to get them looking for family connections. I think I'll see if I can get the folks at the Hoover building to start coordinating with the IRS. I may have to call in a favor or two that a guy in the Washington Office owes me. We've got Claibourne's social security number, which means we can track down his whereabouts through who's been employing him."

"And the Bureau can do that, of course" Matson said. He knew well from previous experience what the FBI could do.....providing it wished to exert itself.

"Yep. Under certain circumstances, they answer requests from below the federal level." Tony answered. "The Bureau and the IRS cooperate with each other pretty closely. Bank robbery and kidnapping are two examples. Shucks," he continued, "While it's usually easier and quicker if the FBI is involved, the IRS will help just about any law enforcement agency, especially in cases involving bank robberies, mail theft, and national security interests. In fact..."

"Huh?" Matson said, in response to Tony's incomplete statement.

"Just thinking," Tony replied. If I can't get hold of Howard, I can also go through the OSI's duty officer. Chances are just about a hundred percent that I'll know whoever's on the desk anyhow, and a lot of people there still owe me a few favors. Or I could get really lucky and my buddy Corky will be in the office."

"Won't that get you into trouble?" Matson asked.

"Not really," Tony answered. "Agent Howard promised complete cooperation. It's in the Bureau's interests to crack this case. In fact," he continued, "when I get hold of Howard, I'll just ask him for authorization to access FBI's investigating authority. If he agrees, any questions I ask will be as if the FBI were asking them. If he doesn't agree, then I'll officially ask for an agent to be assigned here full-time to work on the case."

"Hell, Tony," Matson exclaimed. "The Durango office only has under a dozen special agents assigned as investigators right now! There are maybe three times as many paper pushers there than there are investigators. The ASAC, a guy named Herrin, makes maybe over a dozen, but the SAC's stuck with administration, for the most part. Believe me, the Durango office is small potatoes as far as the FBI is concerned. Their manning is awful.....it's sort of a training site for junior agents. They can't put someone on this full-time!"

"I know. That's why I figure Howard will give us anything we want," Tony replied, a wicked smile crossing his face. "He's smart enough to know what his SAC will want him to do. Now," he continued, "let me tell you about a couple ideas I had this morning. I," he said with considerable satisfaction, "have a plan. Of course, there are a few details that still have to check out, but if they work out the way I'm starting to think they will, I think my plan just might work."

Tony explained in detail, a task that took nearly twenty minutes and involved them making two trips to the wall map. When he finished, Matson laughed and said, "Shades of the wild, wild, west! The sheriff's posse rides again! You know, if we pull this off, the media will go wild. If you think you're a celebrity now, just wait!"

Tony groaned again, then said, "Damn! I didn't think of that." He looked thoughtful for a second, then continued, "There's one major problem, Jack."

Matson thought a second. "Right," he said. "How do we figure out where they'd come down out of the mountains." He thought another second. "It makes sense that they'd come out the same way they went in, wouldn't it?" he asked. "And I bet the same people we need to help us get in there can help us find out where that was." He quickly explained what he had in mind.

"Can you set it up? Tony asked.

"I sure as hell can try!" Matson answered. "And there's no reason the people we need help from would refuse. If it works, it'll be terrific PR for them." He paused briefly. "All right, I've got a couple of calls to make, and I may have to go visit a couple of people in person to do a little arm twisting." Matson headed for the door.

"And," Tony said, "I've got to call Jill, call Agent Howard, and do some shopping. Want to sit down over lunch and see what we've got?"

"Great!" Matson called from halfway down the hall. "I'll order..."

"Pizza," Tony made a wild guess and finished the sentence for him.

CHAPTER SIX

Tony spent a busy three hours, first making sure he'd called Jill before doing anything else. Special Agent Howard of the FBI cheerfully agreed to go in to his office and work on Tony's requests. When Tony explained the urgency, Howard promised he'd be in the office in less than half an hour and have at least partial results before noon. After talking with Howard, Tony went to Durango's best-stocked sporting goods store and purchased several items he needed to execute his plan, all of which went on his personal charge card. Fortunately, the card had a very high spending limit on it.

Finally, he went to Animas Air Park and saw Logan Bennett, the owner of the charter and aircraft rental firm he'd done business with the day before. He explained his needs to Bennett, and found that getting the service he wanted would be no problem at all. Expensive, maybe, but not a problem that couldn't be solved with a long checkbook. And Tony certainly had a very long checkbook. Shortly before noon, his tasks complete, he returned to the office. Matson was waiting for him.

"How'd it go with Agent Howard?" the sheriff asked.

"Great," Tony answered. "He's all hot to do whatever he can to help us on this. The Bureau really wants those bank robbers. So Agent Howard called Washington, told the people there what he wanted and explained to them that any questions I might ask were to be considered being asked by the FBI, and then asked that everything be faxed directly to us immediately. He said for the folks in the Hoover Building not to even bother putting the information together neatly because we could do it at this end just as well, and doing it quick and dirty would give us what we need just a little sooner. And I sort of get the impression that if the robbers get caught, even without a lot of active bureau involvement, Howard'll end up looking pretty good. Beside," he added, "it can all be done while he's sitting at his desk."

"Super," Matson said, taking a sip from his coffee mug. "I told you he was a pretty good guy.....for a FBI agent, at least. My chores went just as well. I did have to catch a man at home, but that was no problem. As soon as I explained what we'd need, he jumped at the chance to give it to us...and I do mean *give*. No charge at all for services rendered. He said the company would get super publicity from it, the kind of publicity no amount of money could buy. So the company writes off the cost as a community service."

Matson thought for a moment before going on. "There's one thing I'm concerned about, Tony," he continued. "You're spending a lot of money out of pocket. With the budget the way it is, and considering how stingy the county commissioners have been about spending money on public safety lately, I don't know how the department is going to pay you back. *How!* Hell, I don't know *if!* It may come down to me giving you a personal check."

Tony laughed. "Jack, don't sweat it. I have more money than I know what to do with. If I get the money back from the county, that's fine. If not, I donate the cost to the department and take a tax write-off as an employee business expense. That's legitimate. I'm on the department payroll and every single thing I've spent legally qualifies as an employee business expense, at least the way I look at it. Actually," he laughed again, "my accountants would probably tell me to go for the write-off. Now what about lunch?"

"I was going to get pizza, but we had that yesterday," Matson replied. "Then I thought about sandwiches. And then I decided maybe it'd be nice to go in to town. We could meet Pat and Jill for lunch....unless, of course, you'd rather not," he said with a sly grin.

Tony brightened up. "Super! Let's go, and it's my treat." The thought of seeing Jill Matson again was something he had absolutely no trouble with. He continued, "Maybe she'll tell me where I'm taking her for dinner tonight."

"I figured you wouldn't object," Matson laughed. "I'll call Pat on her cell phone and tell her we'll meet them in about fifteen minutes. There's not much more we can do here today, so I'm planning on going out and driving the highways for a couple hours after we eat. That'll let some of the taxpayers of LaPlata County see that their sheriff is out watching over them. Heck, I might even write a speeding ticket or two. Then I'm going to call it a day."

"Right," Tony said. "Until we hear from the Bureau, there's not much more I can do either, except be at the airport in the morning to pick up tonight's recce photos. Guess I'll head back to the ranch after lunch and see what I can accomplish before I have to pick Jill up." Both men got up and walked through the building and out into the parking lot.

Lunch was most enjoyable. Tony and Jack met Jill and Pat at the corner of Main and Eighth, then went to Lady Falconberg's Barley Exchange, a nice restaurant a block further south on Main. After they were seated, Jill got started on stories about her students and some of the crazy stunts kids had pulled over the years. This got Tony started on some of the dumb things he'd seen people doing in the Washington, D.C., area. The ones that caused the most laughter were Tony's stories of the person who drove through a bank's drive-through window.....going in the wrong direction.....and the person who parked a compact car in a shopping cart corral at a shopping center.....and then couldn't get out of the car. Jack and Pat sat more or less quietly during the meal, watching the two young people obviously enjoying each other's company.

After lunch, the four of them walked up the steps from Lady Falconberg's basement dining room to Main Street's sidewalk. Jack and Pat said goodbye and left to take care of some errands that needed doing before that evening's political soiree. Then Jill said, "I'm off to get my hair done for tonight."

"On a holiday weekend Saturday? Who do you know? Aren't beauticians usually closed on a holiday weekend"?

Normally, they are," she replied. "But I have a hairdresser friend who owes me a big favor. I babysat for her and her husband for a whole weekend last month so they could go to Phoenix for a wedding. She rightfully figures she owes me big time, so she's doing my hair today, and doing it for free at that."

"Gee, Jill," Tony responded, "it looks wonderful to me just the way it is."

"Why thank you, kind sir," Jill replied. "But I wouldn't dream of showing up at the theater tonight without having it done. Too many catty remarks would be made." She chuckled, "And on the subject of catty remarks, I expect to hear a few because of being with you. Some of the local social climbers are going to be awfully jealous of me."

"And you, young sir," she continued, "should expect to be the center of attention. I gather that this evening I'll be in the company of Durango's most famous law enforcement officer, from what the paper said today. There's almost a half page about you in today's paper, you know...front page, at that, and above the fold."

"Oh, shi.......Oh shoot!" Tony exclaimed.

"It's not that bad," Jill said. "They've got a nice picture of you....in Air Force uniform, no less. And lots of background material, things about you staying with your grandfather and going to school off and on in Bayfield, an interview with your father, and...."

"Oh, God!" Tony groaned. "And I suppose the story will be picked up by the D.C. paper, too."

Oh, no, Tony," Jill said. "It's a story from the Washington *Post* that the Durango paper picked up off the AP wire. At a guess, I'd say that the *Post* took yesterday's story from our paper, and then some enterprising reporter made some connections and did some digging. By now, darn near everybody in Durango has seen it." She paused a moment. "You're famous, Mister Frye. Tonight," she continued with a chuckle, "could be really interesting."

"Do you want to back out?" Tony asked, a note of concern in his voice. "If you decide you don't want to go tonight.....

"Only if you don't think you're up to it," Jill answered with a smile. "I can take the heat. Actually it should be very educational, and a lot of fun, too. Of course," she continued, "if you'd rather avoid the spotlight, we could stay home, make hamburgers or order out for a pizza, and just watch a movie on TV."

Tony thought for just a second. "Thanks for giving me an out, Jill," he replied. "I guess I can take the heat, too.....I hope. I certainly won't run from the publicity, much as I'd probably like to. Besides, I love *Guys and Dolls*, and I don't think too many people will be watching me tonight anyhow. Not that hamburgers or pizza and an evening of watching TV doesn't sound attractive. Maybe I could have a rain check on that?"

"It could probably be arranged," she said with a smile, "And why do you think you won't be the center of attention tonight? By now darn near every person in this county who can read has read the article, and a lot of the illiterate ones will no doubt have looked at the pictures. "

"Simple. I figure I'm going to be with the best-looking girl in the county. They'll be too busy looking at you to pay any attention to me. The men will, at least."

Jill laughed and blushed slightly. "Why, thank you, kind sir. After that bit of blarney I have no choice but to wear my most striking dress in hopes of distracting just a little attention away from....as the newspaper put it.....the 'Millionaire Cowboy Cop.' Be prepared for a busy night, bucko. I figure I'm going to have to introduce you to half of what passes for Durango's high society tonight. They'll all be stampeding to meet you."

Tony stood silently for a second, a worried look on his face. Then he spoke. "Jill, I think we have a problem."

Jill ceased smiling. "What's wrong, Tony?

Then he smiled. "Durango's high society may be shocked. I think I have a choice of picking you up in a La Plata County sheriff's department Cherokee or in my pickup, which is only a month or so old, or the ranch pickup, which is pretty rusty and decrepit, not to mention ancient. Grandpa Pete liked his old pickup. He didn't own a car, though he'd rent one, if need be. I don't think I can buy a car between now and five o'clock." He hesitated a second, "I probably could buy one, or at least I think I could, but I don't think I could take delivery on a car by then. Not on a Sunday."

For a moment Tony regretted that Grandpa Pete hadn't believed in mixing cars and ranches; he'd driven a pickup, an old one that had more than its share of dings and a considerable amount of rust on the body. So Tony only had a choice of two trucks, one of which was pretty disreputable, though it was in good mechanical repair, and a police car.

"Consider the problem solved, Tony," Jill laughed. "When you come to pick me up, you can drive my car, if you want. I wouldn't worry about the pickup truck, though. I mean, after all, this is Colorado! Probably a quarter of the people at the play tonight will be driving them. You probably know the joke: a Colorado Cadillac is a pickup with a gun rack. On the other hand," she laughed again, "we'd certainly have no problem getting a parking space if we arrived in Unit Six. You could park it anywhere in town and no city cop would dare to ticket it."

"And dinner? Where would you like to eat?" Tony asked.

"Ahhh, I'm taking advantage of you, Tony. I hope you don't mind." Jill smiled as she put her hand on Tony's arm. "I made reservations at a place called The Bank. It's relatively new, and I've wanted to eat there ever since it opened. The food is supposed to be fantastic, especially the prime rib, anything beef, for that matter. Word has it that this place only serves beef from cows that died a happy and gentle death."

"We have reservations for quarter of six, and the play starts at eight fifteen. It's in an old bank building, which accounts for the name, and it's only about four blocks from the restaurant to the theater, so we don't have to worry about driving there after dinner, not to mention not having to worry about finding a parking place near the theater. It's not much more than maybe a ten minute walk, and that's if we walk slowly. I hope that's OK with you? Can you be at the house by a quarter after five or a little earlier?"

"Sure, he said. "And I kind of like the fact that I'll be the first person to take you to this place. I just hope the food's as good as the newspaper says it is. And," he continued shyly after a brief pause, "I certainly wouldn't object if a certain redhead would prove willing to introduce me to several of Durango's other good restaurants."

"Why Mister Frye," Jill said, "are you asking me out again already?" Her voice had a happy tinkle in it. "And now," she said, looking at her watch, "I really have to run. I have about five minutes to get to the hairdresser's, which, lucky for me, is just around the corner and up the hill half a block." She brushed her fingertips lightly on Tony's cheek, turned, and started to run up the sidewalk. She was about ten feet away from Tony when she stopped, turned, and called to him. "And I want you to tell me how you acquired a liking for *Guys & Dolls*. As musicals go, it's almost an antique!" Before Tony could reply, she turned and started running again.

Tony held his left hand to the spot Jill had touched and watched her run up the street. . "Wow!" he said. "I think she likes me!" With a grin on his face, he crossed Main Street and walked down Seventh to Narrow Gauge Alley, then walked next to the railroad track for a block to the parking lot. Before he got into his Cherokee, he picked up a copy of the day's Durango newspaper from a coin-operated rack. When he got into the vehicle, he scanned the front page, then groaned as he put the paper on the seat beside him. "I don't believe it. Why me?" He started the jeep, then headed for the ranch.

When Tony got home, he found several messages on his answering machine. One was from his father, asking what Tony had managed to do to get involved in investigating a bank robbery. Tony could tell from the tone of his father's voice that Deputy Secretary of State Robert Frye was not amused. Seven messages were from Marissa. Tony could tell both from the tone of her voice and the language she used that Marissa was extremely upset. When provoked, the congressman's daughter could swear like a Marine drill instructor.

In most colorful and profane terms, she demanded repeatedly that Tony call her *immediately*! She also demanded that he drop what he was doing in Colorado and return to Washington, again *immediately*. "Hell would have to freeze over," Tony muttered, "as he deleted the final message from Marissa from the answering machine. I was never really happy in D.C., except when I was working. I should call Marissa tomorrow and tell her that I'm staying here permanently. She'll tell me that if that's the case, I can forget about her."

He smiled. "I think the last couple days have taught me that Marissa just isn't for me. I could never make her happy without making myself miserable," he thought. He gave an affirmative nod of his head. "Yep!" he said. "Tomorrow I call Marissa and tell her I'm staying here. I may even tell her to go to hell. I know that's what she'll tell me to do."

Satisfied at his decision, Tony looked at his watch. he decided he had enough time to poke around the ranch a bit, and decided to start with the horse barn. He walked out of the house, stepped off the porch, and walked the couple hundred feet down the lane top the horse barn. As he walked around the corner of the barn, he saw Lew Barnes, wearing old, faded blue jeans, an old work shirt, and traditional western headgear, working on one of the corral fence posts.

"Hi, Uncle Lew," Tony called.

Barnes put the hammer he'd been using down and pushed his stetson back off his head, revealing a shock of silver hair as he did so. "Afternoon, Junior," Lew answered. "Have you seen today's paper? There's quite an art....."

"Yeah, I've seen it. Haven't read all of it yet, though. I think I'll put that questionable pleasure off until tomorrow."

"Didn't figure it'd make your day. That young lady friend of yours in Washington, the one they interviewed, sounded downright upset. Did you see that part?" the old man asked.

"Oh, no!" Tony exclaimed. "They didn't interview Marissa!"

"Marissa?" Barnes replied. "Yep, that's what the paper said her name was. Some candy ass congressman's daughter, too." Barnes grinned. He had a really low tolerance level for most politicians, especially those on the federal level. "You been moving in some pretty fast company, I reckon."

"And," Tony muttered, "I'm probably going to have to explain Marissa to Jill." He thought for a second, then realized that, even though he'd known Jill Matson a very short time, he realized that he'd pick her over Marissa Montgomery any day of the week.

Then Tony's mind snapped back to matters at hand. "Lew," he began, "I've got a little problem. You see..."

"Kind of like being a deputy, don't you, Junior?" Lew asked, interrupting Tony in mid-sentence.

"Huh?" Barnes' question caught Tony by surprise. He thought for a moment before answering. "Well, yes, I guess I do," he admitted, "not that I'm a real deputy or anything," Tony answered without hesitation. "I'm mostly just going to be doing the investigation end on this bank robbery thing, that and some planning. Maybe it's not that I like it, though. I'm kind of torn right now. I know I promised you after Grandpa Pete's funeral that I'd take an active part in working around the ranch, and I sure want to, but I feel pretty obliged to finish this bank robbery job. And I guess I sort of told the sheriff I'd kind of help out a bit until that wounded deputy recovers." Tony paused.

"Guess you've got your grandpappy's sense of civic responsibility, Son," Barnes said, chuckling a bit. "Tony, you do what you need to do. Pete didn't do much around here the last year or two he was alive, except handle the business end of runnin' the spread. Me 'n' the hands did most everything else. You know I have Pedro Martinez and Ben Warrenton working full time now, along with Buster Jiggs, and Buster's worked here for years and years. Had Pedro and Ben for nigh on to two years now, and they're both damn good workers."

"And Pete had me hire one or two high school boys every summer for the last five or six years," he continued. "You knew that, of course." Lew took his hat off, pulled his bandana from his hip pocket, and wiped his forehead before he continued. "Tony, if you want to actually *work* this ranch full time, that's fine. You want to do what you have time for around here and work for the sheriff, that's fine, too. Me, I'm just happy to have you home where you belong instead of you being back east. Didn't seem right being here without having a Frye in residence."

Tony put his arms around the old man and gave him a hug. "Thanks, Uncle Lew," he said. "I really needed to hear that." He sniffed. "Been feelin' guilty all day about not pulling my weight here. Guess I figured that Grandpa Pete'd be looking down on me with a displeased look on his face."

Barnes chuckled. "Don't see that happenin', Junior," he said. "Your grandpappy always was right proud of the kind of work you did. He'd tell durn near everybody he'd meet about his grandson the Air Force captain but not say hardly a word about his one and only son being a high and mighty gollywhumpus in the State Department and a leadin' light in the D.C. social whirl. . I 'spect he'd be real pleased to find you trying to bring those bank robbers in. He always said you had a strong sense of civic duty. And that, Sonny, sure makes you your grandpa's kin."

Tony wasn't totally convinced. "Well, maybe," he said. "Anyhow, I'm committed to seeing this thing through, Lew, and I'm glad you understand. Any extra help you need, you just let me know. If it takes that, you hire another hand full-time, or even more than one. Now," he said, "let's see what we've got for horses these days. There's only one or two that I seem to remember from the last time I was out here and had time to ride."

The two men walked into the horse barn. Tony looked around and asked several questions. Barnes pointed out where the horses were, down by the river taking advantage of the shade from the trees that grew along the Pine River. Then they went into the tack room, and Tony checked out the saddle his grandfather had given him years ago for his sixteenth birthday. He was very pleased to find it well-oiled and the leather in excellent shape.

"I need to get on a horse, Lew," Tony said, resting his left hand on the pommel of the saddle. "It's been a long time. Trying to ride around Washington was a major pain. All most of those dudes do is ride English and no self-respecting cowboy would even think of doing that." He paused for a second. "You know," he continued, "I made a bunch of enemies back East by saying that only wimps, sissies, and wimmen rode English."

Lew Barnes laughed for close to a minute. "Well, ain't it the truth? I guess Pete and I brought you up right. Won't take much to get you up on a proper saddle. Pete and I took real good care of yours. And, like always, you'll end up stiff and sore until you get used to it again, Junior," Barnes answered with a laugh, calling Tony the name he'd used on him when Tony was a wet-behind-the-ears kid. "Just like every other time you came back here from the East. But," he slapped Tony on the back, "you'll get used to it again, I reckon. Leastways you always did. Anyhow, take your pick of any of the critters. They're all fit to ride and your old saddle's all oiled and ready any time you want to use it.."

"Good," Tony said. "I'll ride around the ranch for an hour or so tomorrow, if I can work it in. Need to get back in practice," he commented. "And now," looking at his watch, "I've got to feed a cat, shower, and get ready to go out. Got a date tonight with the boss's daughter." He laughed as he turned and headed back toward the ranch house.

"Good for him," Barnes said softly to himself as Tony walked up the steps to the ranch house porch. "That Marissa woman didn't sound like she'd do for old Pete's boy. Now, the sheriff's daughter........that's sure 'nuf another story. She's really somethin'." Barnes smiled with satisfaction.

CHAPTER SEVEN

"What if they made a connection between Tolliver and your brother?" County Commissioner Webber asked his wife as he tied his necktie for the second time. The second effort ended up looking as bad as had the first. Webber swore, undid the tie, and started over.

Gladys Webber put down her hair brush and turned to face her husband. "Don't be an ass, Jim," she replied.

"Damn!" The third attempt at tying the necktie ended up as badly as the previous two tries. "But you heard the news broadcast, Gladys," Webber said. "They've identified Tolliver by name and know he's done time in jail. And he swore to us that he didn't have a record, that bastard! If they know that much, wouldn't they know he and Mike are friends?

"Now I'd think that would be quite a stretch, Jim. So Jim Bob did jail time, so what? Mike's never been arrested, even as a kid. Yes, he and Tolliver knew each other back home, but they weren't even from the same town, for Pete's sake, or from the same part of the state if you go back that far!" Gladys Webber was getting a little exasperated with her husband. "And even if they do connect Mike and Jim Bob, Mike's a Claibourne. What is there to connect him with us?" Mrs. Webber turned back to her dresser mirror, picked up her hair brush and went back to doing her hair.

"Damn it, Gladys! The fact that your maiden name is Claibourne isn't exactly a secret," her husband exclaimed.

"So? I think it's unlikely anyone would make a connection. Just remember, when my parents got divorced, my father got custody of Mike. I lived with my mother. We didn't even live in the same county. The only times I saw Mike for close to ten years before we got married was at our grandparents' ranch during school vacation. Do you think there's a police record of that? I'll say it again. Don't be an ass, James!"

County Commissioner Webber did not take his wife's nagging at him lightly. "And wasn't it your grandfather that got us all involved with the Militia? Don't you think there just might be some record of your family's involvement with the movement?"

This last question was too much for Gladys Webber. She slammed the hair brush down on the dresser and turned to face her husband again. "James Webber," she said through clenched teeth, "nobody in my family, absolutely *nobody*, has ever so much as spoken out in a way to attract unfavorable attention to ourselves. Yes, people have known that we disagree with some of the government's policies concerning land use, among other things. But we've always maintained a really low profile. That way we don't attract unfavorable attention. And that, my dear husband, is why I always keep after you not to lose your temper and shoot your damn mouth off in public. And tonight you are going to keep your temper under control and keep your feet and your mouth as far away from each other as possible." Her anger passed almost as quickly as it started. She reached up and gently patted her husband's cheek. "Besides, even if somebody makes a connection between us and Mike, we can say we haven't seen him in years. There's no record of him being anywhere near here. Now finish getting ready. We have to meet the Yarbroughs for dinner before the play and we're running short on time."

****

***

Tony took care of showering and all the other things that had to be done to prepare for dinner and the theater with Jill. The big question he had to address was what to wear. He finally decided on a dark grey suit with a faint light blue pinstripe on the grounds that he could tuck his pistol in to the waistband of the pants relatively discretely. He expected some discomfort when he sat down. In this, he was correct; the pistol pressed against his back whenever he leaned back in the chair he used for a test.

When he walked out of the ranch house to head to town to pick her up, he looked at the two vehicles parked in the ranch yard. His perverse sense of humor wanted to take the county Cherokee, but he decided on his pickup on the grounds that it would fit in more. Then he made a mental note to shop for a car, or maybe a van or station wagon, as soon as possible.

The drive to what Tony thought of as 'Durango West', the upscale residential neighborhood where the Matson residence was located, took about forty-five minutes. Tony pulled in to the driveway a few minutes early, got out of the truck, and walked up to the front door. He knocked, and a few seconds later Pat Matson, wearing a black cocktail dress and a string of pearls, opened the door.

"Come in, Tony," she said. "Jill's almost ready." Mrs. Matson looked at Tony carefully, then said, "My, don't you look nice. That suit really looks good on you."

"Thanks, Mrs. Matson," Tony answered. "You sure look nice tonight, too. I hope Jill approves of what I dragged out of the closet," he said, gesturing to his suit coat. "Took me a while to decide if it was sufficiently formal for tonight. I gather tonight's affair is a couple notches above 'Colorado casual'."

Pat Matson laughed. "I see you know the joke," she said. "Colorado casual: defined as scraping the cow flop off your second best pair of cowboy boots and putting on a clean pair of Levis. You're absolutely right, though. A lot of people around here think a little theater performance is a pretty classy social occasion, and they dress accordingly. That's especially true of us women. We don't have all that many occasions for dressing up out here. So we tend to take advantage of opportunities as they happen." She patted the lapels of his suit to smooth them and said, "Trust me. You certainly won't appear out of place."

"To tell the truth, I was wondering if I shouldn't maybe wear my tux. For the last few years it's been almost a required item of clothing, especially for things at the Kennedy Center, a lot of which, to tell the truth, I'd just as soon have skipped."

Pat laughed again. "I think a tux might be a slight case of overkill, Tony, at least in this part of the world, but I understand what D.C. society can be for unattached junior officers. Senior officers sort of impose on them any time a daughter or some high society young lady doesn't have an escort to some important social function. Thankfully we were married and somewhat older when Jack was stationed there."

She saw from the look on Tony's face that she hit the nail right on the head with her remark about unattached young females in the nation's capital. She took a deep breath, then continued, "Jack's in the bedroom trying to get his necktie tied straight. We've got this sort of formal political thing we sort of have to go to tonight, and he'd just as soon stay home. That man hates suits. It just about takes the threat of a violent application of a rolling pin or a cast iron skillet to get him dressed for the theater. Twenty plus years in the Army and he hated any occasion that he couldn't wear fatigues or BDU's for. The two years he spent at the Pentagon were sheer hell for him. And," she said, turning around, "here's Jill. I'm going to go check on Jack. You kids have fun, and enjoy the show." She hurried off, as her daughter crossed the living room toward Tony.

Tony stared at Jill, his mouth half open. She was wearing a mint green cocktail dress with black lace trim, a black belt, and a scoop neck. The dress was short enough to give Tony a view of what he mentally ranked as a world-class pair of legs. And, like her mother, she wore a pearl necklace, one single strand. The net effect of this, combined with her red hair, lovely face and figure, and fair complexion, was striking. All he could think of to say was, "Hi." And he had trouble getting that out without stuttering.

"Well," she said, spinning around once so the dress flared out slightly, "what do you think?"

Tony thought a second, still admiring the very lovely young lady standing opposite him, then said, "Maybe it's a good thing I've got a pistol tucked in the back of my waistband, Jill. I have a hunch I may have to shoot every second unmarried male in Durango tonight, and maybe more."

This prompted a laugh from Jill. "I hope it doesn't reach that point, Tony. Think of all the bad things the newspapers would print." Her smile faded a bit, then she continued, "I really wish you didn't have to be armed, though."

"Are you upset that I'm carrying?" he asked.

"Oh, heck, no!" she exclaimed. "Just that it might be a bit uncomfortable sitting in the theater chair. I know department policy. Daddy had a pistol tucked in his belt last night when the two of you were playing chess and while we were eating, and I know you had one in the pocket of your jean jacket. Guns don't bother me, Tony. I grew up with them, and I know how to use them, too. Some day you can take me to the pistol range and..."

"And don't bet that she won't clobber you, Tony," Jack Matson said as he walked in to the living room. "You know that line in *Guys and Dolls* about the ear full of cider? This brat's been shooting, both rifle and pistol, since she was six. She shot competitively in college and coaches the marksmanship team at Durango High in her spare time. She's as good a shot as I am."

"Actually, Daddy," Jill said with a smirk, "I'm just a little bit better, at least with a target pistol and small bore rifle. And now, handsome young Mister Frye, shall we depart? Our reservation is for twenty-five minutes from now and we're going to have to hurry to make it to the restaurant on time."

"Don't think it's a problem, Jill. I seem to remember that restaurants generally hold reservations for fifteen minutes, at least back East," Tony answered as he took her arm and led her toward the door.

"Same here," she replied, "but we don't want to rush dinner, do we?"

"Have fun, kids," the sheriff said as Jill and Tony walked to the door. "Like

the Motel 6 ad says, 'We'll leave the light on for you.'"

As Jill and Tony walked to the driveway, Jill tossed him a set of car keys and said, "Drive my Pontiac if you want, Tony."

He caught the proffered keys, "Thanks, Jill. I'd feel terribly awkward escorting a lovely young lady like you in my truck." He laughed, "Really high up on my list of personal chores for next week is to buy another set of wheels." He opened the passenger door of the car for Jill, closed it once she was seated, and walked around to the driver's side. He got in, fastened his seatbelt, looked to make sure that Jill's was fastened, started the car and drove off.

As he pulled out onto U.S. 160 and turned left toward Durango, he said, "Where am I going?"

"See if you can find a parking spot on Narrow Gauge somewhere between Eighth and Tenth," Jill answered. If not, park in the town lot and we'll walk to the restaurant. It's on Main just north of the corner of Ninth." She continued, "I just hope the food's as good as the write-up in the newspaper."

"You shouldn't believe everything you read in newspapers," Tony answered, a remark that prompted a discussion of the article on Tony that had appeared in that day's news-paper. Both of them avoided the topic of Marissa Montgomery and what the article quoted her as saying.

Tony, through simple good luck, was able to find a parking space just around the corner from the restaurant. They were seated promptly, at a table for two in a corner of the main dining room. Each ordered a cocktail, followed by French onion soup, salad and entree. Jill ordered the New York sirloin, medium rare with a side of horseradish and Tony followed suit. Both passed on high calorie desserts, ordering decaf coffee instead. The mealtime portion of their evening together went exceptionally well. They spent much of their time at table laughing at each other's stories.

"That," Tony said with a sigh of contentment as they walked out of the restaurant into the evening twilight, compounded with light from the streetlamps, "was absolutely wonderful, especially the onion soup. It's the second best meal I've had since I left D.C."

"And what, pray tell, was the best?" Jill responded, right on cue. She was virtually certain she knew what Tony's answer was going to be.

"The one you and your mother fixed last night, of course," Tony answered. "What else?"

Jill elbowed him lightly in the ribs, while saying, "Flattery will get you anywhere, Tony. Well, almost anywhere," she amended, after a second's hesitation. "Now," she continued in a more serious tone, "we've got a couple block walk to the theater. We'll be a little early, and you're probably going to have to suffer being introduced to half of Durango. I guarantee every person in the lobby tonight is going to want to meet you."

A small price to pay, fair maiden, for the pleasure of your company," he responded, a comment that earned him another soft elbow in the ribs.

The lobby of the theater was well populated when Jill and Tony arrived, nearly a half hour before curtain time. Jill introduced Tony to several people, mostly couples of about their age, while they waited for the house doors to open. It gave Tony a small sense of satisfaction to actually be able to introduce two people to Jill....Ed Hall, one of his high school classmates at Bayfield High, and his wife, Mary, who graduated a year behind Tony and Ed. Tony and Jill agreed to meet Ed, his wife, and another couple, Bob and Mae Clark, after the play. Intermission promised to be more socializing with the younger crowd until Jill saw an older couple approaching from the far side of the lobby.

"Oh," she whispered. "Heads up, Tony. The enemy is in sight." Then she turned and smiled at the older couple. "Why Mister and Mrs. Webber, how nice to see you," she said. "May I introduce Tony Frye, La Plata's newest deputy? Tony, meet Gladys and James Webber. Mister Webber is one of our county commissioners."

"Mister Frye, it's a real pleasure," Webber said in a booming voice. "Jill's father convinced us to hire you, and of course, we've read all about you in the paper. Haven't we, Dear," he said to his wife.

"Oh, yes," Gladys Webber gushed. "And, of course, we knew your grandfather. Welcome back to Durango, Mr. Frye. As my husband said, we have read about you, indeed."

"Tell me, Deputy Frye," Webber said, "what's going on with tracking down the bank robbers? Is there anything the papers and TV haven't reported?"

Tony thought for a moment, then said, "Actually, not an awful lot. We've got two deputies tracking the robbers up in the national forest. Of course, the big problem is that the robbers have a head start and the deputies can only travel about as fast as the people they're chasing, actually a little slower as they have to go slower to make sure they're following the robbers' trail. If we could just figure out where they were heading, we could get a posse in front of them. But there's twenty or thirty places they could end up, and the department just doesn't have the manpower to cover them all, not even with the extra men from the State Patrol."

"Or, if we knew who they were, we could just work on nailing them after they leave that confounded national forest," he continued. "The problem is we don't know who they are, except for the dead man." Tony paused for a second, then continued, "We do have a set of fingerprints, but no identity to go with them." Tony let his voice fall, "This hasn't been released for public consumption yet, but the prints do match up with a John Doe in the FBI's file in Washington. It could be that we're dealing with a gang from Oklahoma. That's where the dead robber came from, and the prints came from a robbery scene in the same state."

The lights in the lobby flashed several times, signaling the end of the intermission. Jill took Tony's arm. "Time to get back to our seats," she said lightly. "Will you excuse us?"

The Webbers and Tony exchanged the conventional pleasantries, then Tony let Jill lead him back into the theater. As they walked to their seats, he leaned over and whispered in her ear, "'The enemy is in sight'? Just how much do you know about what's going on, Jill?"

When they were seated, Jill put her head on his shoulder and whispered her answer back to him. "Hush! I'll tell you later, when we're alone." She'd no sooner said this than the house lights dimmed and the curtain went up on the second act. They sat in silence for the rest of the show, enjoying the acting and the music, especially "Sit down, you're rocking the boat", as the man playing the part of Nicely Nicely Johnson was an excellent comic actor with a strong singing voice and did a fantastic job with the song.

The play ended, and shortly afterward Jill and Tony met the Clarks and the Halls in the theater lobby. They decided to walk from the theater down to the Strater Hotel and have a drink at the Diamond Belle Saloon. The evening was comfortably warm for May, and the three couples laughed and talked. Jill and Mae, who was one of Jill's teaching colleagues, told a humorous story about an incident that had taken place at the high school a few days earlier. Then Ed Hall recounted a story about Tony falling in a pile of manure as a result of being thrown from a horse when they were high school sophomores on the rodeo team, a tale that made Tony blush, especially as Ed made a point of mentioning that, at the time, Tony had been trying to impress a young lady with his riding ability. The fact that Jill found the story exceptionally funny caused Tony to blush even more.

The time passed quickly, and before they knew it, the three couples were passing through the front door of the grand old Victorian era hotel. They spent the better part of an hour having drinks and munchies in the saloon. Jill broke up the evening when she said, "I hate to say it, but we've got to run. Daddy needs to talk to Tony for a minute tonight before he goes to bed, and he wasn't available when Tony picked me up." Both of the other couples decided they also had to call it a night.

When they left the hotel, the Halls and Clarks parted company at the corner and walked up Main. It was a pleasantly mild night and they walked slowly. Jill steered Tony down Seventh to Narrow Gauge, and then turned north, to walk up the alley to where Tony had parked her car. As they walked, she took Tony's hand and put her head on his arm. Tony waited until there was nobody within hearing, then said, "OK, Jill. What gives? Your dad talked to us before we left and he didn't give me cause to think he'd want to see me later."

"Did you forget you have to be at the airport early in the morning to pick up the next set of reconnaissance photos? I figured you might want to get at least a little sleep tonight. From what Daddy said, you just might be in for a busy day tomorrow."

"Oh," Tony responded, "That's right. I'd almost forgotten about that." He paused for a second as they walked along the narrow sidewalk between the railroad tracks and the street. "Looks like it's gonna be a short night." He paused again, then continued. "Jill, remember the question I asked back at the theater? How the heck much do you know about what's going on?"

"I hope this doesn't upset you," she answered. "I know just about everything that's in the works, Tony. You see, Daddy uses Mom and me as sort of sounding boards. He says it helps him get his thoughts organized. And sometimes one or the other of us will actually come up with a helpful suggestion. So I know that the two of you see the Webbers as suspects."

"And, in case you're worried," she continued, "Mom and I both know how to keep our mouths shut. I know exactly what you have going on tomorrow morning, and I know all about that humdinger of a plan you cooked up. If it works," she said, "the media will go wild! The Durango sheriff's posse rides again! Shades of the old Wild West! Whoopee!"

She thought for a second, then continued, "You think you've got media problems now? Wait 'til you see what happens if the plan you cooked up produces the desired results! If you pull it off, it'll most likely make the news nationwide. Remember what I said about sensationalism being the thing that drives newspaper sales?"

"Just what I need, more publicity," Tony said, a note of distress in his voice.

Jill laughed. Then she said, "Cheer up, Tony. It's not going to hurt that much. You can always fall back on saying 'No comment.' That, or maybe hiding on your ranch."

They walked quietly for a few moments, carefully negotiating the parking meters that partially obstructed passage along the narrow sidewalk. Finally, Jill spoke. "Tony," she said quietly, "is there anything I ought to know about this Marissa person the newspaper article talked about?"

They stopped under a streetlight. Tony said nothing for a moment. "I knew this was going to come up eventually," he said. "I just didn't think it'd be this soon." Tony paused for a moment before he continued. "Look, Jill, when I met you last night, I realized right away that I liked you. You were...," He corrected himself, "You *are* just plain downright enjoyable to be with. Heck, I even enjoyed helping with the dishes last night. Every second I've spent with you since has been wonderful, fun, *happy*."

"As for Marissa....," he hesitated a bit before continuing, ".....there was a time when I thought I might be in love with her. Then a while back, shortly before the time my grandfather died, I realized that we really actually didn't have a whole heck of a lot in common. She's very liberal and I'm fairly conservative. She likes politics and that's something that bores me to tears. Marissa's big on formal social events and I'm more of a casual event person. I'm happy in blue jeans or chinos, even though I don't complain about wearing more formal clothing when I have to......as long as I don't have to on a regular basis.

Tony took a deep breath, then went on. "Looking back on my relationship with Marissa, I guess we really didn't have that much in common, Marissa and me. It did take me some time to realize that, though. Her reaction to me inheriting the ranch was a learning experience", he said as they started walking again.

He paused for a moment, long enough for them to walk past a couple of shuttered storefronts. "You know," he continued, "it wasn't until I was driving out here that I smartened up and fully realized that Marissa is actually a badly spoiled brat. And a major pain in the butt, too, when she doesn't get her way! She's what some people would call a 'control freak'."

"Oh?"

"Yeah. It's kind of hard to explain", he said. She's always been able to get anything she wants, at least from her parents. And a lot of other people are really impressed that her dad's a big wheel in Congress. As a result, she usually ends up getting everything that she wants. Her teachers in the fancy private school she went to let her get away with murder, so she said more than once. She bragged about that a lot, in fact."

"That's part of the problem," he went on, "but it sure isn't all of it. It took a while, but I finally realized that Marissa's impressed by people's social standings, not by whether they're decent people or not. My dad's medium well off in his own right, largely thanks to my grandfather, and 'way up there in the upper level of the State Department. My stepmother's filthy rich. Those things impress Marissa. The fact that my stepmother, in addition to being richer than God, is a member of the First Families of Virginia also impresses her. You don't even want to think about what Marissa said when she found out that I inherited a whole bundle when Grandpa Pete died".

He continued. "In fact, it was my stepmother who first asked me to take Marissa out, to some sort of function at the Kennedy Center. Her father wanted her to attend, and wanted her escorted. So my stepmother, who sits on some sort of board with Marissa's father, volunteered my services. She told me that it'd make a friend in Congress for my dad. I wasn't what you'd call keen on going, but I couldn't think of a good excuse *not* to go. And being drafted to serve as escort is something that goes with being a single junior officer stationed in D.C."

Jill chuckled. "Been through things like that a couple times myself," she said. "I could tell stories about some of the blind dates friends arranged for me when I was in college.....and after."

Tony went on. "Marissa, her parents, my father, and my stepmother, well, they're all.....high society, high *Washington* society, and they're all well-connected in government. Heck, my stepmother's much older first husband - he died close to twenty years ago, more or less - he was a considerable power in the U.S. Senate. I've heard that some people were even talking about him as a potential Presidential candidate not long before he died. High society! I guess for a while that kind of life looked kind of glamorous to me." He grew silent.

Jill hesitated before speaking. "You used the past tense. It doesn't anymore?"

Tony took a moment to compose his thoughts. "Jill," he said, "I liked my job. I was a glorified cop. I spent most of my time sitting at my desk or off in the field somewhere digging for clues, trying to put two and two together in some way so that the answer made sense, and looking for solutions to crimes. I had a slightly fancy-sounding title and wore a military uniform, but basically I was a cop. Correction: I was a criminal investigator. I didn't set out to be one. I really wanted to be a fighter pilot, but when I graduated from the academy, the Air Force seemed to have too many pilots and not enough of a lot of other specialties, criminal investigators being one of them. The 'needs of the service', as the saying has it, came first, so I became a criminal investigator, a glorified cop. As a matter of fact, I suspect my father might have pulled a few strings to make sure I didn't go to flight school. He thinks flying fighters is dangerous."

"Having a big brother who flies one, and having listened to a lot of his stories, I'd say your father is probably right," she said with a chuckle in her voice.

"At the time, I wasn't happy about it, about the OSI assignment, but surprisingly…..at least it was a surprise to me, I found out that I was pretty good at being an investigator. At least that's what the general I worked for said. Must have been true because he fought tooth and nails to get me out of being transferred a couple years ago when the service wanted to give me a career broadening assignment in personnel. And I also found I really liked the work. It was interesting and challenging, so I ended up getting a master's degree in criminology. And I got a very large kick out of solving cases, especially the really tough ones. I was happy, really happy, with the investigative work I was doing. And then Grandpa Pete died. And I inherited the ranch and a bunch of other things. And that's when things really began to change."

He stopped speaking for a moment as they continued walking. "There's another thing, too. I guess I'm just a country boy at heart," he continued, "I spent almost all of my childhood, at least that part after my mother died, living out here with my grandfather. My mother died when I was really young and my father went to a lot of places where he wouldn't, or couldn't, take kids. My sister stayed with my mother's younger sister, but I ended up out here."

"So you spent an awful lot of time with your grandfather," Jill said. "I knew that from listening to him talk about you."

"I have to say this, Jill, much as it's not a nice thing to have to say. My father wasn't much of a father.....no parenting skills despite him being raised by someone who would have earned top grades in that area. We actually don't have a heck of a lot in common. I rarely saw him when I was a kid. That was OK with me because I had Grandpa Pete. I saw more of my father the last few years when I was stationed in D.C. than I ever did in the same amount of time when I was younger." He hesitated, then continued. "We speak, but we're not on the best of terms, especially after Grandpa Pete died."

"How so?" Jill asked.

"I inherited the bulk of Grandpa's estate. Dad got a million dollar trust fund. That was all. I think he resents the fact that I inherited 'way more than he did."

"But you have a sister, too. What about her?"

"My sister's a lot older than I am," he replied. "She was already in medical school when I was finishing grade school. We're civil, but not really close; too much of an age difference. She got the same million dollar inheritance that my father got. And there was no way that Dad could leave me with her while he was off in Darkest Africa some place. So I pretty much grew up on my grandfather's ranch, mostly, especially after my mom died when I was in first grade. Lots of kids play cowboy, but I actually grew up as one. And I liked living there. Liked ranch work, too."

"Something else," he said. "Marissa didn't have any respect for cops, even classy military criminal investigators like me. And she detested the thought of spending time out in 'the sticks', as she called anything rural. Heck, she thinks the outer Philadelphia suburbs are "the sticks"! A half hour on the Diamond F would put her in the nut house. But I'm happy there, really happy. That ranch is *home* to me! Always has been, I guess."

They walked another half block in silence, then Tony went on. "Eventually I realized that Marissa had a real need to *control* people. She insisted that I do what *she* wanted me to do, and I damn well didn't like that. What *I* wanted wasn't important because it didn't fit in with what *she* wanted. After Grandpa Pete died, I started to realize how much she was trying to run my life, her and my stepmother both. That's when I started dragging my heels. And that's why I don't want her in my life any more. I don't want her trying to force her standards on me." He walked another few steps. "And I damn sure am not going to let that happen! I had time to do a lot of thinking as I was driving out here from Washington."

He paused for a couple seconds, then continued. "I took my own sweet time driving out here, largely because doing so gave me a lot of time to think about what I want out of life." He paused a second before adding, "And I took time to play a round of golf, actually several rounds, on the way out here. That's another thing that helped me organize my thoughts. For some reason, chasing that little white ball helps me put things in perspective."

They reached Jill's car. Tony unlocked the passenger door and held it until Jill was seated inside. Then he closed the door, went around to the driver's side, and got in. He started the engine, made sure that Jill had fastened her seatbelt, then backed out of the diagonal parking space.

As he put the car in gear to go forward, Jill said, "If I'm hearing you correctly, Tony, sounds like you really don't like this Marissa person very much at all."

"And that's something I really didn't realize myself until I inherited the ranch," he replied. "When I acquired one heck of a lot of money, I became a lot more attractive to Marissa, at least the image of what she wanted me to be became a lot more attractive to her."

He thought for a moment, then continued. "Maybe that's not a good way to put it. Let's just say that the money gave me more status, and status is a big thing with her......and to her parents and to my step-mother. That bothered me. I like to think the only thing that changed about me when Grandpa Pete died was the size of my bank balance. I'd hate to think that inheriting money could turn me in to a snob, that or a social parasite." He turned south onto Main, then headed west on to Seventh.

They drove a couple of blocks in silence, hitting the traffic light at the corner where they turning on to U.S. 550 and then west on U.S. 160. Finally, as they crossed the bridge over the Animas River, Jill said, "And so you ran away."

Tony thought for a minute before he answered her. "I guess maybe you could say that," he said. "But instead of running *away* from something, I feel like I was running *toward* something. I gave up one way of life for another, and that other way of life, the ranch and living out here in

Colorado, that's a heck of a lot more meaningful to me in a lot of ways. It's what I grew up with. And when I decided to do what I did, to chuck the Air Force and my job, which I did like, and the whole D.C. social scene, which I realized that I really didn't care for that much for at all, I also started to understand that I really didn't like Marissa that much. It's just that what she represented, that D.C. social thing, sort of, well...., seduced me for a while." He reached across the car and took Jill's left hand in his right one. "Am I making any sense?" he asked.

"Yes," she answered simply. "You're making a lot of sense, at least from my point of view."

"And then this bank robbery thing happened and I got a chance to be both a rancher and a cop, at least for a while. Your dad was right. I couldn't turn him down when he offered me this job, but what I really want to do is run the ranch the way my grandfather taught me. He left it to me because he trusted me to do what's right with it. I really appreciate that; it's really sort of a vote of confidence in me."

Tony drove in silence for a couple minutes, finally he spoke softly and in a serious tone. "Jill, where does all this leave us?"

There was a moment's awkward silence. "Where do you want it to leave us, Tony?" she replied.

Tony answered her without so much as a second's hesitation. "I told you that every minute I've spent with you has been terrific. You're a super nice person. You're lots of fun to be with. Shucks," he continued, "I spent the whole day just looking forward to being with you this evening."

"And were you disappointed?" she inquired.

"Nope! Not a darn bit. Everything about this evening just makes me want to see more of you. Heck," he said after a short pause, "meeting you makes getting involved in all that blasted newspaper and television publicity worthwhile."

This statement caused Jill to laugh. When she could speak again, she said, "Tony, I don't know why, but the way you said *that* struck me as funny." She thought for a second. "But you're right. If it weren't for the robbery, we might never have met." She reached over and rested her hand on his shoulder. "You're fun to be with, too. You're not stuck up, nor are you the least bit snobbish, and all things considered, you certainly *could* be, stuck up and snobbish, that is".

Jill paused for a moment to gather her thoughts, then went on, "I probably shouldn't tell you this," she said, "but Daddy invited you to dinner last night partly because he thought I'd enjoy meeting you, though I suspect the other part might have something to do with him really not liking the last person I went out with."

"Something I should know about?" Tony asked. Doing so took mustering up a good bit of courage.

Jill paused for a second. "He's an assistant professor of English up at the college, Fort Lewis. I went out with him three times. That was enough to make me realize that he just wasn't my kind of people. For me, he was sort of like this Marissa person was for you. Talk about shallow and self-centered!"

She hesitated a second, then went on. "And as long as I'm in the mood to make a confession or two, I might as well tell you that a year or so ago, one of the evenings he ate dinner at the house, your grandfather told me the same thing about you that Daddy told me.....more than once, actually.

He said he wanted me to meet you because he thought I'd like you. To tell the truth, when he said that, I was pretty skeptical. First and only time I'd ever had a grandfather talking to me about maybe fixing me up with his grandson. But I did enjoy meeting you, too. Last night was lots of fun, even doing the dishes. If I hadn't enjoyed last night, I wouldn't have asked you to go to the play with me tonight."

"And what about tonight?" Tony asked.

"Well......," Jill started. "You know, you're kind of cute when you blush," she giggled. "I can really visualize you sitting in that pile of manure. And I can just imagine the look on your face as you sat there." She paused for a moment. "Tonight was fun. It was interesting watching you size up the Webbers, and that line of bull you handed them was magnificent. I'd say they swallowed it hook, line, and sinker, as the saying has it. Dinner was certainly a very nice experience, and not just because of the great food, as was going to the Strater after the show...." Jill caught her breath, then continued. "You're fun to be with, too, not to mention being very much of an interesting person."

She turned a bit more toward Tony, as much as the seatbelt allowed, put her left arm in the back of the car's bench seat so she could better see him, and deftly changed the subject. "Now tell me why you like *Guys & Dolls*."

He chuckled. "You know, Runyon once wrote a line that sure fits here, 'a story goes with it'." He thought for a second, then said, "I guess it's because I had a case of the mumps."

"Mumps?" Jill exclaimed. "This I gotta hear."

"Yep, mumps." Tony laughed. "I was in fifth grade, as I remember. Mom had died five years or so earlier and Dad was off in Africa somewhere. So I was staying with Grandpa Pete and going to school in Bayfield. That year virtually the whole fifth grade caught the mumps. Seems there was a problem with vaccination. So there I was, confined to the house and desperate for something to do." He paused. "Did I tell you that I've always been an omnivorous reader? Have been since I was just a kid. In fact, I can't remember not being able to read. I started reading long before I started school."

"No, that's not come up," she said. "So you enjoy reading"?

"That's for sure, but *enjoy* isn't a strong enough word". Tony answered. "I'd say I read a minimum of a hundred books a year, and that's in a year when I don't have much spare time. I'm a fast reader, too. For some reason, I sleep better if I read for an hour before going to bed. I started with Grandpa Pete's library, and picked up a volume of Damon Runyon's Broadway stories. To make a long story short, I read every one of them in two days and then went back and re-read them. And of course, *Guys* & Dolls is based on a couple of Runyon's stories.

"Then I started on Rex Stout's *Nero Wolfe* mysteries; got hung up on those, too. And they sort of got me interested in crime and criminals, not that I ever figured on having anything to do with the subjects up close and personal, you understand. Of course," he admitted, "I'd recovered from the mumps long before I worked my way through all of them."

Jill smiled. "And so reading kept you occupied while you recovered?"

"Yep, the books and learning morse code. Grandpa Pete was a ham radio operator. I decided I wanted to be one, too, so I taught myself the code and learned enough about electronic theory to pass the entry level ham radio license test and get my novice license. Grandpa was so impressed that he gave me transmitter and receiver kits from a company called Heathkit that he'd bought several years before but never put together and helped me build them. By the time we finished with those kits, I sure knew a lot more about electronics than I did when we started working on them. And that's partly why I minored in electrical engineering at the Academy."

Jill sat quietly for a few seconds. "Finally she spoke. "You know," she said, 'it sure shows that you think of your grandfather as a very special person."

This brought a smile to Tony's face. "That's for sure!" he exclaimed. "He was a heck of a good role model. And it wasn't just that he was my grandfather. He was also my best friend. You would have liked him, Jill."

"This is something that might have slipped your mind, young Mister Frye, but I did know your grandfather, not really well, of course, but I knew him because of Daddy. He had dinner at the house several times. And I did like him, even when he was bragging about his one and only grandson, which he did every time I saw him. I told you he kept telling me that he wanted me to meet you. And like I said a moment or two ago, he's the only person I ever met who wanted to fix me up with his grandson."

"Well, now you have met me," Tony said. "I hope it wasn't too bad an experience."

"It was a very nice experience, young sir," she answered, a smile on her face. "As a matter of fact, I've enjoyed every moment I've spent with you, too."

"And if I ask you out for tomorrow night?" Tony said.

"I'd probably decline...," Jill said.

"Oh," Tony said dejectedly.

"But only because I've got a pile of things I really should get done before I go to work on Tuesday and I'm probably going to need more than one evening to get it all done. We're pretty close to the end of the school year and there's a lot I can't put off.....well, that I shouldn't put off, at least. Thank God this is a holiday weekend!"

She looked at Tony. The dejected look on his face was sad to see. "I certainly do want to see you again, but how about just coming over for dinner tomorrow? If I work really hard, I can get a lot of work done in the afternoon. I ought to be able to free up the evening; I'll bet we can find something to do after dinner, too." Jill finished saying as Tony turned the car into the Matson driveway.

Tony put the transmission in park, turned off the engine, and said, "I can sure deal with another home-cooked meal. But maybe we could do something next Saturday, too? How do you feel about going for a horseback ride? I seem to remember that I own a few horses we could use. A horseback ride would be nice, I think. We could ride for a couple hours or so, then maybe run up to Vallecito and have dinner at the Lakeshore. I've always enjoyed eating up there.

Jill opened her door and got out of the car. Tony did the same. "You're tempting me, Tony. I love to ride."

Tony walked around the car and took Jill by the hand. They walked hand in hand up the walkway to the front door of the house. "So yield to temptation," he said. "I could pick you early in the afternoon....."

Jill interrupted him. "About tomorrow," she said. "If I get up early tomorrow morning and get a good bit of school work done before church.....that might work. You're really tempting me, you know."

"So yield to a little temptation," Tony said.

They had reached the front door and were standing on the stoop when the door opened, interrupting Tony just as he was about to put his arms around Jill. Sheriff Matson, pale as a ghost, motioned the two of them in to the house. "I hope I'm not interrupting anything," he said, "but I've got some bad news."

"What's wrong, Daddy?" Jill asked. "Did we do something...."

Her father cut her off. The two of you? Of course not!" he said. It's Barry Morgan. When we got back from our meeting tonight, there was a message on the answering machine for me to call the hospital. Barry died about an hour and a half ago. Doc Evans said blood clots probably worked loose and went to the heart and lungs. By the time the doctor on call got to him, he was gone." He turned to his daughter, "Jill, your mother is going to spend tomorrow with Barry's wife and children. Can you go with her?"

"Of course, Daddy. Poor Pam! She's going to need a lot of help. If need be, I can probably take a few days off from school, not just tomorrow. I've got a pile of comp time coming, as well as a couple of personal days I can use. I have a mess of work to do, but I can let it slip a few days. Then I'll really have to bust to get it done before the academic year ends." She turned to Tony and said, "A rain check on the ride and dinner at the lake, Tony?"

"Absolutely," Tony said. Then, to the sheriff, "Jack, it's not just bank robbery any more. Now we add murder to the list. And I have news for you. Jill introduced me to the Webbers tonight. It didn't seem like an accidental meeting. They had to push their way through a crowded theater lobby to get to us." He paused a moment, then continued, "From the questions they asked, I think they were on a fishing expedition for information about where we are with the investigation. They were not what you'd call even slightly subtle."

"Really? Let's talk about it for a minute. And tomorrow you'll have to start work on a murder book. We need to make sure every step of this investigation is thoroughly documented from here on out. When we nail those responsible, it'll help bring in convictions." The sheriff paused for a minute. "Jill," he said, turning to his daughter, "I'm going to steal Tony away from you."

"I sort of figured that out, Daddy," Jill sighed. "I'll have to call in and get a sub for at least one day after the holiday weekend; maybe more." She touched Tony lightly on the cheek. "Thanks for a wonderful evening, Tony. I'm sorry about tomorrow. We're going to have to postpone horseback riding. When this is over...."

Tony took her left hand in both of his. "Yeah, Jill. When it's over. And I hope that'll be in just a few days. As for tonight, thank you. It's the most enjoyable night I've had in a long time." He watched her as she turned and left the living room, then turned to his boss. "OK, Jack. Let's talk."

Matson motioned for Tony to take a seat, then began to speak. The two men spent the next half hour and more in the sheriff's den, going over various items. One, of course, was Tony's encounter with the Webbers and the implications of it. The second item was what the department needed to do to honor Barry Morgan. Both men took notes on this subject. Morgan's death had come as a profound shock to Sheriff Matson, as it was the first time in his tenure as county sheriff that a La Plata County officer had died in the line of duty. The session ended with the two agreeing to meet for breakfast in the morning after Tony picked up the Sunday night crop of reconnaissance photos.

Tony spent the drive home deep in thought. Part of his thoughts were of Jill and the events of the evening with her. But mostly he thought about Barry Morgan. *He must have been about my age*, Tony thought. *And he's left a wife and two kids behind. Damn!* He thought a few moments more, then muttered, "Jack said he wants to start a fund to help them. And I guess Jill knows his wife pretty well, well enough to refer to her by her first name, at least."

By the time he turned off County 501 and was driving down the ranch lane toward his house, Tony had decided that he'd make a considerable contribution to the fund that the sheriff wanted to set up to help the widow Morgan and her two children. "Other than doing everything I can do to catch those bastards," he muttered to himself, "there's not much else I *can* do. What the hell, it's just money and I have more of that than I know what to do with."

He turned off the county road on to the ranch road, drove past Lew and Mary Barnes' house, and pulled into the spot next to the house where he'd gotten in to the habit of parking. The motion sensor turned the porch light on and Tony noticed that the cat was waiting for him at the door.

****

Gladys Webber poured herself another stiff drink. "Well," she said, her speech slightly slurred, "that deputy didn't sound very impressive. From what he said, I think he has some serious doubts about being able to catch the boys. 'Millionaire Cowboy Cop'," indeed!"

Her husband added another ice cube to his highball glass. "I think you're right, Glad," he giggled. "It sounds like he doesn't have a clue as to where they're going."

"Still," his wife said after she swallowed a mouthful of gin and tonic, "I think we need to speed things up as much as we can. Fortunately we've got a schedule and pretty much know the general areas where the boys will camp and pretty much know when they'll be coming down out of the National Forest. I want you to ride out and intercept them and hustle them back here. Then we'll get them out of the state as quickly as possible. You can take off at first light the morning of the day they're due back here, meet them along the trail, and hustle them along."

James Webber took another sip of his drink. "I can do that," he said. "Guess it's a good thing we tested getting horses through the forest land and locating camp sites last fall. And your idea of using a GPS for navigation was brilliant, Dear. The boys use it to find their way back here, and I can use it to meet them along the way." He thought for a moment, then continued. "Do you think I should have them bury the money out in National Forest land somewhere? If we bury it and mark the location with the GPS, we'd certainly have no trouble finding it again."

Gladys Webber considered this suggestion very carefully before exercising a veto over her husband's idea. Mrs. Webber obviously wanted to keep her eye on the money stolen from the bank.

CHAPTER EIGHT

Tony picked up the photos at the airport about eight, then called the sheriff's home on his cellular phone. Jill answered. Tony asked her to tell her father that he was on his way to the restaurant, and would arrive in about twenty minutes. Jill asked him to hold on for a moment.

When she came back on the phone, she told Tony that his message had been delivered. Then she said, "You'll get there first, Tony. Will you get a table or booth for four, please? A booth would probably be better. We're going to skip church this morning, of course. Mom and I will join you and Daddy, if you don't mind. Then we'll go over to Pam Morgan's and do whatever we can to help. I guess Mom will go with Pam to see the undertaker. Daddy's arranged for him to meet Pam today even though it is a holiday weekend. I gather I'm going to help take care of Pam's two little girls while Pam's working out the funeral details. What a tragedy!" she sighed. By the time she finished saying this, she sounded as if she were on the verge of tears.

Tony told her to hang tough, and said he'd have a table for them when they reached the restaurant. By this time he had turned off the road in from the airport and heading west on 160 on the long grade than wound down past the Farmington Hill turnoff, past the area of the Bodo Industrial Park, where the sheriff's office, the industrial park, and the shopping mall were located. In a few moments more, he negotiated the gentle S turn where 160 ran between the railroad yard and the park next to the Animas River opposite Smelter Hill. Past the traffic light at the junction of routes 160 and 550, then two right turns and he was in the restaurant parking lot.

Tony parked the Cherokee, walked into the restaurant, and asked the waitress for a booth for four. When he saw the size of the booth she took him to, he suggested that something larger would be appropriate, considering the sheriff's size. The waitress nodded agreement; she knew the sheriff. After seating Tony at a large table, she put four menus on the table, and promised that she'd bring the sheriff's party to the table as soon as they arrived. In a moment, she'd returned with a carafe of coffee.

Tony poured a cup while he waited for the Matsons to arrive. "I need this," he thought aloud. "It was a short night.....again." He added a lot of sugar, stirred the coffee, then took a small tentative sip. The coffee was quite hot, so he decided to let it cool for a while before trying to drink any more. Tony sat and waited for the Matsons.....and fidgeted. Part of the fidgeting was due to wanting very much to see the aerial photos that had been taken the previous night. The other part was being anxious to see Jill. Finally, needing something to occupy himself, he got up, crossed to the restaurant entrance, where there was a coin-operated newspaper box, and returned with a copy of the Sunday morning Durango newspaper.

The death of Barry Morgan had made the front page, but the article was very short due to the late hour at which death had occurred. By the time Tony finished reading it, the Matsons were walking across the parking lot toward the front door of the restaurant. The waitress met them at the door and escorted them to the table where Tony was waiting. As the family crossed the dining room, Tony stood. He helped seat Jill as the sheriff did the same for his wife.

The waitress came to take their order and to fill coffee cups for the Matsons, and after doing so, seemed highly attentive to the foursome. The conversation at the table seemed to revolve around things that had to be done as a result of Barry Morgan's death, which didn't surprise Tony. He knew the sheriff would avoid talking about the investigation in a public place. He also knew it was even more unlikely that the sheriff would discuss what they had planned in hopes of catching the bank robbers, who had now become murderers. Tony pretty much stayed out of the conversation, as he did not know Morgan or his family.

Finally the waitress came with the bill, which Tony picked up over Jack's protest. As they walked out of the restaurant, the sheriff said. "Tony, I'll ride up to the office with you. When we're done, I'll get one of the day crew to give me a lift home."

"No problem, Jack," Tony said. "I can give you a lift back to the house. Then I might go back to the ranch and crash for a couple hours, unless you need something done, that is. It was kind of a short night." He paused for a second. "There is something else I'd like to take care of, though."

Pat and Jill Matson thanked Tony for breakfast. Jill patted him gently on the cheek and said, "Call me." Then she and her mother got into Jill's car and drove off, heading toward the north end of town.

Jack and Tony walked to unit six. When they were inside and on the road east heading toward the office, Jack said, "Did you notice how attentive the waitress was?"

"Yeah," Tony answered. "That's the most attention I can ever remember having in a restaurant, except for the times I was out with.....well, with congressmen and generals and such." Jack, who'd read the article about Tony in yesterday's paper, looked at him, knowing that he was referring to Marissa's father, and probably to Marissa, too.

"How much you want to bet the waitress has an in at the newspaper?" he continued.

"No bet," Matson answered. "And she'd probably get a nice juicy check if she could have come up with anything that would look good in print." He changed the subject. "You check the photos out?"

"No," Tony replied. "I was tempted, but I figured it'd wait. Besides," he continued, "if I'd looked at them, I would have been tempted to talk about it at breakfast."

"But you wouldn't," the sheriff said firmly.

"Of course not," Tony responded. "Wouldn't have been smart, with that waitress hovering over us like a vulture. But I admit I sure as heck would have been tempted." He thought for a moment, then said, "Jack, where can I get a uniform?"

"Uniform?" the sheriff replied. "I thought you wanted to work in street clothes."

"Well, that was the original idea. But now I want a uniform. Actually, it's a matter of needing a uniform." He swallowed hard, then continued. "Last night at the house you said you expected the department would turn out in uniform for Barry Morgan's funeral and for calling hours, right?"

"I expect that'll be the case. At least that's what I figure the deputies will want. Barry was well liked."

"So where do I get a uniform?" Tony asked again.

Matson smiled. He'd anticipated Tony's reaction. "At Fishman's Men's Store," he answered, "on the main drag. But alterations'll probably take two days, if not more. And remember, this is Sunday and it's a holiday weekend. The store'll be open at ten this morning, but I don't think you can have one altered by the time calling hours will be held. In fact, I'd bet money on that."

Tony said grimly, "How much you want to bet I can have a uniform custom altered by noon on Monday, at the latest. It's amazing how much quick work the offer of a healthy gratuity can get done. I'm a deputy. Maybe I'm just a temporary, part-time, make-believe deputy, but I'm still officially a deputy. I'll be at the funeral home and the funeral service in uniform if I have to *buy* the damn men's store to get one!"

"Right," Matson said, as Tony drove into the parking lot at the office. Tony's reaction was what he'd hoped and expected it would be. And from the tone of his voice, Matson suspected Tony wasn't kidding when he said he'd buy the store if he had to. The sheriff also suspected doing so wouldn't make more than a tiny dent in Tony's bank balance. By the time Morgan's funeral ended, he half thought maybe he could persuade Tony, assuming the sheriff could catch him in a weak moment, to stay on with the department, at least for a while.

Matson badly needed at least one other full time deputy, now that Barry Morgan was dead. It would be a considerable bonus to acquire not only a deputy, but one who was an experienced criminal investigator, as well, and one who darned well probably had a lot of contacts in the upper levels of federal law enforcement circles. Matson smiled; a smile that could be characterized as *devious*. Maybe if he played his cards just right.....it was starting to look like Jill might make good bait.

The two men walked across the parking lot, entered the building, and sent directly to Tony's office. As soon as the door was closed behind them, Tony opened the package of photos he'd brought in from the vehicle with him. He spread them out on the desk and studied them for a few moments. Finally he pointed to a light spot on one of the photos.

"That's got to be the robbers' campfire," he said. "Anyhow, it's some kind of heat source. Out in the wilderness, it's gotta be a fire of some sort, or maybe a couple cans of Sterno. And here," he pointed to another spot some distance south of the first, this is where your two deputies are." He walked to the map on the wall and stuck pins in it at the locations he'd extrapolated from the photo.

Matson followed him and looked at the locations marked by the pins Tony had placed. "OK," he said. "The boys are camped about a half mile from this trail. They can work their way back to the trail, and then get down to the reservoir. Once they get out of the woods and on the trail, they can make good time. I figure they can be picked up by about five this afternoon. They can take time off until Tuesday night and then, like you planned, they can...."

"No!" Tony interrupted vigorously. "Change in plans."

"Huh?" Matson said.

"Think about it. What if I guessed wrong about where the robbers will go? What if they head somewhere else? If we call off the trackers, we lose them. Probably permanently, and losing them just isn't an option at this point." He gave his head a negative shake. "No, keep them on the trail. Losing a bank robber is one thing, but those bastards are responsible for the death of one of your deputies."

Matson frowned. He thought for a moment, then said slowly, "I guess you're right. If we call them in, we're putting all our eggs in the one basket. But," he continued, "if I don't have those two men, we'll be even shorter..."

Tony anticipated this. "Is there any way," he asked, "that you can borrow a deputy or two, or maybe even more, from other counties?"

Matson stood, mouth open, while he thought about Tony's question. After a few seconds thought, he answered, "We've talked, a bunch of us sheriffs and such, about a multi-county anti-crime task force, even one that could work across state lines. Maybe this would be a good time to informally test the idea. Go grab us each a cup of coffee while I make a couple of quick phone calls."

Tony left the office and went in search of coffee. The coffee maker in Matson's office was empty. Rather than search elsewhere, Tony filled the machine with water, put a filter and coffee in the basket, and switched the machine on. It took the better part of five minutes to brew, and by the time he'd poured two cups, added sugar to both, and walked back to his office with them, Matson was just hanging up the phone.

"Bingo!' The sheriff said with a grin. "We have the loan of four deputies, two from over to Cortez and two from up Silverton way. They are ours for at least a full forty-eight hours, starting Tuesday evening. And Archuleta has promised two more if we need them."

"Tuesday!" Tony said in surprise.

"Yeah," the sheriff answered. "I figure calling hours will be Monday and Tuesday afternoon and evening, with the funeral late Wednesday afternoon. Both Montezuma County and San Juan County will send delegations for calling hours and the funeral. And so will Archuleta. We'll keep two deputies from each delegation for the posse, including Archuleta if we need them. The sheriffs of those counties will pick the men and prep them for what we're doing, at least in a general way, using that cover story you concocted. Of course," he continued, "La Plata County has to pick up the tab for room and board. Another expense for the county commissioners to gripe about."

"Look on the bright side," Tony said. "If our hunch is right, you'll have one less county commissioner to deal with. And on the not so bright side," he continued, "this is our last batch of recce photos. The Air Guard can't fly for us again. Last night was the last support the weekend warriors can give us until next weekend, at the earliest. And by then, hopefully, it'll be too late for them to do anything for us. So I'll fall back on Plan B."

"All right. At least we have a Plan B. I still feel bad, though, about you spending...."

Tony held up his right hand in the classic *stop* sign. "Not your worry, Jack," he said. If you can't come up with funding, then it's a tax write-off, which I sort of need anyhow, according to the tax lawyers I spent a bunch of time with before I left D.C. No problem either way."

"All right," Matson said. "We'll deal with it later. But," he said with a grin, "if you're going to use Plan B, why not come out to the house and have supper afterwards? Or even if you're not using Plan B, for that matter."

Tony didn't have to be asked twice. It was a good excuse to see Jill twice in the same day. He accepted Jack's offer, then picked up the phone to call the charter service and schedule a plane and pilot for late that afternoon. This done, he drove Matson home, then headed for the ranch and a nap. It promised to be a busy evening.

****

****

The bank robbers rode out of the woods and started across a forest service trail, heading straight for the woods on the other side. The voice startled them.

"Hi, guys. What are you three doing 'way out here on horseback?

The riders stopped and looked up the trail, to see a man and woman sitting on a fallen log, each holding a cup. Mike reacted quickly. He drew his pistol and fired two quick shots, hitting both the man and woman in the chest. . The man fell backwards off the log without another sound; the woman screamed repeatedly. Mike spurred his horse uphill, reached her, and fired twice more into her head. Then he fired another shot into the man's head as well.

Cletus hollered, "What the hell'd you do that for? Anybody within a mile of us'll hear those gun shots!"

"They saw us, you damn fool! If we let them live, they could identify us. Now let's get the hell out of here before anyone else sees us!" Mike urged his horse forward back down the hill and turned into the woods. He shouted to the other two, "Hurry up, damn it. We need to get out of here."

A little over a hundred feet back up the trail, hidden from the robbers' view by a big tree, a ten year old boy stood in shocked silence. He'd just seen his parents shot down in cold blood. Without knowing it, Mike and his companions *had* left a witness behind.

CHAPTER NINE

After a good nap, followed by lunch and a couple hours spent taking care of odds and ends around the ranch, Tony was ready to put Plan B to work. He loaded his vehicle, then drove to the small airport on the other side of the Animas River from the office. When he arrived, he took the medium-sized package he'd brought with him, and walked into the charter service office. Logan Bennett was waiting for him. For the first time, Tony looked closely at Bennett. He was, Tony concluded, in his late fifties. But he had old eyes, pilot's eyes, Tony thought, something he really hadn't noticed in their previous meetings. Bennett, or so he guessed, had been flying for a lot of years.

"Evening, Deputy," Bennett said.

"Evening, Mister Bennett," Tony replied. "Are you ready?"

"Yep, and the name's Logan, young fellow. 'Mister' is 'way too formal for around here.

"Thanks, Logan," Tony answered. "And I'm Tony. Tell the truth, I've been away from here so long I just sort of picked up the habit of 'Mister'ing damn near everybody more than six months older than myself."

Bennett laughed as he led Tony out the back door of the office and on to the flight line. He stopped at the same Cessna 172 Tony had chartered the day before. "All preflighted, and set to go," he said, as he climbed into the plane and took the pilot's seat.

"Great," Tony said. "Hopefully, I'll be able to see what I'm looking for and then make it to dinner."

Bennett started the plane's engine, then taxied out for takeoff. A few moments later the plane was in the air and headed north over the town of Durango as it gained altitude. By the time the plane had reached a couple thousand feet above the ground, Tony had opened the box he'd carried with him, removed the infrared vision device the box had contained, put the batteries in it, and put it on his head. He looked down towards the ground.

"Good God!" he exclaimed. "Do these things ever work! And there's a heck of a high heat source down there, one that's moving." He pushed the infrared device up so he could see normally. "Oh," he said. "It's a steam train coming back from Silverton." The device went back down over his eyes. "All right, Logan. Tell me when we're near that campground. I'll use it as a test."

Two or three minutes later, Bennett said, "Do you see the campground, Tony?"

"I see a lot of fairly bright heat sources," Tony answered. He pushed the device up on his forehead again, continuing to look down as he did so. "Yes," he said. "What I saw on infrared is where the campground is. Now let's head for the area I want to check out."

Another ten minutes flying time brought them to the area Tony had mentioned over the phone when he set the flight up that morning. Tony looked and looked, alternately pushing the infrared goggles up so he could see normally. When he did this, he made an occasional notation on the map he'd brought with him. After about five minutes of alternating observations with notations, he took the goggles off his head, put them in the box, and said, "Everything checks out just fine, Logan. We can go back now."

"Roger that," Bennett replied, putting the Cessna in to a gentle turn, then rolling out on a course that would take them back to the Animas Air Park. "And we can both go to dinner."

About forty minutes later, as dusk was deepening, Tony turned into the Matson driveway, parked the Cherokee, and walked to the house. Jack answered the door, ushered Tony in, and escorted him into the kitchen.

"The girls will be here in about a half hour," he said. "They've had one heck of a day, but they've got things pretty well organized. Pam Morgan's a wreck. Thank God her parents are flying up from Phoenix. In fact," he checked his watch, "they should be at the house by now. I had one of the deputies pick them up at the airport. Figured it was the least the department could do."

"How are the children taking it?" Tony asked.

"They're too young to really understand that daddy will never come home again," Matson said. "It's a shame, a damn shame!" He took a pitcher of iced tea from the refrigerator, poured two glasses, handed one to Tony and said, "Can you make a salad?"

"Huh?" Tony responded.

"A salad! Can you make a salad? Pat's got me making supper 'cause they're going to be late. Can you make a salad?"

"Heck, yes," Tony said. "Salads are simple. Just tell me where the stuff is." He gathered from the pained look on Jack's face that cooking was not the sheriff's strong suit.

"Veggies are in the 'frig," Matson replied. The bowls are in the cupboard and the knives are in the top drawer." He pointed twice. "Pat left a cutting board and a salad bowl on the counter. If you make the salad, I'll set the table."

"Can do," Tony said. "By the way, what's for dinner?"

"Lasagna," the sheriff replied.

"Great," Tony answered, as he opened the refrigerator and extracted various salad makings. "I love lasagna." He mentally revised upward his estimate of the sheriff's culinary skills. Making a lasagna was a good few steps above opening cans of pasta sauce and heating them up.

"Me too," Matson answered from the dining room. "Pat makes an extra pan or two every month or so and keeps them in the freezer for emergencies and evenings when she doesn't have time to cook. She said this qualified as an emergency. All I had to do, so she said, was put one of them in the oven. It'll be ready in about a half hour, or maybe a bit more. Jill said maybe I could get you to make the salad. I think they're both afraid I'd slice off a finger or something." So much for Tony's revised assessment of the sheriff's culinary skills. Another revision, downward this time, was obviously needed. The estimate actually dropped even lower than it had been at the beginning. Tony was starting to wonder if the sheriff had to look up the recipe before making a cup of instant coffee.

Jack had finished setting the table and Tony had the salad done and was cleaning up the mess when he heard the front door open and then heard Mrs. Matson speaking to her husband. He also heard footsteps on the hardwood floor of the dining room just before Jill stuck her head around the entryway into the kitchen.

"Hi, Tony," she said softly.

Tony could tell from the sound of her voice that she was tired. "You sound like you had a rough day," he said as he put the plastic cutting board in the dishwasher. This done, he walked to her and took her left hand in both of his. It wasn't difficult to see that she'd had a hard day, but Tony was too much a gentleman to comment on Jill's haggard appearance.

Jill stepped toward him, an act which forced Tony to release her hand so he could put his arms around her. She put her head on Tony's right shoulder and eventually relaxed. He couldn't help notice that she smelled good. After almost a minute, she pulled away. Tony noticed that the shoulder of his shirt was damp. Jill had obviously been crying softly, so softly that Tony hadn't heard her doing so.

"Thanks for giving me a hug and a shoulder to cry on, Tony. I needed that. It sure was a rough day. How the heck do you tell a three year old that her daddy won't be coming home ever again?" A tear rolled down each of Jill's cheeks. "It isn't fair! It just isn't fair!" She began to sob softly again.

Before Tony had a chance to respond, Pat Matson came into the kitchen. If anything, she looked somewhat more haggard than did Jill. And Tony could tell that she, too, had been crying within the last few minutes.

"Hello, Tony," she said quietly.

"Hi, Mrs. M.," Tony replied. "Looks as if the two of you had a rotten day."

"That's an understatement, a classic one," Pat said as she opened the oven to check the lasagna. "It looks OK," she continued. "I guess Jack didn't do too much damage."

"Hey, that's no fair," the sheriff said, coming back into the kitchen. "I'll have you know I fixed a lot of meals when I was in the army. I could have made something tonight besides heating up that frozen lasagna."

"Yes, Dear, I suppose you could have, at that," Pat replied with a weak grin on her face. "But Jill and I wanted something besides K rations or those MRE's you've got stashed in the cellar for hunting and fishing trips; that's about the limit of your cooking abilities, except for making toast and instant coffee.....and sometimes you incinerate the toast. After all, we do have company." This comment produced small laughs from both Jill and Tony and resulted in a mock look of pain on the sheriff's face.

"I don't get no respect," he muttered, doing a fair imitation of Rodney Dangerfield.

"It's just that we know your limitations, Dad," Jill added. "We let you do steaks on the grill, but only with close supervision." She looked at Tony and winked. "Think *incineration*, Tony. Like charred to a crisp," she said with a forced attempt at humor.

"Come on, Tony. Bring your tea and we'll talk in the den. Pat'll call us when supper's done." He turned and walked out of the kitchen, with Tony following.

They sat talking shop for several minutes, Tony commenting on his experiment with the infrared scanning device. Before long Jill appeared in the den doorway and called them to supper. Conversation at the table was restrained. Both women were physically exhausted and emotionally drained, and neither Jack nor Tony wanted to impose on them. And attempts at humor just wouldn't have been appropriate. Finally, when they had all finished eating, Pat said, "You boys go talk. Jill and I will clean this up, and then I'm going to bed. It's not been a good day."

"I'm going to head for bed after we clear the table, too, Mom" Jill said. She turned to Tony. "Do you mind, Tony? I'm really beat."

Before Tony had a chance to reply, he saw the sheriff looking at him, a question on his face. Tony caught the sheriff's eye, then nodded slightly. Jack picked up on this, then said, "You girls go get some rest. Tony and I will take care of the table and we'll clean up in the kitchen, too. We can talk while we're working. My cooking abilities may be limited, as various people around here unkindly keep reminding me, but I am capable of clearing a table and doing dishes."

He rose and began gathering plates and silverware. Tony followed suit. He had empty salad plates in one hand and the salad bowl in the other when Jill came over to him, kissed him lightly on the cheek, and said good night.

"Will you go to the wake tomorrow evening?" she asked.

"I'm going out first thing in the morning to buy a uniform," he answered. "Or to try to buy a uniform," he amended. "I want to be properly dressed for it. Of course, I didn't know Barry, but...."

"Calling hours are two to four and seven to nine," Jill said. "I'm taking a few days off from school even though it's getting near the tail end of the academic year. There are some things that I have to do in the next few days, but there's also things I can postpone. I promised Pam I'd be with her, but I'll have three hours free between..."

"And we could maybe get something to eat and you could rest a little," Tony continued for her. "I'm going to have to get to bed right after we leave the funeral home....."

"I know," Jill interrupted. "You and Daddy won't be able to go out after calling hours. It'll be a short night, and you're probably going to have a busy day Tuesday, but..."

"But when this is over, I'd like to spend a lot more time getting to know you better," he said.

Jill smiled. "I'll hold you to that, Tony. That's about the nicest thing I've heard since breakfast," she said. "You're a lot of fun. I'm happy when I'm with you. Now go help Daddy. I'm going to take a sleepy pill and go to bed." She touched him lightly on the cheek, turned, and headed for the hallway leading to the bedroom wing of the house.

Tony carried the salad plates and the bowl out to the kitchen. Jack was scraping food scraps into the sink and putting dirty dishes into the dishwasher. When Tony put the salad plates on the counter, Matson turned to him.

"She OK?" he asked.

"Guess so," Tony replied. "She's tired and hurting for Barry's wife and kids, but it looks like she's hanging in. How about your wife?"

"Pat's hanging in there, too. It was a rough day for them both," Matson grunted, bending over to put salad plates in the dishwasher. "I'd kind of say she approves of you, Kid."

"Jill or your wife?" Tony asked as they worked on clearing the table and loading the dishwasher.

"Jill, of course, but Pat, too, for that matter," Matson answered.

Tony smiled. "The feeling's mutual, Jack, in both cases. Jill's the nicest thing yet about coming home. I'm looking forward to getting to know her better, a lot better." He changed the subject, so as to address business. "Are we set for tomorrow night?"

"Sure are. Arrangements are all made. The two of us, four outside deputies, and two of our own people. And the horses, too, of course. There'll be eight of us and only three of them."

"Unless Webber sends out a couple more," Tony interjected.

"Or better yet, if he goes out himself," the sheriff responded. "Wouldn't that be just ducky!" he chuckled. "He rides out to join the robbers, and we catch him red-handed with the loot."

"And consorting with the murderers, like providing aid; accessory after the fact, for sure," Tony continued. "But that's hoping for 'way too much."

"It'll never happen," the sheriff sighed, "but we can dream, I guess." He picked up the dishwasher detergent from the counter, filled the soap dispenser, closed the dishwasher door, and activated the machine. "You want another glass of iced tea?"

"No, thanks," Tony answered. I'll head back to the ranch and get some sleep. Tomorrow's probably going to be a busy day. Roll call at half past seven and change of shift at eight?"

"Yep," Matson replied. "That's the schedule."

"Then I'll see you at the office before seven thirty," Tony said. "Thanks for supper. You even did a good job on the lasagna." Tony couldn't resist needling his boss about his cooking skills, or lack thereof.

Matson nearly choked due to trying not to laugh with a mouthful of tea. The good news was that he only narrowly avoided spraying iced tea all over the room. He snorted, then finally swallowed the tea before replying, "I just don't get no respect."

CHAPTER TEN

At seven twenty-five the next morning, after a short night's sleep, Tony was seated in the squad room of the county law enforcement headquarters, in the company of close to a dozen uniformed deputies, all of whom had introduced themselves to him. At exactly half past, Jack Matson strode into the room and walked to the podium in the front center of the room. Once he faced the assembled deputies, the casual murmuring that had echoed softly throughout the room ceased.

Matson spoke, "For those of you who haven't met him, I'd like to introduce Tony Frye." He paused long enough to point at Tony. "Stand up, Tony." Frye rose almost fully erect, waved casually, and then regained his seat. "I don't have to tell you why he's here. If you haven't heard it around the office over the weekend, you've heard it on the radio or on TV, or," he paused for a second and smiled, "maybe some of you intellectual types even read about it in the newspaper." A couple of the deputies laughed; the rest of them grinned. "The rest of you just looked at the pictures," Matson concluded. Two of the deputies gave him a good-natured hissing.

Matson took a sip from his coffee cup, then continued. "You all know your patrol assignments for the day. Calling hours today for Barry are this afternoon and then this evening from seven to nine. I'd like a full turn-out of anyone who is off duty at the funeral home tonight, and then again tomorrow. Pam wants a formal departmental funeral at 5:00 PM on Wednesday. Any volunteers for pallbearers?"

The hand of every uniformed deputy went up. Matson looked around the room briefly. "So be it. Tom," he said, looking at an older deputy who seemed to be in his late forties, "I want you off the road this morning to coordinate with other agencies, the state patrol, the surrounding counties, the fire.... Oh, hell, Tom. You know the drill. And you pick the pallbearers, too. All right, men. Let's go out there to serve and protect or run around in circles or whatever the hell we're supposed to be doing. Dismissed."

Five of the uniformed deputies filed out of the room. The elderly deputy remained. When the others had departed, he walked over to where Jack and Tony were talking. Matson turned to him and spoke, "Tom, you got a chance to meet Tony? Tony, this is Tom Jaffee, chief deputy and departmental training officer."

Jaffee extended his hand to Tony. "We already exchanged a few words before you came in, Jack." He smiled, "Again, welcome aboard, Tony." Then the smile disappeared as he continued, "Just wish it were under more pleasant circumstances."

Tony nodded. "Know what you mean, Tom." He looked at Jack. "Anything you need me for this morning? I need to go buy a uniform and take care of some legal stuff about the ranch, among other chores I should have worked on Friday. Assuming, of course, I can roust one of Grandpa Pete's lawyers out of bed on a long holiday weekend."

"Go ahead and run your errands," Jack answered. "I'll brief Tom in on what you cooked up for tonight. Then we'll pick two of the day shift deputies to go with us. And what you just said reminded me that I need to see a lawyer today, if one's available. Damn all miserable things that go bad on holiday weekends! Got to set up a fund for Barry's family."

"If you want," Tony offered, "I can get that taken care of when I stop at Barret, Gardiner, and MacKenzie, assuming they're open. If not....." He held up his cell phone.

Matson thought for a second, then reached into his breast pocket and pulled out a slip of paper. "OK," he said. "Give it a shot. Considering what those lawyers probably bill to your ranch account, I'm surprised that one or two of them aren't following you around full-time. That'll save me a trip, if you can get one working on this, and I've got a lot I need to do today." He handed the slip of paper to Tony. "Here's the details of what I'd like done. See Blair MacKenzie if you can. He's on retainer as the county attorney anyhow, so he might as well take care of this. You expect to be back before noon?"

"Ought to," Tony said, "unless I run in to complications." He turned and walked out of the squad room.

By half past nine, Tony had completed his legal errand. It being Memorial Day, the banks were closed, so his banking chores were still untouched. Virtually everything else in town was open, holiday or not. Memorial Day weekend, as was true in many parts of the country, marked the start of the summer tourist season. Closing down for the holiday would have deprived many of Durango's business establishments of a splendid opportunity to remove money from the wallets of tourists, an endeavor well thought of by virtually all of the local business owners, given the large number of tourists who flock to southwest Colorado every year.

Some of the city's professional offices were closed, but before he left the sheriff's office, Tony had made arrangements to meet Schuyler Barret, who had served as his uncle's chief Durango lawyer for more years than Tony had been alive. Barret had walked him through all of the papers he'd needed to sign that morning. Barret had also offered to do the work necessary to set up the trust fund for Barry Morgan's family and, as Blair MacKenzie was in Denver on business, to do it *pro bono*, and to have the fund set up with a bank account before noon on Tuesday. Barret remarked that it was the least he could do, as he and his wife and the Morgan family attended the same church. When Tony left the law office, he turned south and walked to Fishman's clothing store. Thankfully, despite the holiday, it was open.

It was just past a quarter before eleven o'clock when Tony finished in Fishman's. His uniforms wouldn't be ready for about two hours and his legal business was finished. He turned right as he left Fishman's and walked south along Durango's main street. By the time he reached the corner, an idea had formed in his mind. He turned the corner and walked past the post office toward the parking lot where he'd left his Cherokee. When he reached the vehicle, he got in, started the engine, and picked up the radio microphone.

"Unit Six to base," he said into the microphone.

"Go ahead, Six," Maggie Miller said from the dispatch center.

"Maggie, could you please tell Sheriff Matson I took care of setting up the fund for Barry's widow. Now I'm going to head out north of town to check traffic and road conditions," Tony said. He knew the sheriff would know he wasn't out on routine patrol and assumed Matson would most likely conclude that he was on some kind of a reconnaissance mission, which was exactly what Tony had in mind.

Once Tony got out well past the business district and where the old rodeo grounds were, the Durango city traffic thinned out a good bit. The rodeo grounds buildings, obviously empty, looked to still be in fairly good shape. Tony wondered if the town would ever find another use for the large tract of land where he'd attended rodeos in his youth. He wondered if there weren't some kind of legal entanglement regarding other uses for the old rodeo grounds. If so, that might explain why the land wasn't in use.

He enjoyed the drive through the Animas Valley, and checked out some of the other things he remembered from his teenage years. Seeing the Dalton Ranch golf course between the right side of the highway and the Animas River reminded him that he hadn't played in several days, his last round being with two of his former faculty members on the Air Force Academy's course. He resolved to get a round of golf in as soon as he could manage it. The thought of golfing made him wonder if Jill played.

The sign for the Trimble Hot Springs turn off brought back good memories of high school swimming parties and picnics there. One thought followed another, and in a matter of seconds he found himself wondering what Jill would look like in a swim suit. He mentally bet she'd be an absolute knock-out wearing one, and resolved to ask her to go to the springs for a picnic and a swim some weekend, some weekend very soon, if he could swing it.

A few minutes later he reached Hermosa, where the tracks of the tourist-hauling railroad crossed from the east to the west side of the highway and began to climb the long grade that would eventually take it to Silverton. The highway dropped in elevation, then began to rise again, and soon crossed the railroad tracks again, this time on an overpass. Eight miles or so further up the road, Tony reached the driveway leading eastward to the Webber guest ranch. He continued north a hundred feet or so, then pulled the Cherokee off the road and onto the shoulder, switched on the emergency flashers as well as the flashing red and blue lights on the light bar on the vehicle's roof, stopped the vehicle, and got out.

To remain relatively inconspicuous, he put the hood of the Cherokee up and poked his head under it for a moment. He even went so far as to put both hands down in to the engine compartment, though he was careful not to touch anything that might be hot. After a few moments, satisfied that he'd put on a good enough show to satisfy the suspicions of anyone who might have been watching, he closed the hood, took a pack of cigarettes out of his shirt pocket, and lit one. Then he leaned up against the right side of the vehicle and relaxed.

While seeming not to be paying close attention to anything, Tony looked toward where he surmised the ranch buildings would be. The trees made it impossible to see anything more than fifty feet off the highway, except down the driveway and looking down the drive would probably produce nothing worthwhile in the way of visual information. Besides, being seen looking down the driveway would only serve to more draw attention to himself, and Tony wanted to avoid this, if at all possible.

"Oh well," he muttered to himself and he carefully field stripped the cigarette, a neatness habit he'd picked up at his first duty base, and ground the remaining flakes of tobacco in to the gravel, "at least it satisfied my curiosity. It was a good idea, even though nothing came of it, and besides, it's a nice day for a drive." He pocketed the cigarette's filter for later disposal, got back into the vehicle, started the engine, and pulled back on to the highway heading north, not wanting any possible observer to see him turning around so close to the Webber property. A few miles up the road, he pulled in to the entrance of the Purgatory ski area, turned around, and headed back south toward Durango.

The highway from Purgatory back to town was mostly downhill, and was, as Tony remembered from his teen age years, a stretch of road where drivers invariable exceeded the speed limit. It gave him a perverse sense of pleasure to drive just under the limit and watch in his rear view mirror as cars, upon seeing the sheriff's department vehicle, slowed down to stay within the speed allowed by law. By the time he reached the foot of the grade, he had a considerable procession of cars backed up behind him. His perverse sense of humor caused him to start humming *I love a parade.*

He was just crossing the railroad tracks at Hermosa when Maggie Miller's voice came over the radio. "Unit Six, this is base."

Tony picked up the mike. "Roger, base. This is six."

"Six, if you're not doing anything that can't be put off, the sheriff wants to discuss the funeral arrangements with you. Can you meet him for lunch at his house?"

"Can do, base. I'm just cruising 550 north of town looking for speeders." Tony knew there was nothing Jack needed to go over with him concerning Barry's funeral. He figured Maggie's message was a ruse to confuse anyone who might be using a scanner to eavesdrop on the sheriff's department radio frequency. "Tell the boss I should be there in about a half hour or less, most likely less."

"Don't rush, Six. Jack's still here at the office. He won't be leaving here for at least another ten minutes or so. Base out."

"Roger, base. Six out." Tony smiled. With any luck, Jill might be having lunch at home, too. He could always hope.

Tony pressed down on the gas pedal. All the way in to the built-up area of Durango, he kept his speed a good five miles or more over the posted limit. When traffic began to get a bit congested, he dropped his speed. Once he turned right on to U.S. 160, crossed the Animas River, and got out of the downtown area, traffic began to thin out again. Climbing the hill out of the Lightner Creek valley, he got his speed back up. As a result, he beat the sheriff to the house by a few minutes...and was somewhat disappointed to find that no one else was home. He was standing outside Unit Six smoking a cigarette when Matson pulled into the driveway.

"What's up?" Tony asked as the sheriff got out of his Cherokee.

"Not out here." Matson said. "Let's get inside. I don't see anyone around, but I don't want to risk someone being out there somewhere with a parabolic mike." The sheriff gestured toward the hillside across the road from his house. "A reporter pulled that stunt down in Flagstaff not too long ago and was dumb enough to brag about it. What she put in the newspaper ended up blowing an undercover drug operation the local cops had been working on for six months. The bitch paid for her scoop, though. No law enforcement person in the Flagstaff area will so much as speak to her. I heard tell that her newspaper is going to fire her because nobody's willing to talk to her about crime, not even the criminals. Anyhow, it's made most of the law enforcement folks in this whole area close to paranoid about what they say and where they say it." Matson let Tony up the walk, unlocked the door, and motioned him inside.

Tony laughed. "Just because you're paranoid," he said, "doesn't mean that people really aren't out to get you."

Once they were inside, Matson said, "Two more deaths. Three men on horseback killed two hikers, a man and a woman, north and west of the lake. Mike and Eddie called in about an hour ago. They found the bodies, and someone the bad guys missed. The dead couple had a son. He saw what happened from maybe a hundred feet away. The bad guys missed him because he was just off the trail in the tree line. The boy described the three people fairly accurately."

"How old's the boy?" Tony asked.

"Young, but not too young to be a good witness. Mike questioned him quite a bit, and he said the boy's story was lucid and detailed."

"I'm surprised the kid's not in shock," Tony said.

"I guess he probably was, but it must have worn off. The shooting happened yesterday. The boy told Eddie he'd stayed by the bodies all night. Said he didn't want animals getting at his parents' bodies," the sheriff said.

"Damn! This complicates things. They'll have to break off trailing the perps."

"No," Matson replied grimly. "Eddie will stay with the boy. I've ordered the state patrol boys on duty at the dam to get a couple civilian volunteers to go in on four wheelers. There are several licensed hunting guides who live up that way, and any of them would be glad to volunteer for something like this. They'll bring out the bodies. Eddie and the boy will come with them. I told Mike to stay on the bad guys' trail."

"That's risky, Jack. If he catches up with them, it'll be three against one. That's long odds, especially when your deputy would probably be caught by surprise."

Matson smiled grimly. "I said that very thing when I talked to Mike. He told me that if I ordered him to break off following the bad guys, he'd probably have technical difficulties with his cell phone. God knows phone coverage up there is spotty enough so folks'd believe him, too. From the tone of his voice, I don't think I'd want to be the perps if he catches up with them. I have a hunch that they just might be shot while resisting arrest. And if it goes down that way," he continued in a bitter voice, "I flat guarantee that the internal affairs investigation will clear him. That couple was murdered in cold blood. Mike's in a mood to save the state of Colorado the expense of a couple of trials."

Tony nodded his head, indicating that he understood the sheriff, agreed with him, too, for that matter.

Matson continued. "You better forget what I just said. Mike's got a Winchester .308 with him. He's a damned good shot, too. I'm not saying he'd kill the suspects in cold blood, but I suspect he'd kill their horses. They wouldn't travel too fast if they're on foot." He paused a second, then went on. "Put the bad guys on foot in the high country and it'd slow them down a hell of a lot. Mike wouldn't enjoy shooting the horses, but he'd damn well do it if need be."

"Any ID on the couple?" Tony asked.

"A doctor and his wife from down in Santa Fe," Matson answered. "Doctor and Mrs. Harold Longo. The son is Harold, Junior,"

"And they were killed on federal land, too, from the looks of it. At least that's how I remember the map back at the office. That means you have to involve the FBI on this, as well. And the way I figure it, the federal death penalty law will probably apply.....hopefully."

"Right," Matson said grimly. "And I have one very pissed off deputy up there in the mountains that'll gladly serve as executioner if the perps rub him the wrong way. Mike said that he and Eddie were pretty upset about that boy's parents being killed. I'd guess neither of them is in a mood to take prisoners. Maybe it's a good thing that Eddie is staying with the boy. If the two of them caught up with the bad guys, I figure they just might resolve the issue right quick."

How soon do you break this to the press?" Tony asked. "The killing of the boy's parents, that is."

"I don't think we can sit on it," Matson replied. "At least not for too long. Thank God for encrypted cell phones that make it next to impossible for people to eavesdrop I don't want it to mess up your plans for tonight and tomorrow, but word of this is going to get out before sunset." He paused a second, "Besides, once word gets out, somebody might just get careless and do something to attract attention to himself. We're probably going to have to do another press conference".

"Can I go out and chase speeders while that's going on"? Tony asked. "I promise to learn how to write tickets really fast."

Matson laughed. "I'll do the press conference. You don't have to suffer through that again, at least not today," the sheriff replied. Then he continued, "Oh, yeah. Mike said the perps are probably starting to head west instead of north. They went on the west side of one particular hill that they'd have probably stayed on the east side of if they were going to continue on north. Mike said the east side looked like it'd be easier on horses, too, so that's another indication they might be going to swing off to the west. That's the only good news they provided, though. And it wasn't good news for the Longo family. They'd still be alive if the perps hadn't started to turn west."

"And if they've turned west...."

"We just might have a surprise in store for them," Matson finished the sentence for Tony. "I arranged for one of my deputies to ride along on the railroad's speeder run. He kept a real close watch on the ground on either side of the tracks for about a five mile stretch and found a place where several horses crossed the railroad tracks and headed up into the mountains. The tracks were faint, and probably at least a week old. If our thinking is right, and those tracks were made by the horses the robbers used in their getaway that just might be where we need to set up an ambush, assuming they return the same way. They just might. Actually I figure the odds are pretty good. The stream the tracks ran along is one that goes quite a ways up into the mountains. It's called Grasshopper Creek. Following it would make for fairly easy going, most likely." He stopped and thought for a second. "Oh, I got you out here with a promise of lunch. There's leftover ham in the 'frig, How 'bout a sandwich? We got the leftover baked ham and Swiss cheese or peanut butter and jelly." Matson headed for the kitchen; Tony followed.

Gladys Webber turned off the television. The sheriff's news conference caused the deaths of Mr. and Mrs. Longo to make the noon news. "Oh, damn it all to hell. If I get my hands on the idiot who killed those people I'll rip his heart out!"

Her husband slammed his fist down on the coffee table. "A dead deputy and now this!" he shouted. "The FBI and the state and county cops won't stop until they solve this, Glad. What are we going to do?"

"We've got to get the boys out of those mountains and out of sight," she answered.

"Out of sight, hell!" her husband exclaimed. "We've got to get them out of the state, maybe even out of the country."

"You're right, Jim, Gladys said. "And I think you were right about Mike. He is a threat to us. If the authorities lay hands on him......."

"I told you," her husband chortled. "I told you he was a problem." It was obvious that Webber was really worried. So what are we going to do about him?"

"We may have to make him disappear.....permanently," Gladys said, after a moment's thought.

"You mean......," her husband gasped. "But he's your own brother, Gladys!"

"Don't be an ass, James," his wife snapped. "He's my brother. But he's also weak, impulsive, and has a big mouth. I beginning to think I'd feel a lot safer if Michael were somewhere where there's be no risk of him implicating us." She thought for a moment before continuing, "Maybe we could bury him under one of the stalls in the horse barn or......."

CHAPTER ELEVEN

Sheriff Matson invited Tony to have dinner with the family that afternoon before going to calling hours at the funeral home for Barry Morgan. And, given the schedule of events for that evening, he also invited Tony to sleep at the house after calling hours. With the schedule Tony had set up, going back to town, going to calling hours at the funeral home, and then driving back to the ranch for the night would leave little time for sleep.

So Tony drove back to town, picked up his uniforms at Fishman's, and then drove back to the ranch to check last minute details with Lou Barnes, to shower, shave, dress, and pack for spending the night at the Matson house, and also to put out extra cat food. Barnes told him that the preparations were all made, and that he would guarantee that his part in Tony's plan would be carried off without a hitch. Tony believed him. His grandfather kept Barnes on the payroll for years, partly because he knew ranching, could be trusted implicitly, and was a stickler for details and partly because they'd been friends for ages, having worked together in developing some of the newer New Mexico oil and gas fields around Farmington a half century earlier. Lew Barnes and his wife were the next thing to family, as far as Tony was concerned. Grandpa Pete had felt the same way.

Shortly before four o'clock, Tony was back in unit six heading west toward Durango. He had a small overnight bag on the passenger's seat beside him, and a scoped Winchester Model 70 .30-06 and several other items covered with a blanket on the floor in back. The rifle was his, a gift from his grandfather many years earlier, when Tony was a sophomore in high school. He was comfortable with it, selecting it over any of the many other hunting weapons in the gun safe at the ranch, his own as well as weapons collected by his grandfather over many a year. He hadn't fired the Winchester for a couple years so before leaving the ranch to head to town, he fired several rounds through it and adjusted the sights so he knew it was zeroed in perfectly at a hundred yards.

More than once he turned the rear view mirror to look at himself. The deputy sheriff's uniform felt funny. It would take some getting used to before he'd feel comfortable in it, and he reminded himself several times that he didn't plan to wear it long enough to really get used to it, that he'd bought it strictly to be properly turned out for calling hours at the funeral home. "After all," he muttered to himself, "what good's it do to have money if you don't spend it on something useful."

It was just after half past four when he pulled in to the driveway of the Matson home. Jill and Pat were just getting out of Jill's car as he arrived. The women were carrying packages from the car, and Tony walked up to Pat to take the bag she was carrying.

"Thanks, Tony," Mrs. Matson said. "I'll unlock the door. Jill and I stopped at the market to get things for a quick supper." She walked ahead of him, taking the house key from her purse. The phone rang just as she opened the door, and she ran into the house to answer it.

Tony used his free hand to take two bags from Jill. "I'll carry these if you can hold the door."

"Thank you, kind sir," Jill replied grimly. "I think I have strength enough to hold the door open, but just barely. It's been a day from....."

"I can imagine," Tony answered. How'd things go at the funeral home?"

"Not good. Not good at all. I spent a lot of time taking care of the kids. I don't think they stopped crying for more than five minutes the whole two hours we were there, not that I think they really understand that their daddy's dead and won't come home ever again. And there wasn't a darn thing I could do to comfort them." A tear rolled down her cheek as she spoke.

"And the kids weren't the only ones that were crying, Jill. Your eyes are really red."

"I know, damn it!" Her voice trembled. "I could do without people seeing me looking like this. I could really do without *you* seeing me like this. My face must be a mess."

"We're going to get them, Jill. We'll catch them and they'll pay for what they did. I have a gut hunch that it'll all work out."

Jill held the front door for Tony, who had grocery bags in both arms. "I hope you're right, Tony. Daddy says he feels the same way. I just hope the two of you aren't being overly optimistic." She paused for a moment, then continued, "But that's not going to give a widow her husband back, and it won't give two kids their daddy or bring back the Longos. But if we catch them, it's a damn good bet they'll be locked up for the rest of their lives, at least. Two murders on federal land might even bring in the death penalty. Ought to bring it in to consideration is more like it, given society's current dislike for the death penalty.."

Jill closed the door and took one of the grocery bags from Tony. "Something like this can make a person really believe in capital punishment, Tony. I hope you catch them, and I hope they get sentenced to death. It won't make things better, but it'll help make things even. I know it's not Christian, but over the years I've become a real believe in retribution for criminals. An eye for an eye, and things like that."

She changed the subject abruptly as they walked in to the kitchen. "Hey, I forgot to tell you that you look good in the uniform! How'd you get one so quickly? Is it yours, or did you borrow one?"

"It's mine, all mine," Tony answered, "or rather *they* are; I bought two of them. And as to how I got it so fast, it's just amazing what offering a considerable gratuity can do. Custom alterations in well under three hours, and I will not tell you how thoroughly I lubricated the wallet of the woman who does the alterations at Fishmans. The store called her in just to do my alterations. Let's just say that money talks. Talks, heck, in this case it screamed. Bet you can still hear the echos bouncing around in Fishman's back room. I wouldn't be surprised if I didn't put that seamstress in a higher income tax bracket for this year! Her family's going to eat really well this week. Better make that this month." He put the grocery bag down on the counter. "It was worth it," he said. "I was determined to be properly dressed for tonight. What the heck, it's only money!!"

"Daddy will appreciate it, Tony," Jill said. "He doesn't like the idea of losing people like this. Now go sit. Mom and I will make supper."

Tony left the kitchen and went in to the living room. Sheriff Matson walked in just as he was getting ready to sit down. The sheriff had Tony get his overnight bag and the other items Tony had in his car and put them in one of the guest bedrooms. Then the two men sat down and reviewed the plans that they had come up with for the wee hours of the morning.

While they were engaged in conversation, the sheriff's phone rang. He excused himself, then picked up the phone.

"Sheriff Matson," he said into the machine. There was a lengthy pause while he listened to the party on the other end. Then the sheriff spoke again. "Yes sir, Mr. Attorney General. I fully appreciate the governor's concern in this, Sir."

A second pause. "You can be sure that we're doing everything we can on this matter."

Another pause. "No sir, I specifically recommend against doing that, at least I recommend against it unless you can get jump-qualified people from Fort Bragg in North Carolina. It would just cause more problems. Even worst, it might confuse matters to the point that the murderers would escape." Yet another pause. "I would only consider doing that if I thought matters had reached the point where doing it was our only chance to catch these people."

Yet another pause. "Thank you for the offer of extra help from the State Patrol and the Colorado Bureau of Investigation. Right now it looks as if we have sufficient personnel in place to deal with this. But matters could change. How soon could help arrive if I have to take you up on the offer?"

Another pause, abet a very short one. "Oh, really? That soon? That's comforting to know. You can be sure I'll contact you immediately if I need more people."

A final pause. "Thank you, Mr. Attorney General. As I said, I'll call immediately if need be." He looked at the telephone handset as if it were a large and ugly snake, then gently replaced it on its base. Having done so, he made a highly impolite gesture toward the phone, a gesture usually referred to as 'flipping the bird'. Then he exclaimed, "Great scout and cat house Thursday! What an idiot!"

"We get more help?" Tony asked.

"I do not believe this," the sheriff said. "I plain flat do not believe it!"

Tony raised his eyebrows as if expressing a question.

"It turns out that Doctor Longo's wife is, or should I say *was*, a second cousin of the governor of New Mexico," the sheriff said, a tone of serious exasperation in his voice. "And not only that, she is also distantly related to the wife of New Mexico's senior member of the United States Senate. Within less than a half hour after news of the Longo murders broke on CNN, both of these illustrious political nabobs phoned the governor of Colorado to express their outrage and their concern about the killings, not to mention demanding that the perps be apprehended, or better yet, that they be killed wherever they're found."

"Now let me guess," Tony said. "I bet our governor got on the phone to the attorney general, who then called you."

Good guess, but there were a few other phone calls as well, Tony," the sheriff said. "One apparently was to the head of the Colorado Army National Guard. Our illustrious governor, displaying the kind of ignorance you'd expect from someone who's never served so much as a day in the military in his whole life and has probably never fired a firearm of any kind to boot, told the general who heads the Guard that he wanted a full company of military police parachuted into the mountains in front of the bad guys."

"He *what!* Jack, you've got to be kidding! Why, that's just about the dumbest.......!"

"It sure is," the sheriff said, shaking his head. "I'd bet that maybe only one or two of the Guard MPs were ever parachute qualified, if that many, even. I can just imagine the kind of rescue operation we'd have to mount to get people down out of trees and evacuate all those MPs with broken arms, legs, and backs. And most likely one or two would even get themselves killed." Sheriff Matson was obviously not pleased with the disastrous potential inherent in the governor's crackpot idea.

"Damn," Tony said. "It wouldn't just be broken bones. Kick an untrained platoon out of a plane in that kind of country is just begging for at least a couple people to be killed. I sure agree with you there! A couple? Hell, Jack, worst case scenario just might be that there'd be a lot more than a couple killed."

"Yeah, you're right on that count. But fortunately the Guard chief talked some sense into the governor's head. The good news is we get extra help if needed. The bad news is that the governor wants to keep the parachute idea open as an option. But maybe we can mention the governor's hairbrained idea later tonight to certain people. Of course, we wouldn't have to tell those certain people how idiotic the idea really is. If the nut case that's responsible for running this state wants to 'chute soldiers in ahead to the bad guys, he'd better see if he can borrow a platoon from the 82nd Airborne at Fort Bragg." Matson scowled. I told the attorney general that, too, and he agreed. What I didn't say was that helicopters could be used to put troops from the Guard ahead of the bad guys. If the governor heard that idea, he'd probably insist that it be done." Matson wiped his forehead." And now," Matson said, changing the topic, "is there anything else we need to consider for later?"

The two men went over their plans for the upcoming attempt to apprehend the bank robbers. Before too long, however, they were called to the table for dinner. Both Pat and Jill apologized for dinner not being up to what they considered their usual standard. Jack and Tony praised the meal, a chicken casserole, regardless. When they had eaten and the table was cleared, Sheriff Matson and his wife left for the funeral home in Pat's vehicle. Tony and Jill followed in Jill's car.

They arrived at the funeral home shortly before six thirty to find several other law enforcement officials present. Sheriff Matson circulated among his deputies, posting two at the entrance as honor guards, two more in the parking lot, and two inside the building as ceremonial attendants at the open casket. Once he had his personnel posted, he rejoined Tony and his wife and daughter. The sheriff put his hand on Tony's elbow and said, "Let me introduce you to the rest of the law enforcement fraternity. If you ladies will excuse us..."

He steered Tony toward where a number of men and a handful of women stood, all dressed in uniform and wearing handguns. Matson introduced Tony to each member of the group, Colorado, Arizona, Utah and New Mexico state police, Durango city officers, the Bayfield and Ignacio town marshals, two members of the Ute Tribal Police, one member each from the Apache and Navaho tribal police, and deputies from four other Colorado counties. And three of Durango's FBI agents were in attendance, plus the SAC as well. In total, it amounted to a considerable contingent of law enforcement personnel.

Once introductions were completed, the collection of officers stood talking shop as the room filled with people who had come to pay their last respects to the fallen deputy and offer condolences to his family. As Tony stood talking with his fellow officers, he mentally evaluated the deputies from San Juan and Montezuma counties, trying to guess which ones would be joining the deputies from La Plata County later that night, or, to be totally accurate, early the following morning.

Perhaps fifteen minutes had passed before Jill came to Tony's side. She touched his arm gently and whispered in his ear, "Can you come with me for a few moments? Pam Morgan wants to meet you."

Tony excused himself and accompanied Jill across the room to where a young woman, dressed in black, sat with two young children. They stopped in front of the woman and Jill said, "Pam, this is Tony Frye. He's the one...."

Pamela Morgan, eyes red from crying and clutching a damp kerchief in her left hand, stood and held her hand out to Tony. "I know," she said. "I'm so glad to meet you, Mr. Frye. I know what you did to help my husband, and I really appreciate that." She wiped her eyes again with the kerchief. "I'm just so...."

"I did what I could, Mrs. Morgan," Tony said. "I only wish things had turned out differently. I just don't know what to say, other than to say we're doing everything we can to find the men who are responsible for his death. We won't stop until they're captured and locked up."

Pamela Morgan smiled sadly. "I know you won't, and I hope you're right," she said. "Sheriff Matson has told me about you, and of course I've also read the newspapers. And Jill speaks highly of you, too. She says you and her father feel there's a good chance you'll catch the men who shot Barry. I know you already killed one just after my husband was...." Her voice broke as she began to sob softly again. She managed a few more words before an elderly man came to her side. "Catch them, Mr. Frye. Catch them and kill them! I hope you can kill every last one of them!'"

The elderly man took her arm. "I know, Pam. Right now you feel the Old Testament punishment: an eye for an eye..." He turned toward Jill and Tony, "If you will excuse us, Pam's family is just arriving." Without waiting for an answer, he turned and steered Pamela Morgan and her children toward the other side of the room, to the entry way from the foyer.

Jill watched them walk away, then turned to Tony and said, "I can understand how she feels. If anything like this happened to Daddy, I'd be willing to kill the people responsible. I've never shot anything other than targets and two deer, but I sure would be willing to make an exception."

"I know what you mean," Tony answered. "I don't like the idea of killing another person. The first one, a couple years ago, was more than enough. But under the circumstances, I'm kind of glad I killed one of those scum the other day." He looked across the room to where Sheriff Matson stood, and caught the look the sheriff was giving him. "Jill," he said, "I think your dad wants one or both of us. Look at who he's talking to."

Jill looked across the room. "Well, I'll be!" she exclaimed. "It's Mr. and Mrs. Webber, along with the rest of the county commissioners and other assorted local political bigwigs. Let's join Daddy, but watch what you say, Tony."

They walked across the room to where the sheriff stood, talking to the Webbers and several other people. "....and we'll have horses waiting in Lake City," the sheriff said. "The plan is to head south from there and try to head the robbers off."

He turned as his daughter and Tony walked up to the group. "Oh, I'm glad you're here, kids," he said. Turning to the others, he said, "You folks all know Jill. This young man she's with is Tony Frye. I'm sure you recognize him from seeing his picture in the paper." Matson introduced each member of the group to Tony, then said, "Tony, I was just telling the county commissioners about your plan to take a posse to Lake City and try heading off the bank robbers. I also told them about the governor's offer to air drop national guard troops ahead of where we think the robbers would be. I also told them why I didn't like the idea. The Guard commander didn't like it either, I gather, but he's working on borrowing a platoon of paratroopers from the 82nd Airborne at Fort Bragg, North Carolina, along with air support to drop them where we'd need them."

"Oh," Tony said, picking up on the sheriff's lie without so much as batting an eyelash. There was no such plan to take a posse to Lake City. "Well, it's about all we can do," he said. "There's no way we can catch up to them from behind. They have too much of a head start. It's fortunate that they're traveling through some awfully rough country. That'll slow them down enough so we can position our people across their line of travel."

He lowered his voice. "Please don't repeat this to anyone else. Earlier today, as the sheriff said, the governor phoned Sheriff Matson and offered to send in a company of military police by parachute. His idea was to drop a hundred or so combat-armed National Guardsmen across the route the robbers seem to be taking. Sheriff Matson said he didn't think matters had quite reached the point where soldiers would be needed, but he did ask the governor to keep the option open. The Guard commander, like the sheriff just said, is working to borrow some paratroopers from the 82nd Airborne in North Carolina, just in case. We just don't want any of the plans we've discussed to become common knowledge."

Commissioner Webber spoke. "I certainly understand the need to keep your plans quiet. But what if the robbers don't keep heading in the direction you think they're going? Then what? If they change direction, would soldiers be used? And if they keep heading generally north toward the Lake City area, would sending a large posse to Lake City and then have them head south to intercept the crooks be sufficient?"

"Sir," Tony answered, "I really don't know how to answer that, other than to say the sheriff will consider our actions as circumstances dictate. I don't think it's likely they'd change directions now, and I'd say the use of a parachute force would be seen as a last resort, but it is an option. As for where the robbers will go, it's awful rough country to the east and it's too close to roads and lots of traffic on the west. North is the only way that makes sense. My bet is we'll catch them in the mountains somewhere south of Lake City. We'll have half the available law officers in southwest Colorado in this posse, more than enough to block off every trail heading into the Lake City area from the national forest without bringing in the Guard. But, like I said a moment ago, it certainly is an option." He thought for a second, then went on. "Don't think it'd be really smart to drop troops in country that rough, but I guess it could be done. Risky, though."

"How sure are you that this plan of sending a posse to Lake City will work, Mr. Frye?" a short, portly man wearing a much rumpled blue suit asked. He'd been in the group when the sheriff was talking about the false plans, so Tony assumed Matson was comfortable with him hearing what they were discussing.

"Excuse me, sir," Tony replied. "I hate to admit it, but I've forgotten your name; too many names and faces in a real short period of time, I'm afraid."

"Huh?" A puzzled look flashed across the short man's face. "Oh," he said. "That's understandable, lad. I know how it feels; I've have the same trouble myself, and more than once. I'm August Wilkins, one of the county commissioners. I knew your grandfather, of course. Everyone knew Pete." He held his right hand out.

Tony shook the proffered hand. "Thanks, Mr. Wilkins." He paused a second before continuing. "How sure am I that the plan'll work? I'd say there's a real good chance it will. But there are a lot of variables. *If* they head the way we figure and *if* we get into the mountains in front of them and *if* we are blocking whatever trail they're using and *if* nothing happens to spook them before we can surprise them, chances are pretty darn good that we'll bag them. I wish I could offer a guarantee, but that's something none of us can do. The odds might be a bit long, but it's our best bet."

The sheriff broke in. "Tony's right. We have a good chance, providing nothing goes wrong and also providing that we've guessed right on what those birds are going to do. There's no way we can guarantee success, but what we're going to do is the only thing that gives us even half a chance of catching the murderers." A movement across the room caught his eye. "Looks like Father Paul wants to start the prayer service. Guess we'd better go sit down." He motioned for Tony and Jill to follow him, turned, and walked toward the front of the room, near where the casket was placed.

The prayer service lasted close to fifteen minutes. When it was over, the sheriff moved to be near Pam Morgan and her family while Tony took the place of one of the deputies standing honor guard at the foot of the casket. This effectively placed both of them where they would not be forced to answer questions from politicians or anybody else. It also gave Tony a chance to mull over what the two members of the county commissioners had said, and *how* they'd said it. Upon careful consideration, he concluded that neither had said anything that seemed out of the ordinary. Webber was a prime suspect and as such, Tony was less than objective in his viewpoint. But Wilkins seemed to be a very open and pleasant person. Tony got the impression the man really wanted to see the robbers captured as soon as possible. He also concluded that he'd better check his reactions with both the sheriff and Jill.

Much of the crowd at the funeral home waited until almost nine o'clock before leaving. Among the last to leave were the law officers. Tony left his post at the foot of the casket and found Jill and her family. They walked to the parking lot behind the funeral home. The sheriff and his wife got into their vehicle and left; Tony and Jill followed in Jill's car, with Tony at the wheel. Once he had the car in motion and heading out of the parking lot, Tony spoke.

"Well, what did you think?" he asked.

"I gather that Daddy's really pleased with your prowess as a liar," Jill answered. "He was positively beaming when you were spinning your share of that whopper I half expected him to start laughing. Tell the truth.....I was hard put not to really break out in a major grin."

Tony chuckled as he braked for a stop sign. "He told a few whoppers himself tonight", he said, as he made a right turn on to Durango's main street. "You were watching faces while I was talking. Did you notice anything interesting?"

Jill nodded her head. "Our friend Webber liked to choke trying to swallow a grin while you were explaining the dummy plan to Augie Wilkins. I'd say the thought of a horde of law officers going all the way up to Lake City by plane and then charging south on horseback into the mountains pleased him greatly. I'm glad I was prepped to watch him. Everybody else was hanging on your every word and nobody would have noticed his expression if you and Daddy hadn't alerted me to keep my eyes on him." She thought for a second, then went on. "If he'd been alone, I think he'd have busted a gut laughing."

Tony smiled grimly. "That's just another indication that he's up to his eyeballs in this mess," he said. He thought for a moment as he turned the corner at the intersection that led to U.S. highway west out of town. "What about this Mr. Wilkins?" he continued. "Could he be connected with Webber?"

"Absolutely not! Augie Wilkins is a sweetheart," she said emphatically. "He's the one person on the County Commission that Daddy can count on for unquestioned support. Daddy hasn't a single doubt about his integrity. Besides," she concluded, "he's not rich and he donated a thousand dollars to the fund that's been set up for Barry's family. He's even been pushing the other commissioners to keep Pam and the children covered on the county's health insurance policy until the kids finish school, no matter how long that is. Augie's as honest a person as you'll find in this county. He's also smarter than average, a lot smarter, according to Daddy. Just don't let that bumbling behavior and the wrinkled blue suit fool you. Daddy says he's got a mind like a steel trap. I guess if he were a cop he'd be sort of like Lieutenant Columbo on that TV program." Jill paused for a second, obviously thinking. "And did I mention that your grandfather liked him?"

Tony scratched a small itch on his chin. "Good," he said. "I kind of liked him, too......seemed like a nice person."

"He is," Jill replied. She sat quietly for a moment. "Tony.....," she hesitated.

"What, Jill?"

Jill waited another few seconds before she spoke, "Tomorrow could be dangerous, couldn't it?" she said quietly.

Tony considered how best to answer her question before he replied. He decided that being totally honest was the only thing he could do, under the circumstances; Jill was no dummy. "Could be," he said. "If we get lucky and get across the bad guys' trail, it sure could. They've killed three people, Jill. They're armed, and we certainly have to consider them dangerous. If we run into them, I wouldn't figure on them surrendering without a fight."

Jill hesitated again before continuing. "Tony, please try to keep an eye on Daddy. He makes an awfully big target." She paused again. "And you be careful, too. I've already told

Daddy I expect him to bring you back standing up, in one piece, and with no added holes. You do the same for him, please."

Tony laughed, then reached across the car and patted Jill's hand. "I appreciate that. And I promise to watch out for your dad. He's a good guy, Jill, and I sure don't want anything to happen to him. And it's not as if he's not had combat experience." He hesitated a second, then continued.

"I can't lie to you, Jill," he said. "There's a risk, but there are only three of them, at least only three that we know of. We'll have them outnumbered; at least we should have them outnumbered. And if my guess is right, we'll also have the surprise factor on our side. We expect to see them; they don't expect us to be there waiting for them. Besides, I don't think there's a lawman in this end of Colorado who'd hesitate to put any of those three down for keeps. They're responsible for a deputy's death; no lawman around here is going to cut them any slack. One wrong move and there'll be dead bank robbers all over the landscape."

She took Tony's hand in hers. "I know all that," she said. "But I can't help but worry. You just be damn careful, Tony Frye. There are a few more restaurants I want to introduce you to. And you owe me a riding date, too, not to mention a lunch."

"And maybe a swim and a picnic at Trimble? At the hot springs?"

"You pick the day this summer; I'll pack the food," Jill replied.

"You wouldn't happen to play golf, would you?" Tony asked hopefully.

"I sure do," she replied. "I'm not really good, but I do enjoy playing."

"And," Tony said, "how 'bout a day touring Mesa Verde. I haven't done that in years."

"I love it there," Jill answered. "I try to go at least once a year. I always learn something new about the Ancient Ones."

"Pick a day," Tony said. "And maybe pushing my luck a bit, how would you feel about riding the train up to Silverton and back?

"Oh, Tony," she said, smiling. "That's one of my favorite things. The scenery is absolutely magnificent, especially when you ride over the high line above the river. That's something I don't think I'd ever get tired of. And Silverton's a fun place to go to. I especially like walking Blair Street and going in to the shops. And there are some pretty good places to have lunch, too."

"Then how about the two of us doing it right after you get out of school?" he asked.

"That would be wonderful," she answered, without the slightest hesitation. "We'll need to get tickets a week or so in advance, at least. Tourist traffic is pretty heavy in the summer so maybe we ought to pick a date soon and reserve tickets. And it's better to go up on the second trip of the day," she said. "The light's better for taking pictures then. And we just have to have seats on the right side of the train when it heads north." She paused, "Lots of people take the bus back. It's quicker. So we could probably get seats on the river gorge side coming back, too."

"Right," Tony said. "No sense on being on the cliff side of the car when we go through the high line, not that we wouldn't be on the scenic side on the return trip. But if we can be on that side going both ways...... Maybe in the next couple days you can look at your summer vacation schedule and we can decide on a day for the trip."

"We'll do just that," she answered. "I'll check my calendar before I go to bed tonight. You do the same and we'll schedule the train ride and get our tickets as soon as possible."

The two young people sat quietly until Tony turned into the driveway of the Matson house. During that time, Jill kept tight hold of Tony's right hand. Despite the difficulty of driving one-handed, Tony made not the slightest effort to regain the use of the hand Jill clutched so firmly. Tony's mind was on Jill, not on the expectations for the next day's events. He could not help comparing her with Marissa Montgomery; Marissa did not come off at all well in the comparison.

****
***

"Oh, my God," Commissioner Webber exclaimed to his wife as he drove their car north along U.S. 550 toward their ranch later that evening. "A hundred combat-armed paratroops. What can the boys hope to do against a force like that?"

"James, I'm frightened," his wife replied. "I'm starting to wish we hadn't sent them out to rob that bank."

Glad," her husband answered, "it's not the robbery that's the problem. It's the three murders. Why did those to damned tourists have to be friends and family members of both a governor and a U.S. senator?"

"We've got to get them back to the ranch as soon as possible," she said grimly. "And I think things have reached the point where all three of them need to disappear.....and to disappear permanently. Why should we kill my brother and let the other two live."

"Because your brother is a weak, chicken-hearted coward," the commissioner answered. "And you're the one who came up with the bright idea of killing him, not me."

"I know that, you fool," she snapped. "If there's room for one grave in the horse barn, then there's room for three. If all three of them vanish, what's left to connect us with the bank robbery, the dead deputy, and the two dead tourists?"

"Nothing," her husband said, "except for the money, of course."

"So at first light to head out, meet them, and get them straight back to the ranch in one hell of a hurry. Bring them in to the stable. I'll be there with a pistol, and you'll have one with you. We'll kill them there, and bury them pretty much where they drop. Then we'll hide the graves under a layer of straw and walk horses back and forth for a half hour or so. Nobody'll ever find them. We'll hide the money the same way. Later, maybe in a year or two, we can start using the money, but slowly and carefully. Very carefully!"

CHAPTER TWELVE

The gigantic insect, or whatever it was, emitted a loud and very annoying buzzing noise, one that Tony found intensely irritating. After a moment, he woke up enough to figure out that the noise came not from an insect, but rather from the alarm clock on the nightstand next to his bed in one of the Matsons' guest bedrooms. He shook the cobwebs from his mind, groaned, and looked at the illuminated digits of the digital alarm: 2:40 AM. The muffled noise of a running shower in another room was the only sound audible once the alarm had been squelched. Tony got up and headed for the bathroom adjacent to the guest bedroom he'd occupied for all too few hours. He shaved, then showered quickly and got dressed, except for his uniform boots. Holding his boots in one hand and his gun belt in the other, he tiptoed quietly down the hallway to the living room and then into the kitchen, following the smell of fresh coffee. The first person he saw as he entered the kitchen was Jill.

"What are you doing up at this ungodly hour?" he said.

"Someone's got to make coffee for you and Daddy," she answered.

"Yes," Pat Matson chimed in from the kitchen counter where she was cracking eggs into a bowl. "And someone's got to fix breakfast for the two of you. Everybody else is getting breakfast in town, but they all slept in town last night, in a motel right down the street from the Denny's, which fortunately happens to stay open all night. The rest of the boys will eat at Denny's. You and Jack don't have that luxury. So....you get a homemade breakfast, you lucky people."

Jill chimed in, "Yeah, and the wait staff here is a lot prettier, too."

"And it's probably a better breakfast than the rest of the crew are getting in town," the sheriff said as he entered the kitchen. "Much as I like Denny's, home cooking has it beat every day. Morning, Dear," he said, kissing his wife. "Morning, Jill," he continued.

"Good morning, Jack," his wife answered. "You boys sit down and we'll get you fed so you can get on the road."

"Yeah," Jill continued as she poured coffee for Tony and her father. "And after which, I'll get a couple hours more sleep before I go for an airplane ride to play radio relay."

"What? You're going to do what?" The surprise in Tony's voice was evident.

"I," Jill said slowly, as if speaking to one of somewhat diminished mental capacity, "am going to be in an airplane about nine o'clock this morning, and will be flying within radio range of where you'll be. Someone has to do it. You're the one who pointed out that your tactical radios only work line-of-sight. And it'll be back up for your cell phones. Redundancy's the word, Tony. And I have a hunch that the cell phones won't work too well. Darned few towers up that way. Besides, it's not my idea. Daddy asked me to do it."

Pat Matson slid scrambled eggs, sausage, and home fries on to two plates before continuing. "And I will be manning both a radio and a cell phone at the Bodo office. At least that's one possibility. Jack said the only way to ensure security on this is to put people he absolutely trusts in the communications chain. Maggie Miller can be trusted as much as any person in this state, but she just might be too busy with her normal duties to babysit the radio, too. And every deputy Jack has available is going to be busy with one thing or another. We just happen to be available. Besides, we work cheap."

"And like the lady said, we work cheap," Jill said with a smile. "Very cheap, like in *free*."

"Now wait a minute," the sheriff said. "You each have a consulting contract that pays you a whole dollar for today's work. And there aren't that many people around here that I'm a hundred per cent sure aren't involved in the militia, or that have friends who are," Jack continued, speaking around a mouthful of toast. He looked at his watch. "Hey, it's getting about time. Finish your food, Tony. We gotta boogie into town."

Before the sheriff could rise from the table, his wife said, "The dollar is our salary for the year, Tony. Jack's too cheap to pay us a dollar a day." The sheriff nearly choked on the food he was trying to swallow, much as he knew his wife and daughter were just jerking his chain.

Both men quickly finished their breakfasts, then stood up. The older Matsons headed for the living room but Jill motioned for Tony to wait. After her parents had left the room, she spoke quietly. "Remember to watch out for Daddy, please, Tony. He sometimes gets a bit careless about his personal safety and has the purple hearts to prove it." She hesitated, then continued. "You remember to be careful, too." She rubbed two fingertips of her right hand down Tony's left cheek, then kissed him. "You're nice, and like I said, there are a few more restaurants I wouldn't mind showing you." Then, for good measure, she planted a major kiss on Tony's lips.

Tony reached up and covered her hand with his. "Careful is my middle name. And it wouldn't look good if I let my boss get himself hurt my first week on the job. Could we maybe do another restaurant this weekend?"

Jill laughed softly. "I think I might be able to work it into my busy social calendar, Deputy Frye. Now you better scoot. Don't want to keep Daddy waiting, do you?" She leaned close and gave him another quick kiss on the cheek.

On the drive to town, Tony and Jack passed a single car and two trucks heading west on highway 160. It was so early, even by Colorado standards   that there wasn't even the slightest hint of pink in the eastern sky. Sunrise, early as it came in late springtime Colorado, was well over an hour and a half away by the time they turned off U.S. 550 on to 6th Street. Three sheriff's patrol vehicles, one each from LaPlata, San Juan, and Montezuema Counties, were parked on the street next to the Denny's restaurant. Six uniformed officers were standing in a tight cluster. Matson stopped his vehicle and Tony rolled his window down so Matson could speak to the congregated deputies.

"Park your cars over in the city lot, boys," he said. "Then we'll just walk to where we're catching our ride." The officers quickly got into their cars, then followed the sheriff's car to the parking lot. When the four cars were parked all in a line and the officers were out of them, the sheriff spoke again. "Bring your weapons and your camouflage clothing and follow us."

He and Tony watched as the deputies gathered their gear, and when everyone was ready, they turned and led the procession of law officers a half block east along 6th Street. When they group reached the railroad crossing, the sheriff led them across the street. Just as the officers reached the south side of the street, a man wearing overalls, a jean jacket, and a engineer's cotton cap opened the big metal gate to the Durango & Silverton Railroad yard, which was normally closed off to public access. Just inside the gate, headlight turned on, a steam engine sat chuffing softly, two cattle cars, a passenger coach, and a caboose coupled behind its tender.

CHAPTER THIRTEEN

Except for street lamps and the headlights of occasional passing cars, and there weren't many of those, downtown Durango was still darker than the Earl of Hell's riding boots when the various officers of the sheriff's posse began to congregate at the Durango and Silverton Narrow Gauge station. A few lights, very few, were visible in houses and apartment buildings on the hillsides east and west of downtown, along, of course, with the city's street lights. Other than these, the only light visible was the headlight shining from above the smoke box of D & S steam locomotive number 476. Matson and Tony parked their car in the parking lot across the street from where the track entered the fenced-in area of the station grounds and walked up to the man at the gate. The other officers followed them.

"Good morning, Sheriff Matson," the man said cheerfully. "I have everything ready for you."

"And good morning to you, Mr. Connelly," the sheriff said. "Tony," he continued, "this is Bud Connelly, general manager of the railroad. When Tony and Connelly finished shaking hands, the sheriff proceeded to introduce the other officers. Once this was completed, he said, "I need to talk to the engineer for a moment, Bud."

"You're talking to him, Jack," Connelly said. "You don't think I'd miss this, do you? If what you're trying to do works, the railroad's going to get a million bucks worth of free publicity. It'll make history, and I damn well want to be there when it happens!" Even in the dark, the smile on Connelly's face was plainly evident.

Matson stifled a groan. All he needed now was for some thumb-fingered amateur playing railroad engineer to ruin the plan that he and Tony had so carefully worked out.

Perhaps Connelly sensed the sheriff's displeasure, for he said, "Don't worry, Jack. I'm the one that does all the practical instruction when we break in a new engineer. I make at least one trip a week at the throttle to Silverton and back just to keep my hand in. Truth is, in addition to being the railroad's boss, I'm also the most qualified engineer working for this outfit. You said you wanted the best; I'm it, damn it! I'll get you where you want to be, and do it just a mite better than any other person available. You need it done right, and I'm the best person to do it."

Matson smiled and accepted the inevitable. "All right, Bud. I do recall you promised me the very best engineer on your payroll," he chuckled. "Is the train all set?"

"You bet, Sheriff," Connelly answered enthusiastically. "The horses are loaded in the two stock cars, as you wanted. I also assigned a couple railroad employees to ride in each of the stock cars. As far as they know, this is a delivery to the Ah Wilderness dude ranch up the line. They won't know any different until they see your people boarding the train so they won't have a chance to spread the news to anybody. When you want those horses unloaded, I figure we can do the job for you in between sixty to ninety seconds."

He turned to Tony and said, "That elderly fellow that brought the two horses in for you and the sheriff? Well, he asked me to tell you to be careful." Then he turned to the sheriff again. "The coach you wanted is behind the stock cars, and I took the liberty of tacking on our caboose at the very end. You'll find one of our hostesses back there, with coffee on the stove and plenty of sandwiches and homemade pies. The coffee and sandwiches are compliments of the D&S, and I had my wife bake four pies for this morning.....didn't tell her why, either."

Matson reached out and patted Connelly on the shoulder. "Thanks, Bud," he said. "Sounds like you've given us everything I wanted, and a bunch extra to boot." He paused, then said, "Sorry I had doubts, but..."

Connelly cut him off before he could finish the apology. "I'd have doubts, too, if I were in your place, I guess. But I don't. I've thought this through six ways from Saturday. This railroad is going to give you everything you want and then some. This'll be a chance to give something back to the community. All you have to do is get your men on board and let me know when you want to head north." Connelly turned, walked to the steps up to the engine cab, and climbed them. He settled himself in the engineer's seat on the right hand side of the locomotive and flashed Matson a "thumbs up" sign.

Matson turned to the seven law officers standing behind him. "Well," he said, "you heard the man. Coffee and food in the caboose. Climb aboard and let's get this circus rolling!" He turned again and led his posse down the concrete walkway that paralleled the tracks, past the engine, tender, stock cars loaded with horses, the coach, and finally to the caboose. He ushered six of his men up the steps and into the car. Then came Tony's turn, but before he could begin the short climb, Matson stopped him and said, "I'll ride the engine. You brief the others. Tell them where we're going and what we expect of run in to." Without waiting for a reply, he turned and headed back toward the front of the train.

Tony climbed the steps and entered the caboose to find the six deputies getting food and coffee and chatting with the pretty young blond girl who was pouring cups of coffee for them. Tony looked at the girl, then spoke to her. "Miss, are you making this trip with us?"

"No sir," she answered. As soon as the last person boards, I'm supposed to make sure this is all set up, and then get off the train. There's three more pots of coffee over there, all set to go on the stove, and coal in the coal box to keep the stove going. More food in the ice box, too." She nodded toward the ice box beside the coal stove.

"Then you'd best leave, Miss," Tony said. "We're about to head out." He watched as the girl put down the cup of coffee she'd just poured and headed toward the rear door of the caboose.

Just as she opened the door, she turned, smiled sweetly, and said, "Have a good trip, guys, and.....and good hunting." Then she closed the door, climbed down the steps to track level, and disappeared in the darkness between the train and the still-darkened depot.

When she was gone, Tony said, "So much for keeping this secret. Hope she keeps her mouth shut. Oh, well, maybe she just guessed. With all the law enforcement people on this train, you don't have to be a rocket scientist........." He didn't finish the sentence, starting another one instead. "All right, men, here's...." He was interrupted by the train starting in to motion, which threw him slightly off balance. Grabbing the edge of the counter to steady himself for a moment as the locomotive took out slack, he continued, "the plan."

Quickly but concisely he explained where they were going and what they would do when they arrived. Then he began to list the rules they would operate by. "We're an ambush team," he said. "We don't talk and we don't smoke. We move as little as possible. We're wearing cammo, and we're just going to blend into the brush until the bad guys come. Then we jump them."

One of the Montezuma County deputies, and older, burly man named Bob Castle, interrupted. "*If* they come, don't you mean?"

Tony scratched his chin with a forefinger as the engineer blew two longs, a short, and another long on the train's whistle for a street crossing. "I'm an optimist so I'll say *when* they come." He paused, then continued. "Everything we have points to them coming down out of the mountains by following one particular creek bed, and that's where we'll be waiting for them. It is possible we figured wrong, and that's why we have eight saddled horses in the stock cars at the front of the train. The train drops us, then runs a mile and a half or so further north, turns around at Cascade Canyon wye, and waits. If we need the horses, we can have the train back to where we'll be inside of five minutes."

Hank Ormond, one of the La Plata deputies, looked up and asked, "But how would we let the folks on the train know we need the horses? Radio coverage out in the area where we're going isn't good, and I'd guess the same is true with cell phones. Basically, it's line of sight and the train isn't going to be in sight of a whole hell of a lot." The engineer blew for another crossing as Ormond finished speaking.

"Good question, Hank," Tony said. "By some undetermined time, but between eight and nine o'clock, we'll have a plane overhead, a plane which can fly five hours on a full load of fuel. There'll be someone in the plane to relay radio messages from us to the train and to headquarters. Communications won't be a problem, except for the half hour or so it'll take the plane to land, refuel, and get back here, and that's if this turns into an all day affair. We hope it doesn't."

He looked around. "Any more questions?" Hearing none, he continued. "Nope? OK, let's fill up on food, especially the pies - lots of sugar to keep us awake, but try to go easy on the coffee. You're probably going to have to hold your water for several hours. Don't make yourselves too uncomfortable by drinking too much." He thought for a second, then said, "And you might want to drain your bladders before we leave the train, just to be on the safe side."

By this time the little train had reached the first bridge over the Animas River and crossed it, picking up speed as it chugged through the darkened town. The seven men in the swaying caboose began to look for seats. As the car was small, one of them opened the door leading to the platform at the front of the car and, accompanied by two others, crossed to the dimly lit coach, where ample seating existed. The men talked softly, smoked, ate, and drank as the train worked its way the first few miles north of town, building up to a respectable speed as it did so.

Up in the cab of locomotive number 476, Sheriff Matson stood behind the engineer's seat on the right side of the locomotive, leaving plenty of space for the fireman to wield his coal scoop. Each time the fireman stepped on the foot pedal that opened the butterfly doors so he could throw another scoop into the fire box, an orange gleam filled the cab. Engineer Connelly finally turned to Matson and, using a loud voice to carry over the mechanical noise level in the cab, spoke. "How in heck are you going to know where to tell me to stop?" he asked.

"Your speeder driver dropped a deputy along the line on his way back from Silverton today, didn't he?" Matson asked in return.

"Yes," the engineer answered. "But what's that..........?"

"About a quarter mile, or probably less, from where we need to get off, he'll be waiting with an infrared signal light. I'll be wearing infrared goggles." Matson patted his jacket pocket. "When I see the light, I'll tell you to stop. It'll be not too far north of the water stop at Tank Creek, so you won't be going too fast, will you?"

"I wasn't planning on watering at Tank Creek," Connelly said. "It's a light train and we won't need to take on water there."

"Better fill the tender anyhow, don't you think? Matson said. "You don't know how long you'll be waiting, and you'll have to keep steam up, won't you?"

"Whoops! Plans just changed," Connelly replied. "I forgot we'll be stopped at the wye and waiting. In an emergency I can pump creek water if I have to, but it'd be smart to take on water at the tank instead. It'd be quicker, for sure. Plus if we pump creek water, we sometimes end up with assorted wildlife sucked up in to the tender. Hadn't thought of running low on water." He considered the situation, then went on. "There'll be river water at the wye. I'll make damned sure I keep the tender's water tank full while we're sitting and waiting, regardless of what the pump sucks up."

CHAPTER FOURTEEN

The three men in the engine cab, engineer, fireman, and sheriff, lapsed into silence as the small train quickly moved through the dark across the plain of the Animas River. The only noises were the clickety-clack of the train's wheels passing over the rail joints, the chugging noise made by steam working the cylinders driving the 44 " diameter driving wheels of the locomotive, the noise made by the opening and closing of the butterfly doors as the fireman threw scoop after scoop of coal on to the fire, and the sound of the train's whistle as the engineer blew the required two longs, a short, and another long whistle signal required by law for each highway crossing. Occasionally the train crew and sheriff's posse would see the lights of a vehicle on U.S. 550 or a light in a house along the highway to the left of the tracks or in the Dalton Ranch residential and golf community on the right side of the train.

Not long after passing Dalton Ranch, the train passed the railroad's storage facility and the old water tank at Hermosa, crossed the U.S. highway, and began the climb up from the river valley. This point pretty well marked the end of the sort of box canyon through which the Animas gently flowed. The rest of the trip would be pretty much upgrade, and slowed both by the grade itself as well as by the requirement to slow to a crawl while crossing the "high line", the high shelf carved out of a sheer cliff above the Animas River gorge more than a century before by the Denver and Rio Grande construction crew. This part of the train trip was the scenic highlight of the trip between Durango and Silverton, but the members of the posse would see virtually nothing of the scenery due to the darkness, though they would have plenty of scenery to admire on the return trip, providing, of course, that success put them in the mood to admire said scenery.

Climbing the grade not only slowed the train's progress, it also increased the noise the engine made, as it had to work harder climbing the grade. The men on the train watched in amusement as light after light in the condominiums on the downhill slope between the tracks and the highway came on, occupants of the residences no doubt awakened by the noise of an unexpected very early train running along the rail line that ran practically through their back yards.

Once the train transited the high line above the Animas River gorge, it began to pick up a little speed. Sheriff Matson leaned out of the engine cab, looked back toward the passenger car and caboose, and flicked the power button on his flashlight so he could see the mile markers. When he found the one he was looking for, he turned back to engineer Connelly and loudly said, "It's only about five miles from here to where we're going to drop off."

"And not much more than three to Tank Creek," Connelly responded over the engine noises. We'll pass the dude ranch at Ah Wilderness in a couple minutes, then stop for water. I figure I'll head out from the water stop at a crawl, probably under five miles an hour, then slow to half that or less when you get your signal. Can you and your men safely jump off a real slow moving train in the dark? I can get the speed down to about one mile per hour if need be."

"We sure can," Matson answered. While you stop to fill the tender's water tank, I'll run back and tell my men to jump off at my signal."

"Jump, hell!" answered Connelly. This train'll be moving so slow they can just step off. Only thing they'll need to do is try not to turn an ankle by stepping on a loose piece of ballast. Of course, it's just starting to get a little bit light, so that'll help."

In a few moments the train halted where Tank Creek came rushing down the side of the steep hill to the east side of the tracks. Connelly expertly brought the train to a halt with the tender's water hatch directly under the water tank's spout. While the fireman climbed up on the tender's deck to open the hatch, pull he spout down, and fill the tank, Matson ran back along the train, climbed into the coach, and quickly instructed his posse on the procedure for leaving the train. Then he ran back to the engine, getting aboard just as the fireman finished filling the water tank.

Once the tank was filled and the hatch closed, the fireman climbed down from the tender, grabbed his coal scoop, and began feeding the fire once more. Connelly gently opened the throttle, applied sand for adhesion on the upgrade, and the train slowly began to move. Matson put on a set of infrared goggles and carefully watched ahead. The train rounded a slight bend and there, several hundred feet ahead of the engine, Matson saw the signal light.

"Slow down, Bud. This is it," he called to the engineer. Without speaking, Connelly eased off on the Johnson bar a notch and made a gentle application of the air brakes. The train slowed to barely a walk as Matson flashed his flashlight toward the coach and caboose. Then he climbed down the steps of the engine. When he was on the bottom step, he flicked the flashlight on and pointed it toward the ground. Carefully calculating the speed and distance to the ground, he shut off the light and stepped off the train and away from it. Looking back toward the rear of the slowly moving train, he could just make out the dark forms of his seven deputies, barely visible in the dim light of the coming dawn, leaving the coach and caboose platforms and stepping off the creeping train. Only one of the deputies missed his step. He rolled and bounced back up on his feet, swearing softly but basically uninjured, save for a small loss of dignity and some minor contusions.

Matson gathered up his men, making sure that each had successfully exited the train without even a slight injury that would limit their effectiveness. Then he led his posse north along the tracks a hundred feet or so to where a dim form was barely visible. "Morning, Hal," Matson called out softly, his voice little more than a whisper.

"Howdy, Boss," the man said, rising from the crouched position he'd been holding a few feet from the railroad track.

Matson turned to his men. "For you that don't know him, this is Hal West, Deputy West. He's been here since yesterday." He turned back. "Report, Hal."

"Yes sir," West said softly. Horse tracks, lots of them, heading east up Grasshopper Creek. Nothing coming back this way. The tracks are at least a week old, maybe older, but certainly not too much older. There's horse droppings, too. They're about the same age. Nothing fresh, except for wild animals.....like elk and bear. One bear I thought might give me some trouble, but it decided to go away peacefully.....thank God!"

"You got us an ambush site picked out?" Matson asked.

"You bet your backside I do. It's a beaut! We'll set up where the creek runs along a steep hillside and leaves less than ten feet of level ground between the south bank of the stream and the hillside where we'll be hidden. That's ten feet max. A lot of it the ledge is maybe six feet. If the baddies come this way, they'll have to go single file on this stretch. The west bank can't be used; no space between the stream and a cliff. Lots of trees and rocks and brush for us to disappear in to. In cammo, we can blend in to the landscape and not be seen from ten feet away if we pick and choose our spots carefully," West said. "And," he continued, "anybody riding a horse along this stretch is going to be watching the trail, not looking uphill to where we'll be hiding."

"Right," Matson said. "Lead off and let's get hidden. Oh," he said as an afterthought, "better drain our bladders. It's liable to be a long day. And go uphill to do it. " Moments later, after the posse members had tended to their personal comfort, Matson added a few more words. "Remember," he said, "anyone that pulls a gun is a fair target. Shoot to kill. Don't talk above a whisper, and then only if you absolutely have to, and otherwise keep as still as possible. You all hunt, and that's what we're doing today, hunting. Let's get into position." He turned to West. "Hal, lead us out and get us set where you think best. The rest of you", Matson commanded, "put your feet exactly where Hal steps. I don't want anyone who passes this way to pick out our trail."

West nodded his head, then motioned for the others to follow him. He lead them up the hill on the south bank of Grasshopper Creek, keeping well above where horses would travel so as to leave no sign of the presence of people. He carefully picked where he put each foot, so as not to leave clumps of bent-over grass to mark his passing. The rest of the deputies did likewise. Perhaps a hundred yards upstream from where the creek crossed under the tracks, he began to indicate hiding places for posse members. He placed them under overhanging tree limbs or behind rock outcroppings, but each place had three things in common.

First, each was far enough above the flat ground along the stream that a rider on horseback, especially one watching an unfamiliar trail, would be unlikely to lift his head near enough to have a chance to seeing one or more of the hidden men. Second, each hiding spot was close enough to the edge of the steep hillside so that any of the men could leap on to the back of a rider and knock the individual off his horse. Finally, each deputy would have a clear pistol or rifle shot at anybody riding or walking along the flat ground beside the stream. Finally, he took up his own chosen position, at the point furthest upstream in the line of officers.

The sheriff and Tony Frye had been placed at about the mid point of the line, and were close enough to speak to each other in a whisper, Matson was under a pine tree, shielded from sight by drooping pine boughs, and Tony in a dark space between two boulders just a few feet from the tree that sheltered the sheriff. By the time all nine men were in position, there was enough light in the sky to clearly see features to the west, but the eastern hillside and the narrow valley created by Grasshopper Creek was still dark. Matson hissed, "We'll have deep shadow here for at least another two hours. It'll help hide us even better. And even at high noon, I doubt much sunlight will filter down through the tree canopy. We could hide a whole company of troops here."

Tony nodded agreement, then whispered, "And we'll have a good view of anything once it moves past us."

"Or anything that comes upstream from the tracks and beyond," Matson said softly. "Damned if I don't think this is just about the perfect ambush spot. Hal picked a good one." The sheriff was smiling broadly as he looked around.

CHAPTER FIFTEEN

The nine men remained almost motionless, except for the small movements necessary to relieve cramped muscles. Occasionally, one member or another would slip off in to the deeper woods to relieve a full bladder, but only as a matter of absolute necessity. More than one of them cursed inwardly for having, despite having been warned, over-indulged in coffee on the train.

Eventually, birds and small animals began to disregard their presence and forest life returned to normal. Time passed, abet slowly, and the sky got lighter. Shortly after seven o'clock, the men heard the sound of the railroad's gasoline speeder heading north along the line, making the daily safety check before the first tourist train would be allowed to depart Durango for the run up to Silverton. About fifteen minutes passed, then the sheriff's posse began to hear unusual sounds coming from downstream.

A single rider astride a rangy bay horse came in to view. The man on horseback kept his eyes on the faint trail of bent grass that marked the passage of numerous horses some days previously. And on the hillside above, nine law officers froze in their positions and held their collective breath until horse and rider were well out of sight.

Matson waited another five minutes, then, with a smile on his face, whispered to Tony, "You recognize that guy?"

Frye nodded his head and whispered back, "Well, well. Mister County Commissioner Webber. Now I wonder just what could be bringing him out here on horseback this fine spring morning?" If Tony had not been so well hidden in the shadows of the rocks, Matson could have seen the big grin that creased his face.

Matson moved slightly out from his hiding place under the pine tree and made a thumbs up gesture in both the upstream and downstream directions. Once he finished, he moved back in to hiding and settled down to wait.

More time passed. By now, there was not a single posse member that was not suffering at least a little from aching arms, legs, and backs. Flexing muscles helped, but all nine men realized that the passing of Commissioner Webber meant they were almost certainly guaranteed to be able to spring their ambush. To a man they were willing to endure whatever discomfort necessary to bring that about. And, despite being willing to endure discomfort, all of them prayed for a speedy resolution to their day's work. Bladders were filling up again.

Finally, a few minutes after ten thirty, they began to hear the faint sounds of several horses, along with muted voices, coming from further up the creek. Then, some minutes later, four men on horseback and three additional pack animals came in to view. One was Commissioner Webber. Neither Matson nor Tony recognized any of the others.

When the men on horseback were just about even with his position on the hillside above them, Matson stood up, automatic pistol in hand and pointed in the general direction of the men on horseback, and hollered, "Halt. Put your hands up in the air. You are all under arrest on a charge of......."

The sheriff didn't get a chance to finish telling the four riders why they were under arrest. The man bringing up the rear began reaching for his pistol immediately upon seeing the sheriff and hearing his voice. He did manage to remove the pistol from the holster he wore around his waist, but never managed to raise it above waist level. Three shots sounded as one, and all slammed in to the suspected outlaw, one in the chest and two through his head. The impact of the three rifle bullets lifted him out of the saddle and dropped him, his head a bloody shambles, on the ground behind his horse, which, badly startled, bolted across the creek, up the steep hill, and in to the woods on the other side of the stream. It didn't take too long for the horse's reins to tangle in undergrowth, which brought the animal to a halt.

The two men in front of the man who'd attempted to draw a weapon wisely complied with Matson's order, but Commissioner Webber, who was leading the procession, made to spur his horse in an attempt to escape. This, as it turned out, was an exercise in futility, because no sooner had Sheriff Matson began shouting his order to halt than Tony Frye jumped up from his hiding place in the rocks, and, after running a few steps parallel to the ledge upon which Commissioner Webber was riding, launched himself over the side of the hill at Webber. The impact of Tony coming down and across horse and rider knocked Webber from the saddle and deposited him on the ground with Tony on top of him.

The impact knocked Webber's breath from his lungs. He started to reach for the pistol at his waist when Tony shoved its barrel of his own weapon into the commissioner's open mouth. "Move that hand another inch, Mister Webber, and I'll spatter what little brains you have all over this forest! Believe me, that'd just make my day!" Having the barrel of a nine millimeter Browning pistol rammed in his mouth made it impossible for the county commissioner to speak, but his hand stopped moving and his body went limp. Fear set in and he messed himself.

Tony disarmed the man, then removed his pistol from Webber's mouth, rolled him on his stomach, handcuffed his hands behind his back, and then stood and pulled Webber erect. Then he realized the significance of the stench he's just noticed. "Guys," he said, "I think Mr. Webber just soiled his body linen."

Matson called out, "Serves him right." Then he issued instructions to his team. "Work in pairs. Read each of these people their Miranda rights. I want it done so it can be documented. And somebody help Tony take Mr. Webber to the stream to get him and his britches cleaned. I don't want him riding in the train in the disgusting condition he's in."

By the time Tony regained his feet, other deputies had secured the other two men and Deputy West was running to assist Tony, a set of unneeded handcuffs in his right hand. They dragged Webber to the stream, stripped him, removed the handcuffs from his wrists, and made him clean both his clothes and himself. When he was reasonably clean and shivering from the cold water he'd bathed in, they made him put his wet clothes back on and handcuffed his hands behind his back again.

Another deputy stood guard over the dead body of the rearmost rider. As pairs of deputies recited the Miranda warning to each of the captives, Sheriff Matson climbed further up the hillside, removed a cellular phone from his pocket, looked at the sky in search of an airplane, and punched in a number. The phone had no coverage. He swore, then took from another pocket the small radio Tony had given him earlier. He turned it on, then in a few seconds, he said, "Jill, it's done. Call your mother on her phone. Tell her to call the FBI and have them carry out their raid." He listened for a moment, then said, "Yes, we're both fine, we're all fine except for one of the bandits, whose day has just been totally ruined..... ruined forever. Luckily I had the foresight to put some body bags on the train. Now call your mother, then call the train on the other radio and tell Mister

Connelly to head back to Grasshopper Creek bridge as soon as he can."

Then, almost as an afterthought he said, "And have the newspaper and radio and television news people alerted to be at a press conference at the railroad station when we get back. Your mother has a list of people to call about this." He listened a moment more, then said, "I will not! You'll have to kiss him yourself." Then he turned off the radio and slipped it back in the pocket of his camouflage fatigue jacket.

Tony looked up the hill at his boss, a question on his face. Matson looked down at him and said, "I'll be dammed if I'm going to kiss you. I told Jill she's going to have to do it herself!" This statement provoked gales of laughter from the posse members. Tony blushed beet red. And then, a few minutes later and from a distance, came the shrill screech of a train whistle blowing repeatedly.

CHAPTER SIXTEEN

The trip back to Durango quickly became very much a public celebration. From what they could see as they passed under the highway 550 overpass a couple miles north of Hermosa, the members of the posse quickly concluded that Pat Matson had wasted no time in calling the media to inform them that there had been arrests and giving them at least some details on the posse and prisoners returning to town via rail. The radio and television stations must have cut in to their normal scheduled programming to announce the news because there were more than a dozen cars parked in the parking area just north of the overpass, and at least twenty people cheering and waving as the train passed by.

As the train slowly dropped downgrade through a wooded area as it approached the valley of the Animas, it passed the cluster of condominiums on the hillside just on the east side of the tracks, the buildings they'd passed earlier that morning. Many of the back balconies of the condo units held people. Except for two individuals, they were all cheering and waving; one of the exceptions was vigorously giving the "thumbs up" sign with both hands; the other, for some reason none of the posse members could fathom, was wearing a kilt and playing the bagpipes as he marched back and forth on his balcony.

From the moment the train came to the bottom of the grade and crossed to the east side of the highway at the small railroad maintenance yard at Hermosa, motorists on highway 550, which ran parallel and quite close to the tracks were waving at the train and honking their horns. More people gathered at every grade crossing, waving and cheering as the train passed. One of the sheriff's deputies, apparently patrolling highway 550, drove parallel to the railroad tracks, light bar and siren on, and waving madly with his left hand out the vehicle's window on the driver's side as he used his right to hold the steering wheel. Other motorists fell in behind him, honking their horns and waving as well. These vehicles quickly took on the nature of an honor procession celebrating the good news as the vehicles escorted the train toward Durango.

Sheriff Matson looked out the window of the caboose at the procession of cars. "It's got to be Cooter," he muttered, shaking his head from side to side as he spoke.

"I don't think I've met Cooter yet," Tony said in response, "whoever he is."

Matson chuckled. "Let's just say that if the sheriff's department were a village, some folks could make a strong case for Cooter Marshall being our resident village idiot," he said. "I inherited Cooter from the previous sheriff, who inherited him from his predecessor. Cooter is the classic 'redneck good ol' boy."

This remark caused the two other men riding in the caboose to laugh; they both knew Cooter well. One of them, when he'd finished laughing, said, "Cooter means well, Boss. He means well. And it could be worse. He could be called the town drunk. At least he doesn't drink."

"As I said, I inherited Cooter from the previous administrations," Matson said softly to Tony. "He's been a deputy close to forever and is dumber than a box of rocks. I'd try getting rid of him, but he *is* a hard worker. He does real well on writing tickets on speeders and such. He'll also work a lot of overtime without complaining. So I guess I'll keep him, not that I have much choice, what with Civil Service and all that. Anyhow," he continued, "thankfully he's old enough to retire but he's also grandfathered against the twenty year service limit. That means I'm pretty well stuck with him." Matson raised the window beside him and waved back at Cooter.

The train slowed down as it reached the developed area of Durango. And as the speed decreased, the number of people gathered at grade crossings increased. Hundreds of cheering people were gathered at the Main Avenue railroad crossing at the north end of Durango's business district. Scores more were standing at every street intersection along Narrow Gauge Alley and many more lined the narrow sidewalk that ran parallel to the track.

It was obvious to everyone concerned that the capture of the bank robbers was becoming a community celebration of considerable magnitude. And at Sixth Street, where the track crossed the street and entered the fenced-in railroad yard and station grounds, there must have been close to a thousand people, and maybe even more, crowding the street and sidewalks, not to mention climbing on cars and pickup trucks for better views. One young man had even climbed up a telephone pole to get a better view of the train as it entered the rail yard.

A half dozen Durango city police were on hand to keep the crowd from blocking the track. Two athletic teenagers had climbed the lamp posts on either side of the gate controlling access to the tracks at the station. Matson wondered if the entire population of the town had turned out. It certainly looked that way. The Durango city police, Matson concluded, were really earning their pay this day. It seemed like a considerable chunk of the population of all of southwest Colorado had turned out to celebrate.

Sheriff Matson mentally gave thanks that the railroad grounds were fenced in and that access to the place where the train would stop was tightly controlled. Without the fence, he figured that his men would practically have to fight their way through a cheering mob to exit the train. In actual fact, the fence, and the efforts of a half dozen city policemen, barely kept the crowd out of the station grounds and railroad yard. And on sidings, as Matson realized, stood the morning's two scheduled tourist trains to Silverton. Matson concluded that Connelly had their boarding and departures delayed so as not to interfere with the posse and its special train.

The train slowly pulled around the balloon track and up to the platform of the Durango railroad station. As it did so, the tourist train on the track closest to the station platform pulled out for Silverton, making space at the platform for the sheriff's train. A horde of news media people stood anxiously awaiting for the train to stop and for the posse members and prisoners to appear. It looked as if all of the television news crews and other reporters in the entire Four Corners area were set up to video the event. The sheriff and the three deputies who had been riding in the caboose crossed the platform between the caboose and the coach in which the rest of the law enforcement officers and the prisoners were riding. The dead body of the man, identity as yet unknown, who had attempted to draw his weapon was wrapped in large plastic garbage bags. It had been necessary to put the body in a rubber body bag before loading it on to the railroad car.

After the four men had entered the coach, Tony Frye signaled for quiet, then spoke to the sheriff and the other posse members. "I think we need to celebrate, guys," he said. "I'd like to throw a party this Saturday evening. Every one of you, wives and girlfriends, too, are invited for dinner, drinks, and whatever. Same for everyone else that's contributed to this, even the FBI." This last remark caused a few soft laughs. FBI agents were not well thought of by most local law enforcement types. Town and county officers in southwest Colorado were no exception; they generally had a low opinion of the FBI.

Then Tony continued, "I'll get word to you all in the next day or two as to where and what time. Today was a team effort and I think we need to celebrate as a team. And I pick up the whole tab. It's time to party!"

He turned to the sheriff. "Jack," he said softly, "isn't there some way I can talk you into doing all the speaking? I'd really just as soon not get any more publicity out of this."

Matson smiled. He was NOT going to let Tony off the hook. "Sorry, kid. You did almost all the planning and you deserve the credit, especially since you personally collared the leader, and with him in possession of a bag of the loot, too. Besides," he continued with a grin, "your involvement is going to be super publicity for the department. It just might help me get the funding we need to meet the demands the county is dropping on us. This 'do more with less' shit just doesn't work." The sheriff could tell by the look on his face that Tony was considerably less than thrilled at the prospect of being the subject of yet another episode of media attention, especially one that was almost guaranteed to get much wider exposure than the first one did.

"Look, Tony," the sheriff went on, "you were in on this at the very beginning. It's only proper for you to wrap it all up. Besides," he smiled, "just think of the headlines! The reporters from the Durango *Herald* will just eat this up. They're going to have to put a real favorable spin on this, and that's going to net the department a lot of friends come election day this fall. The big city papers like the New York *Times* and the Washington *Post* will pick the story up, and it'll get a lot of publicity for this end of Colorado. Wouldn't surprise me one bit if the big TV networks don't put this on the afternoon and evening news. Tourism will probably jump, and the county government sure can use the extra tax revenue that more tourists will bring in, not to mention the money a surge in tourism will put in the cash registers of lots of area businesses."

"There'll be a lot of TV news crews there," the sheriff went on, "and I bet this story makes both local and network news broadcasts tonight. Like it or not, Tony, you've made a big impression on the press. It's not just that I need you to do this, it's that this whole county and the surrounding area can get a big boost by you filling in as department spokesperson for fifteen minutes."

"Oh, joy," Tony groaned. "I guess I have to do it, whether I want to or not." He grinned ruefully. "You're a sneaky and devious man, Jack Matson. That's why I suspect you of having arranged for a TV news crew in a plane shooting footage of this train heading back to town?"

"Guilty as charged!" the sheriff chortled. "It's going to be great P.R., Tony," Matson said gleefully. "Trust me on this one. The way I figure it, right now the better the department looks in the eyes of the public, the better the department is going to fare in the county budget process. The more people who get exposed to this neck of the woods as a vacation spot by news coverage today, the more tourists that will visit this area. The more tourists who come here, the more money the county has to play with. The more money the county has, the bigger the piece of pie we may end up with. Like I said, think of the headlines."

"And," he continued, "you are really going to be super on the witness stand when those slimeballs go on trial. That'll be even more good publicity for the department. I can see it now.....you in court dressed up better than the sleazy criminal lawyers that bunch is liable to hire.....and probably speaking more literate English, too. I can't wait!" Matson chortled.

Tony muttered something Matson didn't quite hear, which was probably just as well, even though he'd muttered it in Russian, and shook his head. The phrase he'd uttered was not an uncommon one in military circles. The sheriff probably was familiar with it. He couldn't blame the sheriff. To tell the truth, he admitted to himself that the media was going to be lying in wait for him anyhow. Maybe if he grabbed the initiative, the end result wouldn't be as bad as the last time he made the news. Maybe he could even mend a fence or two. He shook his head again and muttered, "Damn it, I *am* thinking of the headlines!"

The train came to a stop. Sheriff Matson stepped down on to the platform, followed by Tony, the other posse members, and three handcuffed criminals. They'd deal with the dead body later, and do it as discretely as possible.

Jack Matson began the presentation. "Ladies and gentlemen," he said to the assembled media representatives and bystanders in a loud, firm voice. The people failed to quiet down, so he again said, "Ladies and Gentlemen." There was still too much noise to start the presentation. He held up both hands and eventually people shut up.

"Thank you," Matson said. "I am pleased to announce that we have closed the bank robbery/murder case you have all been following these past several days. This morning we made three arrests in connection with this matter, one of those arrested being County Commissioner James Webber, who you see here in handcuffs. In addition, one individual was shot and killed while attempting to use a firearm to resist arrest. As of this minute, we do not know his identity. His body is on the train and will not, with emphasis on *NOT*, be put on display. Trust me, you don't want to see it. It's not a pretty sight."

"Other arrests in this matter are quite likely. You can probably safely assume that one of the persons who will be arrested and charged as an accomplice before and after the fact will be Commissioner Webber's wife. Actually, the Federal Bureau of Investigation may very well have already arrested her and one or more additional people. We also have a witness to two murders we suspect were committed by one or more of the suspects. I hope to have more to say about this in a day or two. Deputy Tony Frye of the La Plata County Sheriff's Office conducted the investigation and planned the operation that led to a successful conclusion of this sad case. Deputy Frye?"

The sheriff stepped back and, very reluctantly, Tony stepped forward. For the last few minutes he'd been planning how to say what needed to be said in as few words and as quickly as possible.

"This office received considerable assistance from other law enforcement agencies," he began. "Special thanks must be given to the sheriff's offices of Montezuma, Archuleta, and San Juan Counties as well as to a variety of state and federal agencies, including the Department of Defense and the F.B.I. We also especially wish to honor La Plata County sheriff's deputy Barry Morgan, who died as a result of wounds received in the line of duty on the first day of this ordeal and who will be buried with full honors later today. As further investigation uncovers more information concerning this case, which I am sure it will, that information will be given to you as quickly as possible." Tony noticed the sheriff speaking into his cell phone and frantically waving his hand in Tony's direction.

"Ladies and gentlemen, "Tony said. "I believe the sheriff might already have some additional information for you. One moment please."

Sheriff Matson pushed through the crowd of reporters gathered in front of Tony. When he reached Tony's side, he turned and faced the crowd. "Folks," he said, "I just spoke with the SAC of Durango's FBI office. Two FBI agents, accompanied by two of my deputies, went to the Webber ranch to arrest Mrs. Gladys Webber, the wife of County Commissioner Webber. When they got there, Mrs. Webber was in the ranch's large horse barn. One of the agents called for her to come out, saying that they had a federal warrant for her arrest as an accessory to bank robbery and murder. Mrs. Webber made no reply, so the SAC called out that the agents were about to enter the barn and take her in to custody, by force if need be. Then they heard what sounded like a shot. They rushed in to the barn and found Mrs. Webber dead on the barn floor. She had placed the muzzle of a pistol in her mouth, pulled the trigger, and blew her brains out all over the inside of the barn. As additional information becomes available, I'll make sure you get it." Matson looked at Tony, nodded his head curtly, and walked off.

"Nice graphic description, Boss. Bet that makes the news tonight, too," Tony muttered under his breath. Then he looked at looked at the reporters and the rest of the assembled crowd, crossed the first and second fingers of his left hand behind his back, and said, "Thank you, folks, and that's all."

Well, it was a nice try on Tony's part, but that certainly *wasn't* all. Despite his wishful thinking and a desire to get out of the media hot seat as quickly as possible, a good fifteen minutes of questioning followed, and almost all the questions, most of which came from reporters from the Durango *Herald* and many of which were shamelessly designed to elicit personal information from him, were directed at Tony. As he went through the ordeal of answering them, frequently by saying, "No comment," he was constantly aware of Jill Matson, smiling broadly and with her arms folded, standing on a bench near the doorway in to the station while she watched him contend with the reporters. Tony's grudging dealings with the members of the fourth estate seemed to be causing Jill a great deal of amusement. He, himself, was not amused.....but couldn't really fault Jill for smiling at his discomfort.

Finally, the publicity ordeal was over, and sheriff's department vehicles made off with the prisoners. The dead body, mercifully encased in a rubber body bag, went off in an ambulance to the medical examiner's office. All the law officers except for Tony, were also in the process of leaving. A few reporters and still photographers and one TV news camera crew from KREZ-TV lingered on the platform, hoping for another few last-minute crumbs of information, a hope which Tony profoundly intended to deny to them.

He walked over to Jill, who held out her hands to him so he could help her step down off the bench. "Your dad said earlier today that there was something he absolutely refused to do for you," Tony said with and smiled as he held Jill's hand.

Jill replied softly and without hesitation, "There are a couple cameras pointed this way, Tony. How'd you like a picture of me kissing you to make the front page of this afternoon's Durango *Herald*?"

Tony answered the question by wrapping his arms around her and giving her a long kiss, one which Jill returned with considerable enthusiasm. Behind him, he heard camera shutters click. The TV cameraman cheered. After a moment, he released her and said, "I can think of a lot worse things to see in the paper. And I wouldn't even mind if that kiss makes the TV network news tonight, too."

"In that case," Jill said, "maybe we better give them another photo op."

It took Tony half a second to figure out just what Jill meant. When the light bulb over his head went on, he put his arms around her again and gave her a second kiss, much longer and much steamier than the first. When he released her, he said, "Well, I sure hope that one of those makes the evening news. "

And, as things worked out, both made the evening papers and both local and network television......and made a lot of the big city newspapers, too, even as far away as Washington, D.C. Marissa Montgomery saw both the newspaper photos and network television coverage of the news conference.....including the two kisses.

Marissa was most certainly *not* amused. She threw a major hissy fit in the living room of her parents' apartment. The language she used in describing Tony Frye was certainly not what one would expect of a lady. But then, people who knew her well would certainly never describe Marissa Montgomery as being a lady.

CHAPTER SEVENTEEN

On the following Saturday evening, the sliding wall between the two function rooms at The Cattle King restaurant in downtown Durango had been pushed open. The very large room thus created was full of law officers and assorted spouses and significant others, along with more than a few political figures and their spouses. Tony had conferred at length with Jack and Pat Matson in making up the list of invited guests. A considerable number of people, many of them civic leaders, were in attendance. When Tony and the Matsons had finalized the guest list, Tony realized that it was fortunate the he had a well-stocked checkbook. The bill for the event was going to be pretty hefty. But his attitude was basically 'what the hell, it's only money.' He mentally crossed his fingers and hoped he could write off the cost of the evening as 'business entertainment' on his income tax. Tables were set to accommodate the considerable crowd and the restaurant staff was quietly, and seemingly efficiently, preparing to serve dinner as soon as the social hour ended.

Sheriff Matson had prevailed upon Tony to invite the Durango City Council and the remaining members of the county commission to the celebration. His wife had suggested inviting some of the major shakers and movers of the chamber of commerce. The sheriff and Pat Matson were schmoozing with various political figures, FBI agents, the Durango police chief, and the sheriffs of Montezuma, Archuleta, and San Juan Counties while Tony and Jill socialized with the regular run-of-the-mill law enforcement officers and guests. The working press was barred from the premises under threat of being arrested for criminal trespass. This, of course, was at Tony's suggestion.

Dress for the evening, by Jill's suggestion, was Colorado casual, though many guests of the female persuasion, herself included, cheated and dressed a couple notches above the local casual standard. Females tend to have some difficulty in passing up a chance to show off. Neither of the Matson women were exceptions to this rule.

Spirits were high, the bar was open so spirits of another kind were flowing, and all present were obviously having a very good time. Jack Matson, seeing the general consumption of copious amounts of alcoholic beverages, reverently hoped that many of the attendees had made prior arrangements for designated drivers to transport them home when the function was over. He had already made mental note that he might have to insist on the use of taxi cabs by the heavier drinkers and, even worse, might even have to call a few deputies off night patrol to drive the really intoxicated participants home.

On the opposite side of the room, Jill and several of the deputies were teasing Tony about the headlines that resulted from his speaking to the press at the railroad station. "And they used the 'millionaire cowboy cop' line again," she said gleefully. "I just love it!"

"Actually," Tony said woefully, as he speared a bacon-wrapped broiled chicken liver from a tray in the hands of a passing waitress, "they used it again......and again, and again, and......". After the third *again*, he popped the appetizer in his mouth and began to chew. His woeful comment brought gales of laughter from a number of people, especially from Jill. "I swear the only way I'm going to be able to quit hearing that nickname," Tony said after he'd swallowed the appetizer, "is to go hide on the ranch and be a hermit. Maybe when the press finds out that the Longo boy identified two of the baddies as being involved in killing his parents, it'll take some of the heat off me."

Hank Ormond, one of the deputies from the posse, said, "That's possible, I guess. And that news ought to be released tomorrow, if not later tonight." He thought for a second, smiled, and continued. "Hey, Tony, that KREZ TV camera guy told me that you and Jill kissing generated so much heat he was afraid his camera lens would fog up." More gales of laughter. Both Tony and Jill blushed, which just increased the volume of the laughing.

As the laughter died down, Tony felt a hand on his shoulder and turned to see Augie Wilkins, the county commissioner Jill had spoken so highly of. Wilkins, a large smile on his face, held out his hand to Tony. "Thank you, young man," Wilkins said sincerely as he pumped Tony's right hand up and down. "Your grandfather would be proud of you, very proud, in fact. He looked sat the assembled law officers. "Thanks to all of you," he said to them. "Without your sterling efforts, I honestly believe this sorry mess would still be unresolved and those murderers would be walking around free. Not to mention we'd still have the ringleader of the bad guys as a member of the county commission."

Jill interrupted him. "Actually, Daddy says it looks like Mrs. Webber was the brains behind that collection of baddies, Mr. Wilkins, not her husband. I guess that figures. He never did strike me as being overly bright."

Augie Wilkins pondered that statement for a moment before continuing to speak. "No matter which of them was calling the shots, it's over. The people of this county owe you all a considerable debt of gratitude." He looked at Tony.

"Like I said, Pete surely would be proud if he could be here tonight." He looked around at the other officers again. "Thank you all, boys, every last one of you. We're grateful, believe me. And I'm pushing to see that we recognize your services in a more tangible way."

"Speaking for myself, I'm glad I was able to be of service, Mister Wilkins," Tony replied honestly. "Everyone else involved feels the same way. We're all glad we could put those bad guys in the hoosegow. And it was a nice gesture for you to make sure the reward money will all go to the fund for Barry Morgan's wife and kids."

Wilkins smiled broadly. "That's going to be a tidy sum," he said. "There's a federal reward, as well as a reward from the state of Oklahoma. In fact, I've just been given to understand that what you fellows accomplished the other day has cleared up a goodly number of unsolved cases back in Oklahoma, and Kansas, too, for that matter. Fingerprints from those two criminals produced some quite interesting results, so Sheriff Matson just told me.

And I'm happy to say that last night at the county commission meeting we voted to have the county pay for the Morgan family's health insurance until the children all reach the age of twenty-one or when they finish college, whichever comes later. Mrs. Morgan's medical insurance will be paid for the rest of her life, unless she remarries, of course. Fully paid health insurance for family members, by the way, will now automatically apply to any county police or fire department employee who dies or is disabled in the line of duty. We've also voted a tidy supplemental funding bill to cover increasing the county law enforcement budget. It's not a blank check, young man, but it is a healthy sum, a very healthy sum. Jack Matson is quite pleased, and rightfully so."

"That's great, sir," Tony said. "I know how concerned he's been about having the money he needs for the department to do its job."

"And," Wilkins continued, "a part of that sum is to go toward covering what you spent out of pocket to end this matter. According to Jack, that's a not inconsiderable chunk of change. Aircraft rentals, so Jack tells us, don't come cheap. I sincerely hope you have receipts. I told my fellow commission members that it's a sad thing when a deputy spends his own money, and a lot of it, to get his job done. I'm happy to say it didn't take much arm-twisting to get them to agree with me."

Tony looked at Wilkins. "Mr. Wilkins," he said, "I just have to ask you a real serious personal question," he said. "Is there anyone in this county who *didn't* know my grandfather?"

Wilkins stopped. He thought for a moment and then went on. "Well, probably, but most likely nobody who's anybody important, just Johnny-come-latelies from places like Texas and California." He smiled. "Pete was a good friend to the folks around here, Tony. He was.....damn it, it's more than him being a friend. He was just a really good neighbor. In this part of the world, being a good neighbor counts for a lot. Folks who didn't know him personally certainly knew *of* him and knew some of the things he did to help the people of this county."

Wilkins paused, then went on. "Jack Matson says he's offered you a permanent position as the department's chief criminal investigator and head of this new multi-jurisdictional unit that, without the slightest doubt, is going to be set up. Fact is, Jack said the job description was written in such a way that you're probably the only person in the whole Four

Corners area who's qualified to fill the position. From what I hear, the commissioners and sheriffs of the surrounding counties are very much in favor having such a task force, especially as we have high hopes that we'll have a federal grant or two to cover the costs. Jack also said they also were very happy about the idea of putting you in charge of it."

"It's not a question of whether the position will be set up, it's just how long it's going to take to get it organized. There are quite a few legalities that have to be addressed before it'll become official, but they're just formalities. Believe me, I guarantee that it's a done deed." Wilkins stopped talking and frowned, then continued. "The only question is, are you going to take the position? According to the news reports a few days ago, your mind was very set about wanting to devote all your time to running your ranch, not to being a deputy sheriff.

Jill provided the answer to Wilkins' question. She put her arm through Tony's, put her head on his shoulder, and said, "I took him shopping for more uniforms this morning, Mister Wilkins. There's not a single thing for you to worry about; he's taking the job. If he weren't going to take it, I think Mom would stop cooking ham dinners for him."

Postscript

Augie Wilkins' prediction was right. A considerable number of legal formalities had to be addressed before the Four Corners Multi-jurisdictional Law Enforcement Task Force could formally be put in operation. Those formalities were given high priority at every level. Nobody raised any objection to creating the force. The highly favorable publicity that came about as a result of the successful resolution of the Bayfield bank robbery virtually guaranteed that this would be the case.

Tony Frye accepted the position of full time La Plata County Sheriff's Department chief criminal investigator and head of the multi-jurisdictional task force, despite some mental reservations about probably having to spend the majority of his time 'on the job,' as law enforcement jargon had it, rather than spending it running his ranch. Fortunately, as he observed more than once, Lew Barnes was a damned good ranch foreman and had a crew of well-qualified ranch hands working for him. This took a lot of the burden of running the ranch off his shoulders.

A side effect of the publicity that involved Tony was that there were many messages on Tony's phones, both on his house phone and cell phone, during the next few days. While Tony returned calls from his father, sister, and various Air Force friends and assorted other people he knew, with great glee, he totally refused to return the many nasty calls left on his answering machine by Marissa Montgomery. He cheerfully deleted each and every one of her nasty messages, noting as he did so, that they got even nastier, as time passed, than they'd been when she first started calling him.

One obvious reason that Tony cheerfully accepted full time employment with the sheriff's office was that he guessed that doing so would lead to him being able to spend a lot more time with Jill Matson than would be the case if he'd turned the job down. And, as things turned out, that guess was right on the money!

The End

About the Author

David (Dave) Rotthoff was born in Pittsburgh, PA, in 1940. He spent a year in Carnegie Tech's school of fine arts, where he took two courses in thought and expression with best-selling writer Gladys Schmidt [author of *Rembrandt* and *David the King*]. He transferred to the University of Pittsburgh, graduating in 1963 with majors in education, speech & theater and history and a minor in English.

He is twice retired, once as a USAF lieutenant colonel, having served some 26 years on active duty and in the reserves, and as a high school English and history teacher, with thirty-three years teaching in two Maine schools. Dave is a member of the Baltimore & Ohio RR Historical Society. He was written articles for the society's quarterly *and* for the quarterly of the Western Pennsylvania Historical Society.

Dave and his wife Patricia retired in 2000 and became Florida residents in 2004. He writes fiction and does historical research as forms of amusement, two things he jokingly says keep him off the streets and [mostly] out of trouble. His hobbies include playing bridge and cooking, along with dormant interest in amateur radio [call sign KA1EAP] and stamp collecting. He and his wife live in North Fort Myers.

Made in the USA
Las Vegas, NV
31 October 2022

58520662R20152